A
Thousand
Fibers

Susan M. Szurek

Chapbook Press

Schuler Books
2660 28th Street SE
Grand Rapids, MI 49512
(616) 942-7330
www.schulerbooks.com

A Thousand Fibers

ISBN 13: 9781957169804

eBook ISBN 13: 9781957169811

Library of Congress Control Number: 2024906863

Printed in the United States.

Also by Susan M. Szurek:*

Everstille: A Novel

Everstille's Librarian

Olivia from Everstille

Tomas' Children

Her Cousin Julia

My Brother's Things

**Books available at Chapbook Press,
(https://www.schulerbooks.com/chapbook-press)
at Amazon, and additional online book sellers.*

...**A thousand fibers** connect
us with our fellow men...

Hermann Melville

Det blir som det blir.

Swedish saying

Contents

One

Bonneville, Illinois: 1922

"Maybe you should just stay out of her business," replied Mr. Anderson as he used his cane to maneuver himself up from the wooden kitchen chair, the one he had repaired years ago. "Anyway, I need to get going. The horse and wagon are there, and I'll be at the side of the house when he's ready to leave. Let him know I'm waiting for him."

His wife nodded and handed him the brown-paper wrapped package that had been given to her. "Remember, she said to wait until you drop him off to hand it to him. And as far as her condition is concerned, I *can* help her, you know. She doesn't have to have it, and I know she is early enough along so that it won't be a hard loss. She hasn't said anything to me, but will, once he's gone. And good riddance. Once you leave with him, I'll check those herbs in my case. I expect she'll come down here soon. You better go. I hear him on the stairs."

Mr. Anderson left, holding the package in one hand while using the cane with his other. Mrs. Anderson shut the door behind him and went into the kitchen to deliver the message and make the offer of a breakfast. Today the man wouldn't be eating in the dining room with the lady of the house. She suspected he wouldn't eat at all but would just leave. She was right. After drinking a cup of coffee, he went back up the stairs to pack his things. The woman watched him leave, then walked into the three-room suite she and her husband shared, pulled out the small leather suitcase from under their bed, and began to mull over what was inside.

***

As Ingrid stood behind the curtain, she saw Thomas turn around to stare at the second-floor bedroom window thinking she was there. She knew he would look and was sure he wouldn't think to lift his eyes up one floor, to the third-floor, to the servants' quarters, to connect with her eyes. She watched until the wagon driven by Mr. Anderson turned onto the road to town; the blooming early spring tree branches hid them from her sight.

She stood for a minute longer, and then, feeling faint, sat down in the corner chair. She took deep breaths and willed the morning sickness away. It worked. At least for a time. She would go back to her bedroom, the one on the second-floor, the large, ornately decorated one she had shared with her husband. The one attached to the dressing room which housed the smaller bed, the one in which, years ago, her husband, Fredrick Vogel, died. She would lay down in her bed and sleep a while. Mrs. Anderson had been told to leave her alone until she came downstairs, and she would. She knew Mrs. Anderson suspected. She always knew the secrets.

Ingrid took another breath and rose from the chair. As she passed the other servant's bedroom, the larger one, she saw Thomas had removed the bedding, folded it, left it at the foot of the bed. The sun pressed into the room and lit up the small mirror over the washstand, drawing her attention to it. She noticed something on the stand and walked over to see what it was. Thomas' comb which held a few of his dark hairs had been left. She touched his hairs, brushing her fingers gently against them but did not remove them. Turning, she departed the third-floor room while cradling the comb in her hand and went down one flight of stairs to her bedroom. Walking to the ornate dresser, she opened the top drawer where she kept her jewelry, and placed the comb next to the velvet-covered box containing a special gold and emerald bracelet. She shut the drawer, turned, and went to her bed where she lay down trying to make herself comfortable. She would rest for a time. Then she would find Mrs. Anderson and confide to her the secret she presumed was already known.

Two

Ingrid Winthrop

Despite her grandmother's conscientious ministrations: the academic dictates, the designed tutoring in music, etiquette, and languages (both French and German), the conservative but fashionable clothing, the appropriate age-specific books, toys, and games, the necessary introduction to society and friends, the careful choice of an expensive, elite boarding school, Ingrid was aware of her grandmother's dislike of her. Perhaps not when she was so young, when she was just a couple years old and her parents' horrific deaths placed her into the care of Louisa Winthrop, her paternal grandmother, but certainly as she aged, as she noted the punctilious tone of derision when her grandmother spoke to her, the deliberate stares she was given when Grandmother Louisa didn't realize she was being seen, the lack of physical contact which her friends and their parents often shared. There were enough of these instances that Ingrid, at twelve years old, feeling a bit grown, sought to question the reason for the dislike.

She was home for the summer, having returned from the spring term at boarding school. She and her grandmother were seated at the dining table eating a late summer supper when dessert, always fresh fruit in season, never a sweet which was saved for holidays or birthdays, was served. Ingrid watched her grandmother take a careful bite of the peeled and poached peach placed with care in the everyday blue and white china before she spoke.

"Grandmother, can I ask you something?"

"*May* I ask," Grandmother Louisa corrected. "What is it?"

"Why don't you like me?"

Grandmother Louisa stopped mid-chew and swallowed before placing her spoon down and her hands in the lap folds of her dove-gray dress, the mourning color she had insisted upon wearing years beyond the social expectation of the tradition. She looked at her granddaughter, surprised at the question, shocked at the directness.

"Nonsense, Ingrid. I do love you."

"Not *love*," and Ingrid looked back into her grandmother's eyes, searching for the truth. "I asked about you *liking* me."

Louisa Winthrop hesitated just a moment, almost allowing the sorrow at her only son's death and the dislike of his dead wife who was this girl's mother show through her narrowed eyes and twisted mouth and clutched hands. But she held herself and took in a shallow breath and drew the curtains across her visage, arresting any show of emotion. She picked up her spoon and raised another small piece of the peach to her mouth, wondering if she would be able to move it down her closed throat.

"What silliness you bring up. I love and like you the appropriate amount. Such a question! Now, finish your dessert and then go practice the piano before you get ready for bed."

Louisa replaced the uneaten spoonful, pushed the dish away, and nodded to the standing servant. "Have Cook seep some peppermint tea," she ordered. "My stomach needs a soothing agent." She was soothing the wrong organ. It was her heart that had broken at the death of her son, her only child. It was that organ which wanted soothing, which craved healing, which was past peppermint protection.

*****

The last decades of the nineteenth century held multiple sorrows for Louisa (née Barnard) Winthrop, wife of George Winthrop of the esteemed East Coast Winthrop family. The New York winters were dreadful, and the usual plans were being made for moving to the Winter Colony in Aiken, South Carolina where both George and Louisa would enjoy the comforts of the resort and the splendor of the sun until the snow in the northeast was mostly melted. Their plan was to depart immediately after the usual Christmas Day celebration. But the snow came earlier than expected that year. In early December, as George was returning from a late evening at his club, he and his carriage were caught in an intensely severe and unexpected ice storm. It was late when he left his carriage stuck in the muddied and iced streets, instructing his driver to disengage it, a task which would take some hours. He determined to walk home to his large house which was only four streets down from the Vanderbilt mansion on 57th Street. He arrived cold and soaked and stayed in his wet evening dress while he warmed up with a brandy. But the chill turned to a cold and then a fever, and a mighty, hacking cough took residence in his chest, and the winter plans to travel south were abandoned. For a month, doctors were seen coming and going from the tall brownstone, all of them expressing various opinions and producing an assortment of tonics and tinctures, none of which helped. Christmas at the Winthrop estate that year was a quiet and solemn affair, lacking joy and good will. By the last week in January, a few remote relatives and friends had made the journey to visit George Winthrop a last time, commiserate with his wife, and wipe counterfeit tears decorously, using expensively detailed Irish linen handkerchiefs.

Meticulous funeral traditions and constancies were observed throughout the following weeks and months. George Winthrop was dressed in his newest suit and settled on his bed with a decorated and hidden cooling board beneath him and massive (in both size and expense) floral arrangements surrounding him. This allowed for closest family and intimate friends to say their farewells comfortably. Mourning clothes were ordered and rapidly created, and Louisa's long black public veil was readied. Black crepe was tied to the front door's bell knob as reminder to visitors of the sorrow inside, and black lined notecards and stationery were ordered for required personal correspondence. Eight members of George's club received letters on the black-lined stationery requesting them to act as pallbearers, and all except the one who remained at the Winter Colony in Aiken replied they were honored to assist. Another friend was found. The obituary published in the *New York Times* was, as expected, only a few lines, and the indication of a "private funeral" was understood. Death required traditional specificity, adherence to exactness, and unstated bounty, and no one would have been more cognizant of that than George Winthrop.

In 1877, when Cornelius Vanderbilt died, he was buried in the family plot at the Moravian Cemetery in Staten Island. Because George Winthrop, although he did not know the man personally, admired his wealth, he purchased his own family plots there in 1880 and arranged to be buried as close to the Vanderbilts as possible. Unfortunately for the Winthrops, Cornelius and his family were reburied in 1888 in what became known as the new Vanderbilt Mausoleum in the Vanderbilt Cemetery adjacent to Moravian Cemetery. But plots had been obtained, monument stones had been readied, and the original cemetery purchase became George's final resting place. Louisa Winthrop realized that the distance to the cemetery and the winter weather would necessitate the small procession to travel for a lengthy time. The carriage ride would take close to two hours. Multiple carriages, needed to transport the immediate family, necessary relatives, the minister, pallbearers, and a few friends, were hired. This task was supervised by George's son, Von George Winthrop. Afterwards, a quiet but splendid dinner would be offered to the mourners who would be exhausted after the consuming day and were due refreshment. That too required planning and organizing. Louisa had hoped to be assisted in this task by Von's wife, but the woman, Eliza, claimed her delicate condition precluded her from both the planning and the long cold journey to the cemetery. While Eliza refused kindly and spoke logically to her mother-in-law, and although Louise understood and capitulated to the woman's decision, it did not endear the younger to her elder. It added to the unhappiness that the widow felt. Even when the baby was safely born in early April of 1889, the event provided additional chagrin and sorrow for the grandmother. The child was, unfortunately, female.

***

Von George Winthrop was the third child born to Louisa and George Winthrop, but the only one to survive. Louisa was delighted she had finally produced a son, a living heir to the Winthrop name, money, and estate, and took constant and exacting care in his upbringing. She kept him at home, tutoring him with scrupulous concern far longer than she should have, according to his father. Eventually, the boy's father spoke to his mother, and amid quiet tears, Von was sent away to a proper boarding school where he relished being with other boys and away from his mother's persistent attentions. He was as successful as any other student at the school, and when accepted by the best university the Winthrop money could buy, he flourished and in only one year later than expected, left with an appropriate degree. He resided at home with his parents, and his mother concocted plans for a wedding to one of the delicate specimens of womanhood she continually introduced to him. Louisa never expected that this son, educated at the finest institutions, successful at his father's business, tall and handsome in a way that astounded even her, would fall in love and insist upon marrying a little nobody he met while ice skating with friends at, of all places, Brooklyn's Union Pond.

There was no doubt about Eliza Kenner's beauty, and no uncertainty about her attitude. Her forthrightness and independence were what attracted Von. She was tall for a woman, with hair a burnt – umber color, mixing various browns and a subtle shade of red, and her eyes, a medium sparkling chestnut. She held herself straight, and because her posture was so athletically pronounced, when she spoke face-to-face to Louisa Winthrop, she looked down at her with a mouth in a constant uplift, likened to a smirk, a perceived slight Louisa never forgot or forgave. The facts of her life were simple: she was from Brooklyn, her father owned a small shoe store, Eliza worked there, her parents were immigrants whose families arrived from Prussia before she was born, and she claimed to attend a Lutheran Church. It was the church business which so disturbed Louisa. She looked at Eliza and wondered: is she Jewish? There was a possibility, and she was so disturbed by it that she cornered her husband one evening during his brandy-and-cigar time, mentioning the possibility and forcing him to discuss it.

"Stop it, Louisa," and George took the last sip of his glass and then thought about refilling it, "Eliza is a perfectly delightful young woman. And if she claims to be Lutheran, then she is. There is little difference from what I can tell between the two churches. Lutheran or Episcopalian, what does it matter? Not that we even attend that often," and he found a golden drop left in the glass which he lifted to his lips.

"But she has that look about her, George. I just think there could be some…" and here Louisa looked about the substantial room wondering how loudly she should say the word, *"Jewishness…* in her blood. Her parents are immigrants and from PRUSSIA. You know that. She has told us herself."

George sighed. "Well, I like her. She is pleasant and makes me laugh. And Von is obviously intent upon marrying her. I see nothing wrong with it. After all, the Vanderbilts came over from the Netherlands, and one of them was an indentured servant. Cornelius himself started business as a ferry boat operator and, as I would remind you, did quite well. Now, let it go. This discussion is over. And please, leave me to read my paper. The girl is fine. They have my blessing."

Louisa stopped in shock. "I certainly hope you didn't tell Von that. I intend to speak to him about this entire situation and to get him to see reason."

"Already did," and George shook out his paper and held it up in front of his face. "Start planning for the wedding, my dear. And close the door when you leave."

The wedding was a small one, held in the front parlor of the Saint Thomas Episcopal Church in Manhattan on a spring morning in April, 1888, as Louisa demanded. A lovely wedding breakfast was held at the Winthrop home, and Eliza's parents and younger brother attended along with some intimate friends of the Winthrops. Because Von and his father were so busy with their business, plans for a three-month honeymoon to Europe were put off until that fall, but by then, Eliza and

Von were thrilled to discover they would soon be parents. The trip was delayed again. Then there was the decoration and organization of their recently purchased home just two streets down from Louisa and George, the unexpected death of George Winthrop whose departure involved numerous business and legal transactions, and the much-anticipated birth of their daughter, Ingrid. When the required mourning period was over, and Ingrid was two years old, her parents decided she could be left with her nurse, the governess, and her grandmother as they took the long-delayed honeymoon journey to Europe where they would travel by rail through France and Switzerland and into Germany, then to England before coming home to New York. The honeymoon trip from which they would never return.

***

Gustave Eiffel was well-known for devising the Eiffel Tower in Paris, but his bridge building expertise was not as widely touted. In 1875 he built a bridge over the Birs River in Munchenstein, Switzerland, and it stood strong doing its job for years. At least until June 14, 1891. Repairs had periodically been made to the bridge because seasonal floods disturbed the integrity of the structure and cracks began to appear. A recent spring flood had caused one of the abutments to be destroyed, and a pier sank, causing the bridge to collapse, and the passenger train which traveled over it carrying five-hundred people, to crash. There were nine passenger cars, extra ones having been added, along with an extra engine car, and four of them fell into the Birs River. Almost two-hundred people were injured. Seventy-three were killed. Among the dead were Von George Winthrop and his wife, Eliza.

It was an arduous and lengthy task to untangle the living from the dead, the bodies from the water. The names and identities of the deceased took days to unravel. Louisa read about the tragic train disaster in the newspaper a couple days after it happened. She didn't discover the news about her son and daughter-in-law for three more days and collapsed in a faint upon receiving the telegram. A doctor was called. Her lawyers appeared. A representative of the family was sent to Switzerland, and the decision was made to bury the couple in the *Friedhof Munchenstein*, the closest and largest nearby cemetery. It was best that Louisa not be told it was a Jewish Cemetery. Special permission was sought and obtained, and man and wife were buried there in adjoining plots. A large monument in English was eventually installed, and while Louisa was devastated that her son could not be buried in the Moravian Cemetery plot with his father, she ensured a large memorial to him was placed there with his wife's name engraved in smaller letters near the bottom of the stone. Louisa wore mourning black for years, and only when Ingrid was ten years old, did she decide that dove-gray dresses indicating half-mourning could be ordered. But she saw Eliza in her granddaughter's burnt-umber hair and chestnut eyes and the straightness of her back, and as she grew, the child exhibited her dead mother's distinct individualism. While she treasured Ingrid as the only remnant of her son, she resented the reminder of his wife.

***

Estate and guardianship laws were beyond Louisa Winthrop's understanding, but her personal lawyers and the lawyers for her husband's firm managed it all. Ingrid's permanent and legal home was with her paternal grandmother. Her parents newly purchased and decorated house with all the furniture, her dead father's business interests, the new carriage and horses which had been acquired just before the fated European trip, were all sold. Neither Ingrid nor her grandmother needed to worry about money. The lawyers, who were well educated, well established, well paid, made sure of that. Ingrid and her nurse and the governess moved into the newly renovated second-floor wing of Louisa's house where every comfort was attained. The only problem was the sound of Ingrid's crying and calling out for "Mama" and "Papa" which happened often during the evening and bedtime hours. Luckily the newly decorated wing had large wooden doors which could be closed, and Louisa, while in her own section of the second-floor, was undisturbed.

Eventually the sobbing and crying stopped or at least lessened, and adherence to the nurse and the governess as her substitute parents was established. Ingrid, for a few years, looked forward to that time she and Mama and Papa would meet and play together in Heaven, just as the substitute parents assured her would eventually happen. After a few years, Heaven was almost as forgotten as Mama and Papa, and Ingrid had adjusted to her new life. Of course, she did see her grandmother daily and was counseled that this relative loved her and would always care for her. During the fifteen minutes each afternoon she was in her presence, Ingrid clung to her nurse or governess and would kiss the unfamiliar old woman's cheek only when prompted. The length of time with her grandmother increased little by little, and eventually she spent a full thirty minutes in the front parlor, reciting the stories and poems she had been taught, and, with a surprisingly mature voice, singing the songs she was learning. When it was determined that her nurse was no longer needed, the woman found a position with another family and left, taking with her a carefully written letter of recommendation, a thoughtful set of new handkerchiefs, and a liberal gratuity. Both she and Ingrid sobbed at the farewell. The governess was also sad to see the woman go, partly because it made her aware of her own time limit in the Winthrop household. Louisa Winthrop was busy interviewing tutors for her granddaughter. It was time for Ingrid to stop singing baby songs and playing childish games. She was to begin academic studies: French lessons, (German the following year), piano and voice instruction, and twice monthly etiquette lessons. After all, the child was maturing, and Ingrid was already five years old.

***

There were times Louisa Winthrop felt guilty at her treatment of Ingrid. Her son had received a loving upbringing; she had been caring and maternal to him; she hadn't been aloof in her manner or detached from his physical being as she realized she was towards his daughter. Perhaps if Ingrid had been a boy, someone to carry on the Winthrop name, a remembrance of Von, she would feel a warmth towards this granddaughter. Perhaps if Ingrid did not approximate her mother so boldly, Louisa could have embraced her and held her and rallied a bit in her own sorrow. But there it was. So, Louisa eased her conscience and compensated by making sure this child was well brought up, carefully educated, as polished, proficient, and proper as possible. Luckily, Ingrid took to her studies becoming an adept reader even as a very young child, and her tutors were honest in their substantial praise. Her piano teacher, Mrs. Mildred Clark, was especially laudatory and was delighted when asked to report to Mrs. Winthrop. Inflating Ingrid's talent just a tad, would please Mrs. Winthrop and insure Mrs. Clark's continued position.

"Truly, Mrs. Winthrop, Ingrid is a wonder! At just six-and-a – half years old, she already plays piano quite well with both hands, and is able to accompany herself using her right hand as she sings simple songs. Her sense of rhythm is excellent, and she is capable of sight-reading uncomplicated tunes. That is quite a gift for someone so young."

"I'm pleased to hear this, Mrs. Clark. I wouldn't want to continue if Ingrid didn't show some aptitude." Louisa wanted Mildred Clark to understand she would not spend money and receive nothing in return.

"Ingrid shows much aptitude, and it has only been a bit over a year of lessons. She has almost memorized *Melodie* from Schumann's *Album for the Young*, and in a few months, I believe she can begin the second part of that book as well as work at the simplified, reworked *Inventions* by Bach. Of course, I will not push her as I am aware of her many academic endeavors."

Louisa shook her head, "Push away, Mrs. Clark. Push Ingrid if she has any talent. I have no objection," and she gave a slight, tight smile which accentuated her instructions.

"Very well, Mrs. Winthrop. I am organizing a student recital at the First Episcopalian Church in three months. If you decide that Ingrid should be part of the performance, let me know, and at the next lesson, I will introduce her to a new performance piece."

"Absolutely, Mrs. Clark. Introduce the piece," and Louisa nodded Mildred Clark out of the front parlor. Mrs. Clark left in a servile, unobtrusive manner. She was a slight, timid woman and somewhat daunted by Ingrid's grandmother who was fully aware of her own presence.

For a year, Louisa listened to Ingrid playing the piano and heard her singing as she played. She heard some incorrect notes being played, but was surprised at what she thought might be vocal talent. Ingrid was young, her voice untrained, but the following year, a proper voice instructor was sought. Madame Katherine Duff-Ross was recommended to Louisa and was contacted about lessons. Mrs. Duff-Ross was not slight and timid. She was a proud, haughty woman, and when contacted about teaching a new student at that student's home, was startled. After all, she periodically sang opera with the chorus of the Metropolitan Opera House, had taught at the New York Academy of Music, and was currently a highly regarded professor of voice at the National Conservatory of Music of America. Pupils came to her. She didn't travel to them. But the recompense she was offered was twice the usual amount, and Mrs. Winthrop would send a carriage, a rather nice one, for her travels. She accepted the job and for most of a year, traveled to Louisa Winthrop's home to teach her granddaughter. When asked to attend Mrs. Winthrop in the front parlor after one of the lessons, she was at first angered to be ordered into the front parlor as if she were a common music teacher. It was aggravating. She went anyway.

"Madame Duff-Ross, thank you for coming, and please be seated. I am having tea brought for us. I hope you don't mind staying for a brief conversation. I'd like to discuss Ingrid's progress," and Louisa who knew exactly how to differentiate between the lowly piano teacher and the esteemed voice professional, offered her a chair.

Madame Duff-Ross nodded her acquiescence and arranged herself in the chair across from Louisa. Tea was served and the two women small talked as it was prepared, and then they sipped. Madame Duff-Ross waited for questions. She sat upright, placed her cup and saucer down, and looked into the face of the woman who was sipping her own tea. Louisa placed her cup down and leaned back against her chair. Being in charge, she could be comfortable.

"I would like to know your opinion about my granddaughter's musical ability. Please be forthright in your judgement."

Madame Duff-Ross nodded. "Ingrid has talent, and I am both pleased and surprised at it. She completes her breathing and vocal exercises as if she has done them for years instead of months, and her accurate posture helps. It is too soon to know the extent of her vocal range, but in the simple songs I have given her, she shows a control of dynamics which is remarkable. All in all, she demonstrates ability and talent for one so young."

Louisa nodded. "I know she has played some piano pieces for you. What about that potential?"

"Ingrid is careful in her fingering and shows some ability to sight read. And if you are asking me whether she shows more talent in her vocal abilities or her piano playing, I would say that her voice is yet young, but may be coached and trained, and that is where her talent lies. She should, of course, continue with piano lessons, but I am willing to teach her twice a week if that is what you would like."

Louisa nodded again. "That *is* what I would like. I will reduce her piano lessons to biweekly. You have the same view of her talent as I do," and the two women planned Ingrid's musical future.

Mrs. Clark was surprised and dismayed when informed that she would be required to give Ingrid piano lessons only once every two weeks. She didn't object. She didn't ask for a reason. She simply nodded at the change. She would try to engage another student to make up for the loss.

***

Ingrid was kept busy and involved. She continued her academic tutoring, the language lessons, her piano and voice instruction, her twice monthly etiquette training. At age seven, she began attending St. Thomas Episcopal Sunday Service with her grandmother on those weeks she attended. At age eight, Ingrid spent more time in her grandmother's presence, having luncheon most days with her, putting those etiquette lessons to a test. At age nine, Ingrid and Mrs. Winthrop would have dinner together on Thursdays and Saturdays. By age ten, Ingrid was taking daily luncheon and dinner with her grandmother except for those days her grandmother was otherwise involved with social obligations. Ingrid did not have many friends, but her grandmother ensured she was invited to parties and some dinners with the grandchildren of her friends. Ingrid and her governess were scheduled for daily walks, weather permitting, sometimes to Central Park. In particularly good weather, Ingrid would travel in the carriage with her grandmother who instructed their coachman to drive leisurely up and down Central Park's East Drive where other wealthy friends could be seen doing the same. Louisa would nod in a precise and friendly manner as she passed her friends and instructed Ingrid to sit up straight, keep her gloved hands folded in her lap, and enjoy the view. There were visits to the Metropolitan Museum of Art, the American Museum of Natural History, and a special visit to the Metropolitan Opera House for Ingrid's tenth birthday. Her vocal instructor, Madame Duff-Ross was performing in a minor role in Gounod's *Roméo et Juliette,* an opera sung in French which tested Ingrid's study of that language.

As Ingrid grew, her grandmother became used to her presence, and some of her iciness and sorrow melted. However, there was always the reminder of Eliza in Ingrid's hair and eyes and height. Periodically, she would carefully examine her granddaughter across the dining room table, looking for instances of her son, hoping to catch a ghost of his smile, a shadow of his joy, a fragment of his sparkle. But she was disappointed at only observing Eliza's imprint on the girl. Ingrid would notice Louisa's examination of her and wonder what she had done to bring on such a frown, such a deepening of the lines between her eyes, such a soft, shredded sigh from the lips. Emotions were kept in check, however, and table talk centered on the trivial. Except for that late June Sunday evening when Ingrid was informed that she would be leaving her grandmother's home in the fall to attend the Bennett Academy for Girls, a boarding school located about twenty miles west in an area known as Woodland Park.

***

It was during an early spring afternoon tea with some of her friends that Louisa Winthrop first heard about the school. The women were gathered in the front parlor of Mrs. Crenshaw's house, sipping tea and visiting, and Mrs. Crenshaw mentioned the boarding school that her older granddaughter was attending. Her younger granddaughter would be sent there when she reached the appropriate age, and she spoke about how pleased her son and daughter-in-law were with what they believed was an advanced and modern curriculum.

"The girls have their academics, of course, and besides geography and history and rhetoric, mathematics of some sort is studied. Not that I believe females need to know much, but apparently this study allows for clear and precise thinking, according to my son. The Arts are also part of the curriculum, and each girl studies an instrument and sings in various choirs. Free-hand drawing and sketching is taught. Honestly, my granddaughter, Margaret, does draw the loveliest flowers. She is quite accomplished," and Mrs. Crenshaw inquired if anyone else wanted more tea.

"You know, Louisa," and she poured a bit more of the carefully seeped Oolong into her cup, "why don't you consider sending Ingrid there? I know she is tutored and taught by excellent instructors, but she is ten years old, and don't you think it would help to introduce her to some of the society children who attend? You might look into it. I can give you the information for inquiries if you'd like."

Louisa considered the possibility. She sipped her tea, then placed her cup and saucer down. "Yes, Jacqueline, I think that would be something I might look into. Thank you."

During the following months, there was considerable correspondence between the Winthrop household and the Bennett Academy for Girls. Louisa wrote carefully worded inquiries asking about the availability of a place for Ingrid in the fall term; she wanted a detailed explanation of the curriculum, particularly the music lessons offered; she was curious about the accommodations for the students and desired a specific calendar for the upcoming academic year. She never inquired about the cost. It wasn't important. Her lawyers would see to it. After deciding the school was a suitable option for Ingrid, she sent one of her lawyers to visit and examine the school, and report back. The report was satisfactory. So, on that late June evening, during the dessert of strawberries, she spoke to Ingrid about the plans.

"…and next week you will be fitted for the uniforms all the girls wear." She took another bite of the sweet berry redness, and looked at Ingrid's saucer which remained full. "Why aren't you eating dessert? These are particularly sweet."

Ingrid had no appetite, but she picked up her spoon and ate one of the berries. Then she put the spoon down and looked at her grandmother. "When will I go? How long will I be there? Will I have voice lessons? Why am I going? I won't know anyone, will I? Will I come back here? Where is this school?" and the questions poured out of Ingrid.

"Ingrid, I have looked into this Academy. It is time for you to meet other socially acceptable young women. The fall term is three months, from September to November. You will be home for Thanksgiving. The spring term runs from March to May, and during the months you are here, we will continue your voice lessons. Music and drawing will be taught at the Academy, and you will learn to know the girls there. Many of the girls will have older brothers, and that is certainly a consideration."

"Why? What do you mean?"

"It just is. Never mind. Finish your dessert now. My, it is warm for June," and Louisa was done discussing the matter with her granddaughter.

By the end of August, Ingrid's new uniforms were fitted and completed; her trunk was being packed. When Madame Duff-Ross appeared at the house for her final voice lesson before Bennett Academy took over, Ingrid could not help but tear up at the lesson's end.

"Ingrid," cautioned Madame, "do not shed tears and waste your emotions. Save them for your vocal performances. I will expect you to continue your vocal breathing and exercises and assume you will do your best to outshine other girls at the academy. After all, none have had the training I have given you. I will see you in a few months, and we will resume your lessons. Do you understand?"

"Yes, Madame." And Ingrid held back a sob. She was scared, a bit confused, and sorry to surrender what had been known. When the woman went to the door to leave, Ingrid ran to her and hugged her. To her surprise, she was hugged back. Neither expected the display of emotion. Neither was used to it.

The last task for Ingrid's governess before leaving Mrs. Winthrop's employment was to accompany Ingrid on her carriage ride to the Bennett Academy. She was to ensure Ingrid was deposited in the appropriate room, unpack her trunk, and deliver the instructional letter from Mrs. Winthrop to the headmistress. Once this was completed, she would leave. Ingrid watched as her governess climbed into the carriage to travel back to New York and her next assignment. They waved to each other, and Ingrid stood watching the carriage disappear down the road and around the corner. When there was nothing else to be seen, even when she stood on her tip-toes and squinted her eyes, she turned back to look at the imposing brown brick building where she would spend the next four years. She walked slowly to the door, opened it, and went upstairs to the third floor, to her assigned room, the small space she would share with a stranger at the Bennett Academy for Girls, where an advanced and modern curriculum would be provided. It was perfect for 1899; perfect for the year on the edge of the twentieth century.

***

Louisa Winthrop did not expect to miss her granddaughter. She did not think she would pause her morning newspaper reading to listen for footsteps coming down the stairs or hold her cup of Oolong tea still, waiting for the piano notes which could be faintly heard if the music room door was kept open. She was unaware that she had listened daily for the vocal exercises practiced by Ingrid and was surprised to realize she missed hearing them. She would glance across the dining room table looking to note which color ribbon kept the burnt-umber hair from falling into her granddaughter's face, but seeing no young girl there, would emit a single sigh. Louisa was mindful of the silence in the house, and the stillness which created a restlessness in her, seeming to make the time move more slowly. She continued carriage rides through Central Park's East Drive but did not particularly enjoy them without being able to correct Ingrid's posture or caution her to fold her gloved hands. Visits to museums became boring without a child to monitor. She even missed the attendance of Mrs. Clark and Madame Duff-Ross, and found herself sitting in the front parlor, gazing out the window, looking for a governess and a young girl to return from a daily walk. The months of September, October, and November stretched ponderously in front of her, and for the first time in a long while, she looked forward to the Thanksgiving feast celebration. Despite her reluctance to serve overly sugared desserts, she instructed Cook to make not only the chocolate pudding, but also the cherry angel cake because both were Ingrid's favorites. On the day Ingrid was to return from her first fall term at the Bennett Academy, Louisa woke early after a restless night's sleep, feeling an excitement not observed in years. She waited through the day for the carriage to arrive, finding herself pacing up and down in front of the parlor window, gazing out of it with a tilted head when she heard a close noise.

Finally, the correct carriage pulled into the allotted space, and Ingrid entered the house. Although hugs were not exchanged, her grandmother lowered her cheek so that it could be kissed. She felt an unexpected rush of joy as the youthful lips brushed against her ribbed face.

"Well, Ingrid, are you glad to be back? I have had one of your dresses laid out on your bed. Go upstairs and wash and change and then come down to the dining room. Over dinner you may explain to me the lessons from the past three months. I will see you in one hour," and Louisa fashioned her lips in what she assumed was a smile.

Ingrid did as instructed. One hour later, wearing the dress which was just a bit snug for her growing figure, she joined her grandmother in the dining room where she spoke of her lessons, her newly acquired friends, the teachers, and her anxiousness to return to school in the spring. As she watched and listened to her granddaughter, Louisa had some realizations. Ingrid had become more talkative, quick spirited, much livelier. She had grown taller, and new clothing would be required. But mostly, Louisa realized she welcomed a connection with the girl. She was glad Ingrid was home.

Ingrid did not tell everything to her grandmother. The start of the fall term at Bennett Academy had been difficult. She woke up the first morning in a small bed located in a tiny room, next to a strange girl who had cried herself to sleep. Ingrid did not cry but determined to save her emotions for musical performances as she had been directed. However, she mirrored the depth of her roommate's sorrow. Attempting to comfort then both, Ingrid held the girl's hand as they walked to the dining area where food choices were plentiful and healthy although they lacked the tastiness of Cook's meals. The girls took a few bites and then looked at the faces made by each other and laughed, and the day improved. All the days got better after that first one.

Ingrid found herself happy to be in the company of girls her age. She relished the lessons and absorbed the knowledge imparted by the youthful and progressive female teachers. Rhetoric and elocution, geography and history, and mathematics lessons were tolerable because other girls to whom the concepts were also new, shared in them. Ingrid continued to practice piano and vocal exercises and delighted in singing in a choir. But the best part of being at Bennett Academy was the self-sufficiency and the independence which were encouraged. She was never told what to wear because everyone wore the required uniform. She had choices for her meals although nothing approached the palatableness of remembered meals produced by Cook. Free time was allowed on

Saturday and Sunday afternoons when she could walk the grounds with other girls, indulge in reading a book, or lay in the grass in the yard, something she had never done before. The students could read and discuss and think for themselves, and like the proverbial sponge, Ingrid, soaked up the offered, available, and previously unexplored personal freedom. Emancipation was an edifying sensation.

***

Four years and eight terms later, Ingrid was fourteen years old. When a ceremony was held for students who had completed the Academy's program, her grandmother did not send someone to attend and then accompany Ingrid home. Louisa herself showed up and took a seat in the garden where chairs were arranged so family and friends could see the twenty-two girls being celebrated. Speeches, awards, and honors were distributed, and a recital was given. Violin performances, piano solos, and vocal renderings were delivered, and Ingrid sang a rendition of Duparc's *Chanson triste*. After the tea and cookie reception, the girls gathered to say their good-byes and pledge eternal friendship, although that rarely happened. Most of the girls would attend finishing schools and then be introduced to society. Some knew that within a few years, they would become brides, arrangements having been made by their parents. A smaller number would continue their education elsewhere. Ingrid had an idea about what she wanted to do and hoped to discuss it with her grandmother. The nearly three-hour journey home would be the perfect opportunity.

Once Ingrid's trunk and belongings were stored in the carriage and the two passengers settled inside, Louisa sat back, attempting to get comfortable for the lengthy trip. Ingrid stared out of the carriage window at the buildings and grounds which were no longer her home. She waved to other carriages containing departing friends who waved back. Several modern but noisy and dirty automobiles filled with families and trunks left the schoolgrounds to travel the roads as young boys ran alongside the smoking vehicles delighted at their noise while their mothers fussed at them to get away from the danger. As Ingrid lost sight of the buildings and the grounds, she settled back and thought about what she wanted to discuss with her grandmother. There was a quiet for a time before Louisa spoke.

"I was impressed by your performance today, Ingrid. Your vocal range has shown vast improvement, and you were by far the best one there. Don't let that go to your head. I am simply stating facts. But I did enjoy your song choice. Your French accent shows refinement. Madame Duff-Ross will be pleased," and Louisa cocked her head and nodded to the air.

"Thank you, Grandmother. I'm glad you were able to come today. I know this is a long trip for you, but at least the weather is agreeable. I'm looking forward to studying again with Madame," and Ingrid hesitated, "and I would like to ask you something."

Louisa's eyes were partly shut, but they opened at the comment. She waited for the words.

Ingrid took a breath. She had garnered self-confidence and self-assurance over the past years and had been encouraged to speak carefully and logically, but this was her grandmother. The grandmother who, Ingrid believed, was not particularly fond of her. And she wanted a favor. She knew she was young, but her time at the Bennett Academy had created a taste for schooling. She wanted to continue her education. And she wanted it to be in music. She took another breath.

"Thank you for sending me to Bennett Academy. I believe I've learned many things, and I would like to continue. We never talked about what you expect me to do now, but I'm fourteen and want to continue my education," and Ingrid watched her grandmother's face which was giving nothing away.

"Wonderful! That was exactly what I was thinking, Ingrid, so we have similar thoughts. I want you to be well-rounded and project yourself in a manner that would have pleased both your father and grandfather. I am looking into some special finishing schools for you. There are a number of them in New York which are highly regarded. Of course, the best ones are in Switzerland, but there is no way I could send you there. Certainly not after…" and Louisa stopped, hesitant in sorrow. "Anyway, we shall have some time this summer to…"

"NO!", and Ingrid's tone startled her grandmother into silence. "That is not what I mean. I wish to study music. Perhaps make it a career like Madame Duff-Ross. Maybe even sing opera in one of the New York opera houses. I could study with Madame at the National Conservatory where she teaches. I am old enough to travel there and she could help…"

"What are you thinking, Ingrid? The stage? Opera? No proper New York family would want their son marrying an…*actress*! Music is a wonderful hobby, and while your voice is quite good for your age, there is no way I will allow my granddaughter to set foot on the stage. What are you thinking?"

"I'm thinking that there is no way I will attend a finishing school. This is what I want to do, Grandmother. I have given it much thought, and I know I can be successful. As far as marriage, I am too young to consider that. Look at Madame Duff-Ross. She sings and teaches and is married. Why would being on the stage stop me from doing that one day?"

"Ingrid, that supposition only shows your immaturity and naiveté! Madame Duff-Ross is *not* married. She takes the married title to avoid foolish chatter and gossip. There is much you do not understand, and this conversation is over. Now, my head is beginning to hurt. Please be quiet while I try to rest during this ghastly carriage ride," and Louisa closed her eyes and leaned her head against the back of the seat.

The conversation was over for that day, but Ingrid was determined. Additional discussions were inaugurated by her. She was resolved to wear down her grandmother. She planned and thought. She involved Madame Duff-Ross in her strategy. The summer passed and finally, Louisa was swayed. A compromise was agreed to, and while neither party was totally pleased with it, they were both glad the months of talking and discussing and arguing were over; promises and bargains were made. Ingrid would remain home with her grandmother for one year attending finishing school classes during that time. She would continue her vocal lessons until the fall term of 1904 when she would be fifteen. One year of musical study was agreed to, and if Ingrid did not achieve at the highest of levels, did not follow her grandmother's dictates in dress and fashion and social obligations, did not spend her leisure time in activities her grandmother deemed important, one year would be all that was allowed. After the year of musical study, Louisa would reconsider what to allow. Either Ingrid would do as Louisa wanted: complete an additional year at finishing school and spend the appropriate time at various social activities and meetings searching for a suitable, well-connected and acceptable husband, or continue with musical studies. This was fair. After all, when one year of musical study was done, Ingrid would be sixteen.

***

With all the passion of youth and the fortitude of self-assurance garnered from her time at the Bennett Academy for Girls, Ingrid threw herself into pleasing her grandmother. She attended the finishing school classes and did it with the good grace she knew would please Louisa. She was considerate and pleasant and attentive as her grandmother lectured. She wore what was suggested, ate what was placed before her, attended the dinners and teas required, and did not complain. When the year of finishing school was complete, her year of lessons and schooling began at the National Conservatory, and Ingrid doubled her attempts. To her grandmother's mixture of disappointment and pride, Ingrid was successful at her studies, achieved beyond the required levels and, because Louisa Winthrop kept her word, was allowed to remain a music student. When Madame Duff-Ross was asked to teach at the newly opened Institute of Musical Arts, Ingrid transferred there for her studies. It turned out to be a productive move. A new opera company, the Manhattan Opera Company, was created in 1906, and it advertised for additional singers to perform in the chorus and minor roles. Madame Duff-Ross spoke excitedly to Ingrid about the opportunity.

"It sounds wonderful, Madame, but my grandmother…"

"I believe I will invite your grandmother to join me for tea tomorrow where we can discuss it. It is a grand opportunity for you to put your years of hard work to use, and of course, I will accompany you to the audition next week. Now, let's decide which arias you should prepare for it." The teacher went to the piano to shuffle through the music sheets, Ingrid peering over her shoulder.

***

The New York opera world of the early twentieth century held all the intrigue and drama of any actual opera produced during that time. The rivalry between Oscar Hammerstein's newly formed Manhattan Opera Company and his nemesis, Heinrich Conried's Metropolitan Opera House, was fodder for whispers and rumors. The opening night of the Manhattan Opera Company boasted Belinni's *I Puritani* with Alessandro Bonci singing the title role, and the traffic jam around the theater on opening night made the newspapers' headlines the following day. Hammerstein, a Berlin born, cigar-smoking celebrity, knew what to do and who to obtain for the operas he produced. Every youthful soprano, alto, tenor, and baritone in the city was anxious to be involved in the company, even if only as chorus members. Minor roles were given to those singers, and Ingrid was as anxious as anyone else to get her delicate foot in that door. Madame Duff-Ross worked her magic with Louisa Winthrop, and she accompanied Ingrid to the audition the following week. Madame was delighted to report back to Louisa that her star pupil, Louisa's granddaughter, was the newest member of the Manhattan Opera House chorus. Louisa nodded her head in reluctant agreement. Ingrid was breathless with joy.

And busy. Besides her own practicing and continued vocal studies, the classes she was taking in Italian and *History of the Opera,* and voice lessons to three girls who adored their young and spirited teacher, Ingrid now added practices and rehearsals at the Manhattan Opera House. Louisa was worried about all this activity. Her granddaughter was already eighteen, and she had not shown interest in marriage. There had been some young men callers, but Ingrid did not encourage them.

"Did you enjoy the dinner with the Belmonts?" asked Louisa after one society event. "I thought their son, Jeffery, was beautifully attentive to you, and I wouldn't be surprised if he called on us soon."

Ingrid shrugged. She was looking over the vocal score of the new opera and was not interested in a review of the previous evening. When her grandmother cleared her throat for the third time, she looked up to answer.

"The dinner was splendid, Grandmother, but it was a very late evening, and frankly, Jeffery is rather boring. Please don't think I will be married off to someone like that. I doubt he will call because I discouraged him. I told him I was terribly busy with my studies and work. But don't worry, I was cordial."

"Ingrid! This is not the first time you have done that. You ignored Clarence Coster at the last church social, and I heard from Edward Richards' great-aunt that you turned down his invitation for the charity ball to be held next month. How will you ever find a husband if you refuse to be sociable? Marriage is a duty and responsibility for a young woman like you, and I am trying to assist in this effort. What have you to say for yourself?"

Placing the score down on the settee beside her, Ingrid sighed and stared out the window. Marriage was not on her mind. She was anxious about what she saw as her new profession, and knew her grandmother saw it as a hobby…a brief and foolish interlude before settling down to the life of a society wife. She looked at Louisa's face and smiled, forgiving her.

"I am sure there will be someone for me, and I will not think marriage a duty and responsibility then. You see, Grandmother, I must feel a connection, a special connection with the person I marry. I don't know what that will be, but when it occurs, I will recognize it; I'll understand it. There must be a feeling, a reaction, a sensibility to this connection. I will not endure the dullness and tediousness I do now when talking to Jeffery or being stuck at a table with Clarence or Edward, or any of the other men you would have me marry. I will have a distinct feeling. Then I will know."

Louisa sniffed her disgust. "A connection? Perhaps you are waiting for the hair on your arms to stand up, or your heart to flutter," she disclosed. "Some type of nonsensical romantic sensation which you will consider a sign."

Ingrid nodded. "Actually, that sounds correct. There will be a sign of some sort. Something to let me know this is the one, this is right. I will have a connection to the man. Perhaps a tingly feeling at the nape of my neck, or a quick breath. Something. And in the meanwhile, I will continue to concentrate on my music," and Ingrid took her score, walked over to her grandmother and leaned down to kiss her forehead. "I'll know, Grandmother."

"Humph!" answered Louisa. She glared at the trees in the front of the house.

What could be done? Louisa was growing older. She watched as her friends' grandchildren married and created great-grandchildren, and she acknowledged the jealousy she felt in her soul. Not that she would allow anyone to know that, but she felt she had missed out on so much when her own son died at such a young age. There were times she felt both angry and depressed. And yet, she admired Ingrid's talent and enjoyed hearing her voice. Often, without Ingrid knowing, she attended the Manhattan Opera House to hear her sing and watch her perform. She watched her move on the stage, confident that Ingrid's impressive soprano was superior to anyone else's. Through the years, Louisa had come to secretly adore this granddaughter who was independent and unafraid, talented and accomplished, and, unfortunately, still unmarried.

***

Oscar Hammerstein knew how to draw a crowd. Australia's Nellie Melba sang the role of Mimi in *La boheme* to tremendous acclaim. Ingrid sang in the chorus. Scottish born Mary Garden sang the title role in *Louise*, and Ingrid acted as a resident of Paris, singing with the chorus. Perhaps Mary Garden's greatest triumph was in the American premiere of Debussy's *Pelle`as et Me`lisande*. It was Ingrid's also. She sang the role of Yniola, young son to Golaud, and on the stage by herself, dressed as a youth, a dark boyish wig covering her hair, her soprano voice climbed to the heights of the Manhattan Opera House, and it was difficult to determine whether Madame Duff-Ross, Louisa Winthrop, or Ingrid herself was more pleased. The first performance was breathtaking, and Ingrid became more at ease with each additional rendition. After her third enactment, when she returned to the dressing room, a lush arrangement of dahlias and roses intermixed with celosia and mixed foliage tumbling out of a stone container, was left for Ingrid. She assumed her music teacher or grandmother sent the flowers to her, but they had not. On the attached card the message declared: *You were amazing tonight as you are every night*, and there was no signature. Someone was watching her.

The flowers came for her every time she performed. They were always different and carefully chosen. Some were small, delicate bouquets and others large and flowing arrangements. The attached complimentary cards were never signed, and while she pondered about the sender, Ingrid remained too busy to delve into the mystery. She was engaged with learning roles and practicing them. Ingrid shared the role of Giulietta in Offenbach's *Tales of Hoffmann,* with another young woman in the company. She, at first, feared that singing the role of a courtesan would shock her grandmother, who was, by this time, usually present at most of her performances. But Louisa accepted the fantasy role and praised Ingrid's voice, and the flowers which appeared each time she sang continued to fill the shared dressing room. Ingrid was teased by many of the other singers not receiving the same obviously expensive floral tributes. Their teasing masked jealousy.

Roles continued to be given to Ingrid, and she worked diligently at the tasks assigned her. She was so busy with the opera house through the years of 1908 and 1909, that she had to end her studies at the Institute of Musical Arts and curtail her teaching of the young vocal students. She rehearsed and practiced, and operatic parts, while minor, continued to be offered to her. And the flower bouquets continued to show up, each accompanied by a cryptic note.

***

It was the latter part of March, 1909, and the opera *Salome* staring Mary Garden was coming to the end of its run. It had certainly been a successful one. Also, a scandalous one. Mary Garden's performance of the *dance of the seven veils* had been decried by New York clergymen who called both the opera and the dance "shameful" and "disgraceful" and "wicked" although none of them had actually seen it. Oscar Hammerstein was grateful for their remarks. He chomped on his cigar and raked in the cash from the sold-out performances. Ingrid had been given the role of the female slave who sang a few lines.

She was also part of the royal guests and chorus. She was exhausted from her work, and when the company was due to have a break in a couple weeks, she looked forward to a rest. The evening's performance had been another sold-out one, and she had stayed behind to take her turn sorting out and hanging up costumes. She was late leaving the theater but aware her grandmother was waiting for her. They would ride home in the carriage together. Louise often attended the opera and waited for Ingrid on her late evenings, carefully protecting the reputation of her unmarried granddaughter.

As Ingrid walked down the long hallway behind the stage where the dressing rooms and offices were located, she heard talking and thought she recognized her grandmother's voice. She buttoned the top buttons of her coat and finished pulling on her long gloves. As she came closer to the voices, she knew one of them was Louisa's. She was startled to see her grandmother seated at the small round table which was kept just inside the outer door leading to the carriage, noting that she was not alone. There was a man seated with her, and as Ingrid came closer, she heard her grandmother say, "Here she is now."

The man who was seated at the same table, rose as Ingrid walked towards them. He was not young but was not as old as her grandmother. There was gray in his still mostly brown hair. He was tall and maintained a perfectly straight posture. A fashionable opera cloak was thrown around his shoulders, and his top hat rested on the table. Ingrid looked into his face which contained lines about the eyes. She was uncertain of their color although they were lighter than her own brown ones. A perplexed crease appeared at her forehead. She did not know this person.

Her grandmother gave a slight smile as Ingrid stopped in front of the table. In a voice filled with pride and a bit louder than her usual tone, Louisa Winthrop spoke.

"This is my granddaughter, Miss Ingrid Winthrop. Ingrid, this is Mr. Fredrick Vogel who is anxious to make your acquaintance."

Ingrid held out her gloved hand to shake the man's and spoke. "How do you do, Mr. Vogel?"

Fredrick Vogel took Ingrid's gloved hand in his, and in the classic European manner, bent towards it as he brought it to his lips and said, "*Enchanté*."

Then he raised his eyes, which Ingrid could now tell were hazel, met her chestnut-colored ones, held them with his gaze, and in a muted tone with just the hint of an accent said, "I hope you enjoyed the flowers."

There was a sudden tingly feeling at the nape of Ingrid Winthrop's neck.

Three

Fredrick Vogel

For over one thousand years from Charlemagne to Napoleon, the Holy Roman Empire, made up of dozens and dozens of individual states and countries and principalities, borders fluctuating due to small wars and disagreements, hung together over much of the central European continent. There was a bit of chaos until 1871 when Wilhelm I, King of Prussia, was crowned Emperor of the newly created German Empire. He, assisted by Otto von Bismarck, made Berlin the capital city, modernized Germany, and brought the Empire to international prominence. Modernization comes with its difficulties. When the bank depression known as the Panic of 1873 occurred, Germany's bourgeoning middle class, many of whom had received generous loans to support their businesses, became both alarmed and intimidated. They sought a way out of debt, a path to solvency, a new start. This was the situation Ernst and Agatha Vogel, small business owners whose shop in Berlin offered cheeses and sausages, found themselves. The Vogels sold what they could, gathered all available money, bid farewell to a select few, and left for what they hoped was a way out of debt, a path to solvency, a new start. They boarded a ship and sailed for America taking their ten-year old son, Fredrick, with them.

The journey across the Atlantic was miserable for Ernst and Agatha, partly because violent storms and winds made it a longer trek. The voyage was just over two months. Ernst was sea-sick for the first month and then spent the next month caring for Agatha who almost died when she miscarried the child she didn't know she was bringing with her. She would never be the same, and her son would never have a sibling, but Fredrick was unaware of it all. While his parents were sick and miserable, he adjusted to the rocking and moving of the ship, becoming a leader to other America-bound children with whom he ran and played games, and when the ship finally docked at the Castle Garden depot at Manhattan's edge, the boy could barely contain his excitement. His parents were relieved, and as Ernst used his basic knowledge of English to determine what was happening, his wife, Agatha, held tightly to Fredrick's hand and wiped the tears away from her face. She cried for many reasons.

Ernst Vogel wrested his family to the forefront of the crowd of immigrants in an attempt to expedite the lengthy and torturous required inspections, evaluations, and probing through which everyone was compelled. There was the initial health inspection, the baggage and customs inspection, a second and more thorough health examination, registration of papers, a trip to the baggage delivery line so their possessions could eventually be delivered to their residence, and then a confusing meeting with the exchange brokers who would take the silver they had in exchange for the strange-looking American currency. At last, the Vogels were sent to a large rotunda-shaped room where eventually Ernst found his cousin, Elias Wagner, who would take them to his home. When he found Elias, he threw his arms around the cousin he hadn't seen since boyhood and could not help the tears which he didn't bother to wipe away. Agatha was drained and beyond tears, while Fredrick's enthusiasm for adventure and travel had dissipated after the second health inspection. It would take another two hours to travel from the Castle Garden depot to the New York Community of Yorkville where Elias and his wife, Carla, lived with their two boys. Carla had the foresight to send sandwiches for the travelers, and as they climbed onto Elias' wagon, they were grateful for the prepared food and the jars of water. Fredrick gobbled part of a sandwich before falling asleep in the back. He dreamed that the rocking and moving of the wagon was the sway and lull of the large ship where he had spent the last two months. Exhausted by the extended and tedious trip, he didn't walk into his new home, but was carried by his father and placed on the floor in the blanket which would suffice for his bed. He did not wake up until late afternoon the following day.

The months the Vogels spent with the Wagners were both instructive and baffling. The Upper East Side of Manhattan in New York was a haven for immigrants from Germany. But additional languages such as Czechoslovakian and Hungarian could be heard, and although German was the dominant language, English was almost as prevalent. Breweries and small shops selling German-made foods and goods could be found all along 86th Street, and construction of additional shops and buildings was ongoing. Newly planned and much anticipated elevated train lines which would eventually run along the lengths of Second and then Third Avenues, were cause for excitement and discussion. While Ernst and Fredrick prattled on about the building and the changes happening around them, Agatha paid little attention to goings-on outside of the small apartment. Her time was consumed with organizing and cleaning and attempting to get along with Carla, the American wife of Elias. But her husband and son remained filled with elation, eagerness, and exhilaration at the sights and experiences of this new life.

Ernst wasted no time in obtaining a job. Actually, more than one. He found work in a brewery during the day and worked part of each night as a member of a city construction crew, carrying, stacking, and organizing the building materials to be used for the daily construction of the new elevated trains. Both jobs involved a physical perseverance which the shopkeeper was unused to, but he didn't care since he was earning more money than he ever had in Berlin. He gave a fair part of his earnings to his cousin while he and his family lived with them but was also able to keep a decent amount for himself. He had plans. As Ernst walked along the streets, he noted the additional buildings which were being constructed, and he wanted to move his son and wife into one of them as soon as possible. He insisted his son attend public school with his cousins where the reading and writing of English was taught. Fredrick did not complain. He caught on quickly to the studies, easing into the schoolwork with his native intelligence. Despite the many small frays he faced as the "new kid", Fredrick actually enjoyed school. He didn't back down from the clashes and won as many as he lost. Soon another young immigrant boy came to take his place in the classroom, and Fredrick, changing positions, became the teaser rather than the teased. Survival of the fittest. Both Ernst and Fredrick adapted to their new life, learning the strange language and curious customs of New York. Because they accepted and even welcomed these changes, their time as foreigners eased; their assimilation was straightforward. This was not the case with Agatha.

The voyage to the United States was difficult for her in many ways. It wasn't just the sea-sickness she felt or the horrendous miscarriage or the unknown quality of the adventures she and her family would undertake. Agatha missed her home to such an extent that she would wake up nightly sobbing, having dreamed about not only family and friends left behind, but also the familiar belongings which were gone. She missed her pots and pans, especially the large cast-iron one she used to fry meat, the one her mother and grandmother had used. It had been sold. She missed the blanket she and Ernst had slept under the entire time they had been married. The blanket was from her best friend, Marta, gifted to the Vogels for their wedding. Before leaving, Agatha gave the blanket back to Marta, asking her to remember their friendship; to pray for their safety and success. The Vogels sold the upright piano, Agatha's favorite wedding gift. It just fit in their small parlor when she and Ernst settled in their Berlin home, and the instrument often figured in her dreams. She could hear the tones; she saw the lowest C key which sometimes stuck; she felt the smooth top which she had dusted daily. She heard Fredrick practicing the musical pieces she taught him. All in her dreams, of course. She dreamed about walking the streets in Berlin with her husband and small son, visiting the neighbors during the Christmas holiday, sharing in the *Glühwein mit Schuss,* the only time she allowed herself to indulge in brandied wine. In her dreams, she could taste the drink, could smell the roasting duck, could see the fire throwing small sparks and warming the parlor, could hear the song, *Alle Jahre wieder,* which was her favorite of the season. In her dreams Agatha visited the small church cemetery where her parents and younger sister were buried, sold the cheese and smoked meats in the small shop she and her husband ran, swept the back steps where Fredrick would sit with his friend, Jan, as they talked and laughed and ate the cheese Agatha fed them. All gone now. No cemetery, no piano, no Jan, no cheese. Just this strange land and these relatives of Ernst's, and the woman, Carla, with whom she did not get along. Her husband was gone working much of the time, and Fredrick was busy at school or playing with friends or his cousins, those two boys who were rude and American. Agatha was unhappy.

She gained a small bit of her happiness back when after a year, Ernst had saved enough for the family to rent their own small apartment. It was cramped and on the top floor of the tenement building three streets away from the cousins. Due to the many steep stairs she had to climb, Agatha rarely left their home. But there were advantages to living on the top floor. Because they were so close to the rooftop, she could hang wet clothes outside when the weather allowed, sit on a small wobbly old chair to look out over the buildings, peek up at the sky and around the city when smoke from nearby factories allowed it. She breathed in the high air which offered only a hint of horse droppings, sausage makings, and the multitude of odors from other apartments which were more pervasive in the apartment itself due to the fact that the one window was nailed shut and the other one faced a horse stable. Agatha was happiest on the roof. She had made no real friends in this unfamiliar land but was glad to be away from Carla and her rude boys, visiting them only when holidays were celebrated and she accompanied her husband and son to their house. She assumed Carla was just as happy to see her leave. Two queen bees in a hive and such, according to Ernst.

After a couple more years working both a day and a night job, Ernst had some good fortune. He heard of a new opportunity for a job with the Steinway Pianoforte Company, recently relocated in a vast, rural section of Queens known as *Astoria*. He traveled there, necessarily taking a day off from his job, on the chance of being hired. Being from Germany was an advantage, perhaps even a requirement. Running into William Steinway, son of Heinrich Steinway and builder of the newly constructed Steinway Village in Astoria was pure luck. Of course, Ernst did not know who the older gentleman was as he found himself walking with him along the rural acreage which was being transformed into a town, but they fell into a conversation, a German language one. The older gentleman asked about Ernst's business in the compound, and listened to his dreams about a better life, a new job.

"Ja, ich komne aus Berlin. Meine Familie und ich kamen vier Jahren hierher," answered Ernst to the question asked about his roots.

"Ah, dann wollen Sie hier nicht nur arbeiten sondren hier leben. Kommen. Ich stelle Sie meinem Gebaudemanager vor," and Mr. Steinway took Ernst to the manager of his town where he completed the papers, taking a job as *Arbeiter*, general worker, in the Steinway factory.

In filling out the papers, Ernst was required to swear that he would disavow any interest, support, or connection with a workers' union of any kind. That was not a hardship. Living in the factory town created by Steinway was a small price to pay when there was access to a newly built rowhouse, stores, a public school, a library, a Reformed Church, a firehouse, and a park. Ernst agreed to the stipulations demanded. He wanted his part of this American dream, even if that meant the Vogel family was owned fully and completely by the Steinway Company. He went home that evening and told Agatha about his new job, about his luck in America. They began to organize the few belongings they possessed, placing the clothing and kitchen wares into boxes and bags, and, in the spirit of celebration, broke out the small bottle of *Kirschwisser* kept for special occasions. Agatha did not object when Ernst poured them both a second glass.

The move was a reassuring one for the Vogels, especially Agatha who was comforted to be in the company of other German-speaking immigrants and relieved to not have to learn the harsh and impossible English language with which her husband and son apparently had little trouble. She cleaned the two-story red-bricked rowhouse with a joyful vengeance each day, scrubbing and polishing the old furniture and new floors until it was challenging to determine which was new and which was old. She walked to the Reformed Church daily before visiting the village's store to purchase needed foodstuffs and prayed a thankful prayer to the Reformed Church God that her family was safe and in their own home. Agatha began to find ways to save a small bit of money each month with the idea that eventually she would be able to save enough to purchase one of the used Steinway upright pianos for their small parlor. The three-hundred-dollar price tag did not seem so prohibitive in this grand new world. And when, ten years later, she died of the diphtheria which was raging in parts of New York, she had saved over half that amount. Her husband, who survived his bout with the disease, used part of it for a lovely headstone for her grave to which his name would, sooner than anyone expected, be added.

***

While his parents struggled with the multitude of everyday problems facing new immigrants, Fredrick accepted and learned from them. He had a natural ability to lead and a quickness of thought which earned him the admiration of his older American cousins despite the differences in their ages. Fredrick was unafraid to roam not just his neighborhood, but surrounding ones, discovering which streets were safest and which ones to avoid at all costs. From East 72nd to North 96th; from Third Avenue to the East River, Fredrick traveled the community rarely with other schoolfriends, sometimes with his cousins, often by himself. He visited Central Park where the trees and greenery reminded him of his German homeland, walked along Fifth Avenue admiring the architecture of the many fine buildings, went to the menagerie which was located in Lower Manhattan and would eventually turn into Central Park Zoo. Fredrick stared at the animals there but watched the visiting throngs of humans just as often. He enjoyed listening to the various accents and languages, picking up useful bits of information from his wanderings, watching people at work and at play. He noted the manners and dress of the people, particularly the men, establishing which ones were gentlemen, which ones were fakes, keeping the information locked away, certain he would have a use for it. The American education and the streetwise edification he received was useful to him as he rapidly became the thing with which his parents, in particular his mother, grappled: a New Yorker, an American.

Fredrick did not skip school like his older cousins often did. He was happy to attend daily, and usually went early once he discovered he could sneak into the red-brick building through the back door where the janitor, the hired man who stoked the coal furnace in winter and refilled supplies for the teachers who were responsible for cleaning their own classrooms, entered before the sun came up. Fredrick wandered around quietly viewing the rooms, finding secret hiding places, and, best of all, playing the old upright Aeolian Company piano which was stored in a small room in the school basement. The piano needed tuning; the top octave and the last few bass keys did not work, but most of the middle did. There was a tinny sound when played, but Fredrick did not mind.

When he first came upon the instrument he stood and played as quietly as possible. He had to stand because there was no bench or chair for him. He was worried that the janitor would hear and kick him out, but that did not happen. One morning, after about a month of periodically sneaking into the school to wander and to play the piano, he saw an old chair had been placed directly in front of middle *C*, and he took this as tacit permission to continue his musical performances. He had no sheet music to read since his mother could not bring any with them, so he tried to remember the pieces he had practiced in Germany in the parlor of their home under the guidance of his mother. Sometimes he picked out hymns he remembered singing, and sometimes he made up his own tunes. When his years of education at the school were completed and he would no longer spend a couple mornings alone in the dark basement, he sought out the janitor. Upon finding him, he stood facing the man. Fredrick didn't know what to say, and the janitor was also silent. The two looked at each other, smiled, and nodded heads. It was enough.

Fredrick completed his schooling in the New York public school system before the move to Astoria. When the family moved to Steinway Village, he, at age fourteen and encouraged by his father, began working with two other boys at the workshop of Hans, one of the master craftsmen, who taught them all the intricacies of choosing the proper wood, the laminating, bending, flexing, gluing, and general shaping of it to the exacting proportions which would create the esteemed Steinway pianoforte. Before all this could be mastered, the assistants needed to learn which woods were the most pliable yet strongest; the most robust yet flexible. It was necessary to know the differences between beech and maple and spruce and to understand which to use for various parts and why. They needed to identify the various components of the instrument: the lid, the frame, the soundboard, the ribs, the rods, the pedals, the damper. It helped that because he had learned to play the piano while a child in Germany, Fredrick was familiar with a piano's features. It also helped that Hans was a kindly man, a natural teacher, and rarely physically chastised his assistants for their errors. At fourteen, Fredrick was the largest of the boys, nearly six-feet tall and his developing muscles were clearly visible under his somewhat ragged clothing. He was a quicker learner than were his companions, able to read and write both German and English with competent fluency, and was recognized by Hans as a diligent young worker who could advance in the business. A couple years later, when asked to recommend one of his assistants for a position delivering the splendidly elegant grand pianos, Hans sent Fredrick.

Delivery of the instruments was not just a physical job. It required the skills of reasoning and assessing and judging. When one of the grand pianos was moved to another location, the dismantling and wrapping and packing had to be done with extreme care. The top, the pedal lyre, the legs were removed and packed methodically. The stringed instrument itself was carefully wrapped and settled onto a board using a piano tilter and various handcarts, but it was necessary to know where to place the tools and how and when to physically carry the awkwardly heavy and precious instrument. For a time, Fredrick worked as one of the three movers on a team of four men. Eventually because he was able to not only determine how to turn and move and could instruct the others in doing so, but also because he could read the street signs and building names and invoices, he became the guide and leader of his own group. His adeptness in reading English was handy, and Fredrick's quiet leadership and friendliness belied his youth.

New York City in the latter part of the nineteenth century prided itself on the array of cultural and educational opportunities offered to both inhabitants and visitors crowding the streets of the city. Concerts, musicals, dramas of all sorts were available in the many theaters and halls. The Steinway organization opened their own concert hall in 1866, but additional halls and theaters continued to spring up in the decades following. There was Thalia Theatre offering German plays, Madison Square Garden and Carnegie Hall in the last decade of the century giving concerts and musical entertainment of various kinds. The Metropolitan Opera House and the New York Philharmonic were older, popular institutions. Music schools abounded from the Brooklyn Academy of Music, to the National Conservatory of Music of America, to the New York Academy of Music. Music of all varieties was heard from both small and large venues, and all these places, as well as individuals including New York's Four Hundred and the nouveau riche who yearned to be in that number, wanted only the best of musical instruments. They wanted a Steinway pianoforte. Fredrick Vogel, leading his team of men, delivered the instruments to them, creating a name for himself in the process.

Fredrick took to dressing in an older but serviceable suitcoat when his team delivered the instruments. He decided that looking "professorish" as he called it, would help with his youthful demeanor and make the delivery special. He used his lunchbreak at the factory to practice at the pianos which were stored at various places in the buildings. He prepared and adjusted his speech at home, attempting to modulate his tones, ridding himself of any German or New York accent as much as possible. He spoke clearly and expertly to the individuals accepting the expensive instruments and oversaw the delivery, ensuring it was done correctly. Once the piano parts were moved into place and the instrument was put together, Fredrick would produce a perfectly clean, new, soft cloth, and wipe the piano gently himself. He would adjust the bench, and with everyone watching him, would sit, and just as if he were a concert pianist, would play one of the two pieces he had practiced to perfection: either the first movement of Beethoven's *Moonlight Sonata,* or Johann Bach's *Prelude 1 in C Major*. Both pieces were decidedly showy but surprisingly uncomplicated, and Fredrick was a showman. When finished, he would wipe the bench clean, fold the cloth and lay it back on the bench. He bowed to the polite applause surrounding him, his team being part of the show, presented the invoice to the new owner of the Steinway piano, and pronounced in the painstakingly renovated tones he had practiced, "Mr. Steinway and our entire team hope you will treasure the many years of exquisite music played on this fine and noble instrument." With a motion to the team to leave, he would wait to answer any questions asked of him, shake hands, and bow slightly in an old-fashioned European manner which never failed to impress. Soon, word of Fredrick's delivery method got back to Willian Steinway who called him into his office.

It was 1883; Fredrick was twenty years old, and he was worried. He had just returned from a delivery wearing his worn but serviceable suitcoat as he entered the building which housed William Steinway's office. He was told to wait until Mr. Steinway called for him, and he stood nervously with his cap in his hand, moving from one foot to the other. He feared being fired. How would he face his parents? What job would he be able to do? He felt his heart pound in his chest and wondered if he, even at his young age, was having an attack of some sort. When he was ushered into Mr. Steinway's office he moved slowly as if in a dream, and stood before the desk of this man whose village he had lived in with his parents for the past six years. He waited for the pronouncement.

William Steinway looked up at the young man standing before him. He took in his neatly combed hair and steady hazel eyes. The old suitcoat Fredrick wore did not fit him well, and his shoes were polished but worn. Mr. Steinway was sure that if he were to ask this man to turn over his shoes, there would be holes in the bottom. He waited a full minute and said nothing. Then he spoke.

"Be seated, Mr. Vogel. I will come to the point. Your method of delivery of the Steinway pianos has come to my attention. I understand that after they are delivered and reassembled, you wipe off the instrument, play a piece, and make a speech. Is this correct?"

"Yes, Sir, it is."

Mr. Steinway waited and nodded. "And this was your idea?"

"Yes, Sir, it was."

"Explain why you do this."

Fredrick thought carefully. Why *did* he do it? He wasn't sure he could explain himself. The idea seemed appropriate at the time but perhaps it wasn't. Perhaps it was silly or unbusinesslike. He took a deep breath and looked at the man seated across from him. He stood up before him and began to talk.

"It seems to me that when such a beautiful instrument is delivered, when a person puts out a great amount of money for it, there should be a ceremony with the delivery. To set the instrument up and leave it seems unfitting when so much work had gone into it. I have been here, Mr. Steinway, at your company for six years, since I was fourteen, and I have worked at various departments and know the time and effort and craftsmanship which go into producing these pianos. I want to do a service to the people who work here, and if I could, I would introduce each one who worked on their instrument to the new owner of these pianos. I am not saying this because I think I am in trouble or have done something wrong, although if I have, I apologize, but I am sincere. My family and I belong to this village: your village. I have watched my father work for years becoming a craftsman. My mother is proud of the house we live in and cleans and cares for it. Craftsmanship and care are important, and I want to provide the new owners of these instruments with the assurance that they have purchased something which because of the craftsmanship and care put into it, will last for decades and which will bring them and those who hear it joy. If I have made a mistake, again, I apologize," and Fredrick stopped, fearing he had said too much. Fearing he had not said enough. Fearing he had said the wrong things. He waited in fear.

"Sit down, Fredrick. You have not done anything wrong. In fact, you have done something right. Do you remember delivering the grand piano to the house of Clement Moore on East 34th Street?"

"Yes, I remember."

"Mr. Moore was impressed with your delivery and has since ordered an additional grand piano to be delivered to his Chelsea Estate in the countryside of west Manhattan. He has asked for your team to complete the delivery when the piano is finished. Apparently, there are additional clients who were also impressed, and they recommended their friends purchase a Steinway piano, assuring them that our delivery system is meritorious. I promised those who have ordered new instruments that you and your team will complete the delivery once they are available. So, no, you have not done anything wrong. In fact, I am impressed with your keen judgement and have decided to send you to the office of Mr. Nahum Stetson. He is the manager of the warehouse and has been put in charge of sales and marketing for the company. He is organizing and training a team of salesmen who will travel throughout the United States to take orders for our instruments. I believe you will be a great addition to the team, and he is expecting to speak with you today. Do you think you can handle the job?"

Fredrick was astounded. And relieved. In fact, he had so many feelings he could barely think. But he maintained his composure and said, "Mr. Steinway, I know I can. Thank you for this opportunity."

William Steinway nodded his head and the two men stood up to shake hands. The older man looked over Fredrick once again.

"The suit you are wearing…is that the only one you own?"

"Yes, it is. I only wear it for the deliveries."

William Steinway took a sheet of paper from his desk and wrote something on it. He handed it to Fredrick and said, "This is my tailor, Felix Weber. He is at the Lord and Taylor's building at Broadway and 20th Street. Go there to the Men's Clothing Department and see him. He will make you a fitting suit for the new work you will do, and I will inform him that the bill is to be sent to me. He will outfit you with a shirt and tie and new shoes too. You should look good for your new job."

Fredrick didn't know what to say. "Mr. Steinway, this is very generous, but I can't accept this. I…"

"Nonsense. This is one outfit. The next one you will buy yourself. I have a feeling you will be able to afford to do that. Now, Mr. Stetson is waiting. Go and talk to him."

The two men shook hands once again and Fredrick went to the office one floor below to speak about his new assignment. He and

Mr. Stetson came to an agreement, and within a few months, Fredrick, wearing his new bespoke suit and the shoes with no holes in the bottom, gifts from William Steinway, was one of the team of elite salesmen who sold the carefully crafted and expensive Steinway pianos throughout the United States. Mr. Steinway was right. Fredrick had no difficulty purchasing additional suits and clothing and shoes. In fact, he became a dedicated client to Felix Weber, Lord and Taylor's best and most esteemed men's tailor.

***

The following years were productive and profitable for Fredrick. He traveled to Boston, Philadelphia, and Chicago, learning about those cities, staying in various hotels, eating at acclaimed restaurants. He stayed with his parents in their Steinway Village rowhouse when he was in New York, but after some time, Mr. Stetson decided that Fredrick's talents would best serve the Steinway Company if he remained in New York City, working at the Steinway Showrooms. Because he needed to be close to the Showroom, Fredrick found another salesman who was willing to sublet part of a miniscule apartment on East 14th Street for a reasonably low cost. In this way, Fredrick was near his job, able to take on additional work opportunities, and in a position to save some extra pay. He made bi-monthly visits to his parents who were aging. Agatha Vogel died when Fredrick was twenty-four, and his weakened and saddened father lasted only another year. By his twenty-sixth birthday, Fredrick was alone in New York: an orphan by consequence, an American by chance, and, at age twenty-seven, a married man by choice.

***

Fredrick Vogel and Edith Caroline Peters met at the Steinway Showroom on East 14th Street where her father, John Peters, brought his daughter to choose a grand piano as a present for her twentieth birthday. Mr. Peters claimed a distant family connection to New York's wealthy, cultured, and socially prominent Richard Peters' family although the surname they shared was a common one, and the two men had never met. John Peters had earned his new wealth through speculating on railroads, banking, and iron mills, popular but risky and slightly illicit ventures. He had proven the adage that *it is better to be born lucky than rich,* and with his assets he could easily afford the lovely grand piano Edith chose. However, his luck had not held in obtaining a substantially prestigious society marriage for Edith. He attempted to arrange, through dances and dinners given at his fashionable new mansion, proper introductions for her, but the right people never showed due in part to the gossip surrounding him and his financial dealings. Hopes for entry into New York's high society were fading. Besides, he feared discovery. John Peters, which was not even his real name, was cognizant of his checkered background; of his poverty-stricken Hell's Kitchen beginnings; of the mother and siblings he left there to fend for themselves; of his often illegal although profitable activities; of his secret, undesirable, criminal associations. When he observed an immediate connection between the two young people at the Steinway Showroom, he took note. And when Fredrick made many more additional visits to the Peters' home to ostensibly check on the piano's suitability and fitness than was necessary, Mr. Peters yielded acknowledgement and granted permission for Edith and Fredrick to court. A well-spoken, fashionably dressed, prosperous business man was an acceptable husband for his daughter who had recently turned twenty and had no other prospects. At least none as substantial, successful, and socially privileged as Fredrick seemed to be.

The wedding was not as opulent as Mr. Peters would have wanted. His wife and daughter prevailed upon him to downplay their dubious wealth and have a wedding which displayed *understated decency* as Mrs. Peters explained. "New York society will take note of our restraint and tastefulness. It is elegance and sophistication we should display. Edith's gown, my dress, your suit, and the expensive flowers which will adorn the front parlor will be sufficient," and the scene was set. Mr. Peters insisted upon the wedding breakfast being created by Delmonico's renowned chef, Charles Ranhofer, who would not himself appear, but for an unreasonable cost which was readily paid, would create and organize the meal and send one of his best Sous Chefs to oversee the entire affair. The wedding, as it was described at the bottom of page twenty-eight of the *New-York Tribune* was "overbearing yet modest", an oxymoron about which John Peters was unsure since it created in him a vacillation between annoyance and satisfaction.

Two gifts were bestowed upon the newlyweds by her parents. Fredrick and Edith were gifted a newly built, spacious, elaborate townhouse located on New York's Fifth Avenue, close to many of the socially prominent families John Peters desired to know. Fredrick's new father-in-law caused a blush to form on Fredrick's face as he presented his son-in-law the deed to the house at the wedding breakfast, making his generous gift known to all there, an unequivocal societal *faux pas*. Before moving in, Edith and her mother spent an enormous amount of time and bank notes to decorate the many rooms, creating a grand yet comfortable home for the Vogels. When the townhouse was completed, there were only a few months during which the couple could enjoy their new home and belongings before the second gift was rendered. This was a voyage to Europe which would combine an extended honeymoon with a business trip.

The plan was to travel by ship to France, spending time in Paris, traveling through the countryside into Switzerland, and then to Germany. Fredrick was anxious to visit his home in Berlin where he hoped to see relatives and friends and show Edith where he had been born and lived for the first decade of his life. They would then go to Hamburg where a Steinway piano factory had been built in 1880. Mr. Stetson assigned Fredrick the task of spending time overseeing production of the pianos, the organization of the factory, and returning with a thorough report. He and Edith were to spend a week there before voyaging to England and then back to New York. The trip would last almost four months, and Edith was stupendously excited. This would be her first venture out of the country. To add to her excitement, the Vogels would travel by rail, and Edith adored the movement of a train. She looked forward to dining in the special car created for that purpose, sleeping in the cozy compartments, examining the passing landscape through the large first-class windows. There was excitement as the Vogels boarded the train at the Basel, Switzerland railway station to travel to Delémont, Switzerland. After spending a few days in the area, they would reboard the train and travel northward to Berlin. Edith had insisted upon obtaining seats at the front of the railcar where she could sit next to the wide window and be both charmed by the scenery and exhilarated by the speed as they passed it. The bridge over which they traveled had been built by the famous Gustave Eiffel; they were moving swiftly over the river Birs; they were headed towards Munchenstein; Edith had just turned to her husband to comment enthusiastically about the river below, which she could just view. The date was June 14, 1891.

***

Months later, as the snow fell around the streets surrounding the townhouse on Fifth Avenue, greeting the first week of January in the year 1892, Fredrick decided it was time to unpack Edith's trunks which had been sent to her suite and which remained closed. The locked trunks were waiting for someone to remove the high-necked morning dresses, the afternoon outfits with an open neckline and shorter sleeves, the evening gowns which bared the chest and hugged the hips. There were simple skirts with shirtwaist blouses which had lace down the front and matching jackets. Hats with feathers and large brims, an elegant torque to hug the head, and a jaunty straw boater to match the shirtwaist outfits were removed from their boxes. There was even a bicycling uniform which was new, never having been worn, but Edith thought it smart and wanted to be prepared just in case they decided to try the sport. Underthings, nightdresses, soft, silky robes were spread about the bedroom. Fredrick removed each item and stood holding it, trying to remember when she had worn it, where they had been: in Paris or the French countryside or the Swiss towns and railway system. Not all the clothes had been worn. After last June 14, there was little need. Just a dress she had worn to the hospital. He couldn't find it. And, of course, the best gown, the one she was so fond of, the lovely blue frock in which she had been buried, was not among the others.

The aftermath of a tragedy comes in *what ifs? What if* they hadn't been in the front of the railcar? They would not have been last to be rescued because it had been necessary to remove those in back first. *What if* Fredrick had been able to move the large seat which trapped Edith sooner? If he had not been so trapped himself, she may not have sustained the internal injuries which were not noticed until it was too late. *What if* the young doctor who examined Edith had been more experienced? He should have noticed that she was in shock and could not explain the pain she felt because she didn't realize it until much later. *What if* when he was able to get her to a hospital, the ambulance had not taken that wrong turn and then had to slowly backtrack in the narrow Swiss street? Getting her to the hospital earlier may have helped to save her life. *What if* they had never gone to Europe, or had never taken the railway, or had stayed in Paris that one extra day to visit the Louvre? *What if* they had just plunged into the cold river below, hitting the water together, drowning in the chill, as steel and luggage and parts of the railcar fell upon them, just as it happened to so many others? Then Fredrick would not be standing in Edith's bedroom suite unpacking her clothes which would never be worn by her, wondering what to do with them, where they should be stored, to whom they should be given or sold. The *what ifs* filled his mind, and he could barely see because of the wetness filling his eyes. He stopped after a while, unable to look through the jewelry boxes which contained the diamond bracelets and pearl necklaces and cameo broaches and golden earrings. Those items would need to wait for a different day. A different year when the lovely items would be sold because the memories were too agonizing. The clothes remained hanging in closets for years until he decided that his housekeeper could deal with their dispersal.

Fredrick buried Edith in Switzerland. He telegraphed her parents numerous times, and they finally agreed that would be best. The burial was brief. No one was there to attend. Fredrick was still nursing a broken arm and could barely deal with necessary tasks. He did not travel to Berlin but did get to Hamburg and the Steinway factory where he remained for more weeks than planned. Mr. Stetson was understanding about his situation, and when Fredrick eventually returned to New York in December, there were two men from the Steinway organization to help him get back to his townhouse. His in-laws did not greet him at the dock nor did they appear at the townhouse. In fact, he had received no response to his last three telegrams. When eventually he was well enough to travel out to the Peters' mansion, he found it sealed, closed, and apparently sold. It seems, as rumors would have it, that John Peters and his secret, undesirable, criminal associations had engaged in various financial disagreements which did not end well. John Peters and his wife, one late evening, disappeared to the West, the far West, hauling what money they had in two travel bags, leaving gossip and hearsay and various allegations in their stead. Their daughter was gone. So were they. Fredrick returned to his townhouse to wait out the holidays in seclusion and in grief.

Eventually, he returned to work, throwing himself into his job in an attempt to bury his sorrow, and in doing so, created for himself a stellar reputation. Without any planning on his part, without realizing it, his story as a handsome, sad young widower with an air of mystery began to circulate, intriguing the Fifth Avenue neighbors. These two instances collaborated to forge a new figure, to construct a fresh personage, to render a minor celebrity. Over the next years, Fredrick Vogel would cultivate a presence which would have surprised both his immigrant parents and his outrageous in-laws had any of them been around to witness it. John Peters, especially, would have been bitterly jealous that his son-in-law managed to gain the admiration and appreciation of New York's high society, captivating the very people who disparaged him and at whose tables he was refused a seat.

***

"Yes, Mr. Vogel, this is absolutely the height of fashion. Here, allow me to show you how the back of the suit will fall," and Felix Weber carefully turned Fredrick to the side where they could both admire the cut of the lounge suit, the newest in men's fashions. Then he looked at Fredrick's young and clean-shaven face and suggested that perhaps he grow a moustache or a short, pointed beard. They were becoming fashionable. "Even a trimmed full beard will make you look older, more distinguished. Isn't that what you would like to project?"

The two of them discussed facial hair as the lounge suit was marked and pinned to perfection.

Over the past decade, Fredrick had relied on Felix Weber for more than fashion advice. The man was a fountain of knowledge not only about men's clothing, but also about society in general. Specifically, society in New York with its required etiquette, social relationships, financial dealings. Fredrick was given clues about which people he should cater to, which ones he should be politely impartial to, and which ones were out-of-favor and he should totally ignore. In return for these essential details, Fredrick encouraged his colleagues to patronize Felix Weber, to use his services as much as they were able to. Financially able to. Mr. Weber's services were expensive. Costly, but upscale, elegant, and dashing.

The two men aided each other. Mr. Weber advised Fredrick, suggesting he spend some of his earnings and savings to obtain land. "Land," he said as he straightened the finely tailored evening suit to fit his client, "that's what these men are investing in. Oh, there are stocks and businesses, and fine artwork, rare books, and paintings, but they all have land somewhere. Do it, Mr. Vogel. Find some good land, some wide space which is away from a city. Purchase a large plot. Build a house on it, or find one and renovate it. Believe me, I hear this happening all the time. Land is readily available in the West, and even the Midwest. Look into it," and then he added, "but also make sure you have ready cash. Put some away. Do not put all your money into stocks or the banks. Hide cash for a rainy day." Fredrick did. In exchange, when Mr. Weber wanted a piano for his wife and daughter, Fredrick was able to obtain one of the newly created Model K uprights at a fraction of the actual cost, and supervised the delivery himself. Holidays never passed without Fredrick bringing Felix a bottle of his favorite whiskey. The one he kept in his office so that his wife did not know. Periodically, after a fitting, the two men would go into Felix's small office, close the door, and sip on the amber liquid while Fredrick listened to the latest advice and gossip.

"So, where have you been invited lately? And tell me who was there and what they were wearing," and Felix sipped his whiskey and sat back waiting for the report.

***

Over the years, Fredrick had become the *extra man* at dinners and concerts and dances when one was required. He had been invited to a dinner at the Wilson's, his neighbors just across the street from his townhouse on Fifth Avenue. Once a year of mourning was over, Mr. Wilson called on Fredrick and extended the invitation from his wife. After Fredrick accepted, he made an appointment with Felix to obtain a new evening suit, and that was the first time he and Felix discussed social engagements and expected etiquette. "You know, this is a test," said Felix, making Fredrick a bit nervous, "and should you pass it, and I don't doubt you will, you will be accepted as a proper guest to the posh dinners on Fifth Avenue. You will meet the important people, the wealthy ones whose advice you may solicit. Now, let's go over what you should wear and how you should act." Fredrick passed his test. The handsome, young widower with an air of mystery charmed the Wilsons.

Whenever there was a need for an extra man, and even often when there was not, Fredrick was invited. His wardrobe increased as the need for it did, and he often found himself at a large dining table, toasting the hostess, making small talk to an older aunt or a younger sister, and obtaining financial advice from other men as cigars were puffed and brandy was served in the host's smoking parlor. Because Fredrick held the deed to his townhouse there were no annual payments to be made; therefore, taking Felix's advice, a portion of his salary and commissions was earmarked for investing. By following pointers and tips garnered at various social occasions, he was able to put together a small but viable portfolio. He purchased beautifully bound rare books for his library. He took Felix Weber's additional advice and made a rather large land purchase, finding an acceptable plot of land in the Midwest, not too far from Chicago. And he always had plenty of cash safely hidden for any adversity which could appear. He spent purposefully; he saved judiciously. Eventually, there was a need to hire a young housekeeper who was able to organize his bachelor quarters, to dust the Steinway he played when there was time, to set the clean dishes in the proper cabinets, to arrange fresh flowers on his tables. When it was Fredrick's turn to reciprocate with a dinner party of his own, his housekeeper, Mrs. Anderson, hired a chef and servers, and assigned her own older husband to act as doorman and butler. Fredrick began to rely on the couple, ultimately hiring them as his full-time servants. They stayed with him in his New York Fifth Avenue townhouse, and later, when a move was made to Chicago and then to a small town in Illinois, they moved with him and his new young wife. When additional closet space was needed for the expanded wardrobe Fredrick was collecting, it was Mrs. Anderson who arranged for the removal of the dresses and other clothing belonging to the now, long-dead and mostly forgotten first wife, Edith Vogel.

Travels, sales, dinners, concerts, and social engagements of all sorts kept Fredrick occupied. It all helped to heal his heartbreak, although Fredrick often wondered if the brief courtship and marriage to Edith, the relationship with his nefarious and missing in-laws, the tragic consequences of the railway accident were all just part of a fantastical illusion. Nevertheless, he was busy, and the years passed. In 1893 when the World's Columbian Exposition was held in Chicago, Fredrick was sent to take notes on the pianos exhibited there. Mr. Steinway did not send his pianos due to what he deemed an unfair system of judging them. But he wanted to know what was being shown, and Fredrick spent ten days in that city. A trip to Hamburg, Germany where Fredrick, once again, visited and reported on the Steinway factory, occurred in 1895. This time, Fredrick took time to visit Berlin, looking for lost relatives and friends. He did not find any, but did purchase some lovely antique furniture which he had shipped back to his Fifth Avenue townhouse. He considered visiting Edith's grave in Switzerland, but decided it would be too emotionally upsetting, so he did not. Back in New York, in 1898, the consolidation of the five boroughs was completed, and people celebrated (or mourned), and the popular song, *The Sidewalks of New York,* was on everyone's tongues. Fredrick was often asked to play the piano and lead the group in singing it at various social engagements. The pedigreed society singers laughed, joked, and had a great time as they sang, pretending to be ordinary New Yorkers. They were smugly mindful that they were not.

The early years of the twentieth century fostered a symbiotic relationship between the Steinway organization and Fredrick Vogel. New piano models: the *Model N* upright in 1900, the *Model K* upright in 1904, the *Model A Baby Grand* in 1905, were in such demand that the Steinway factory had difficulty keeping up with all the orders Fredrick wrote. Music schools, theaters, opera houses, as well as individuals wanted the carefully-crafted, beautifully made, luscious-toned instruments for teaching, playing, entertaining. And when in 1905, Heinrich Conreid, the manager of New York's Metropolitan Opera House, ordered ten new Steinways, Fredrick wrote up the order, had lunch with Mr. Conreid, and thanked him profusely for the season opera tickets which he was given. This was Fredrick's introduction to the world of opera, a connection which would, in a couple short years, transform his life.

***

Everyone in the New York music world knew of Oscar Hammerstein, the garish, splashy, brilliant, cigar-smoking, silk-top-hat wearing administrator, executive, organizer of failed theaters, failed opera houses, and failed businesses, none of which ever stopped him from creating new and successful theaters, opera houses and businesses. He had immigrated from Berlin, Germany and made his fortune in America. He lost it multiple times before remaking it multiple times, holding tightly to his American Dream while blowing smoke rings from his cigars. During one of his early theater endeavors, he employed an actor, Heinrich Conreid, with whom, after a tentative friendship, he had numerous arguments, creating a feud lasting for decades. When his old enemy became the Metropolitan Opera House's new manager and administrator, Oscar was determined to outdo whatever the Met, as it became called, planned to do. Oscar Hammerstein formed his own opera company: the Manhattan Opera Company, a venture which would open in December, 1906 and close in 1910. But during the years it was in business, Hammerstein's operation would rival the Met's. Did Conreid hire Enrico Caruso? Hammerstein snagged Nellie Melba, Mary Garden, John McCormack. Did the Met ignore operas which were sung in French? Hammerstein would highlight them. Did Hammerstein find out that Conreid ordered ten Steinway pianos? He would order twelve! A dozen of them! And when he did, he ordered them from Fredrick Vogel.

They connected: these two Berlin-born German immigrants. Fredrick would accompany the pianos as, piecemeal, they were created and delivered to Hammerstein's opera house. During one of these deliveries, Oscar Hammerstein watched as the Steinways were set into their places, then took the younger man by the arm and walked him through his new opera house which was set to open soon.

"Well, Fredrick, what do you think of this? Look at the grandness of the balcony, the richness of the red velvet curtains, the height of the catwalks. The acoustics are amazing! Come, sit here with me and watch as my company walks through the staging of *I Puritani*. I have hired Alessandro Bonci to sing the title role, and, I must tell you exciting news: Nellie Melba will be here soon too. Ha! Let the Met surpass that!" Oscar moved Fredrick to the front of the mezzanine where they sat and watched the stage.

"Mr. Hammerstein, I'm impressed with what you have done here, and look forward to the opening night. Thank you again for the tickets. The last three of the new uprights you ordered are due to be delivered at week's end. I'll be here to see them properly installed into the practice rooms," and Fredrick smiled at the man seated next to him chomping on the cigar he continually had in his mouth.

"Excellent, Fredrick, excellent. Now listen to this chorus." And he leaned forward.

Fredrick paid attention and watched the chorus of singers acting as gentlemen and ladies of the court. He listened and looked, and as the group stepped forward moving into twos and threes across the stage, a young woman, flanked by two of the men, caught his attention. She stood perfectly straight with what Fredrick thought was majesty; her brown hair, hints of red shining in the stage lights, was piled on top of her head. He observed her movements and thought them graceful; he heard her singing and believed it flawless. She stood out from the crowd, and Fredrick noted her. Later in the week, after the delivery of the new pianos and another meeting with Oscar Hammerstein, they watched the current rehearsal once again, and Fredrick would learn the woman's name. It was Ingrid Winthrop.

***

Fredrick, at age forty-three, was a widower who assumed that another marriage was beyond him. But he was no monk. There had been some involvements, one or two liaisons, a fling here and there. Sometimes a widowed younger sister, or older one, of a society family came to visit and was placed next to Fredrick at dinner. Dalliances or flirtations occurred. Nothing was serious. No one was harmed. There was that one instance when someone's elder, widowed sister, after leaving New York, sent Fredrick several frank and somewhat scandalous letters inviting him to visit her in Vermont. Fredrick answered, in the politest terms, that his business kept him from the visit, but should things change, he would most assuredly get in touch. He did not. He remained a bachelor, and the marriage of his youth seemed more distant as time passed; the idea that another marriage would happen became less and less likely; and then he beheld the woman standing on the stage of the Manhattan Opera House, singing in the chorus, moving with grace, and something happened. Something unexpected. Something electrifying. Something fateful.

***

It was not in Hammerstein's nature to do anything that wasn't spectacular, and his new opera venture was, indeed, a spectacular success. World class performers took the Manhattan Opera stage. Crowds filled the streets, and a few times the New York police force was needed to settle the excited opera goers. Newspapers reviewing the grand opera performances called them *truly grand!* Oscar became the darling of society and he was elated and thrilled to be invited to the homes of society's elite. On those evenings, if Fredrick happened to be in attendance, the two of them always spoke and made plans to meet for a lunch. Sometimes Fredrick simply stopped in to say hello to Oscar. He would sit in one of the two large and comfortable leather chairs in his office and the men would enjoy their *Kaffeeklatsch* drinking the hot *Jacobs Kronung* coffee that Oscar imported, and eating the *strudel* which was brought in each day from the nearby German bakery and supplied to the opera company, the stage crew, the musicians, the workers. It was during one of these meetings Fredrick asked about the woman in the company.

"Ah, so you are enthralled with Ingrid, are you?" Oscar wiped his mouth with his handkerchief and looked at Fredrick. "She is a treasure with a marvelously expressive voice. I believe she will be singing a larger role in *Pelle`as et Me`lisande*. If you are interested, perhaps you can be introduced to her grandmother."

"Grandmother? Where is her father? Her family?"

"Miss Winthrop lives with her grandmother, Louisa Winthrop. There was some tragedy which left her an orphan. However, I must warn you: Mrs. Winthrop is a lioness! If she doesn't send a woman to guard her granddaughter and see her home, she shows up herself. If you'd like, I can arrange for you to sit next to her when I know she will be here. The front office will let me know. But Ingrid is young, Fredrick. And she has a career here. I would hate to lose her."

Fredrick smiled and finished his coffee. He placed the cup and saucer down, sat back, and quietly sighed. He nodded his head slowly. "Yes, Oscar, I would appreciate a seat next to Mrs. Winthrop. Let me know when she will next be at a performance. And, is there a florist around here you would recommend?"

***

He stood when Louisa Winthrop entered the center orchestra row. He helped her with her coat and arranged her shawl. He stooped down and picked up her program when she dropped it. And the second and the third time and all the consecutive times they sat together, he, courteously and attentively, did the same things for her. They began to share small confidences, quiet confidentialities. One evening, she pointed out the fact that there, there in the crowd towards the back of the stage, there was her granddaughter singing and laughing and acting.

He looked at Ingrid as if he had never seen her before. He commented on her vibrant and full voice and then apologized for being so forward. She said, "Nonsense, you are correct," and they smiled at each other. He surreptitiously sent flowers to Ingrid's dressing room each time she appeared. He attached a unique note to each floral arrangement, spending time considering what to write, never including his name. He remained attentive to Louisa Winthrop, forming a familiar friendship, and when, after enjoying yet another performance together, she inquired if he would like to meet her granddaughter, he answered that he would be honored. And when they were introduced, and as he bent over Ingrid's gloved hand, holding it to his lips in the European fashion, Fate loomed. Fate, in all her impetuous grandeur, fostered an affinity, created a rapport, effectuated a fusing between them. Fredrick connected with the young woman, looked up into her face, felt an unexplainable tightening in his stomach, and knew he would, at age forty-three, willingly abandon his bachelor life, forego his flirtations and flings, do the thing he was positive would never again occur. He would marry this lovely woman with the burnt-umber hair and the chestnut-colored eyes.

Four

Mr. and Mrs. Fredrick Vogel

"I have invited Mr. Vogel for Sunday supper, Ingrid. He is such a delightful man, and is so attentive to us both," and Louisa Winthrop glanced over at the fresh flowers which had just arrived. The attached note was, as usual, cordial, warm, and not presumptive of anything.

Ingrid smiled and then stretched. She was on hiatus from the opera company which had closed for the season and would not resume rehearsals for another six weeks. She was enjoying her time of rest. She was also enjoying the steady attention from Fredrick Vogel, and while she was unsure about where this relationship was headed, she knew she had her grandmother's approval for it. She nodded at the woman across the breakfast table and smiled.

"It will be good to see Mr. Vogel again."

"Do you have plans for today?"

"Yes. I have an appointment at eleven o'clock for a fitting with the dresses I ordered at Bergdorf Goodman. Would you prefer I don't travel alone? I can take Hilda if you would rather I do that."

Louisa nodded. "Yes, take Hilda. How long will you be gone? Will you return before two o'clock, do you think?"

Ingrid thought. "I should be back by that time. Is there something you need?"

"Oh no," lied Louisa. "I was just wondering. I may take a brief nap this afternoon. It was difficult to sleep last night."

Ingrid got up saying, "I'll let Peter know I need the carriage. I should get ready now. Be back later this afternoon, Grandmother."

Louisa Winthrop nodded. She was aware of Ingrid's appointment today, but there was a specific reason she needed to know about her time of return. Fredrick Vogel had contacted her earlier in the week, asking for an audience. He had something of importance to discuss with her, and she was sure she knew what it was. She was prepared to give her consent because it was time for Ingrid to be married. This opera singing diversion had run its course. Ingrid had been active in the Manhattan Opera Company for three seasons, and she was not getting younger. There were few suitable society men for Ingrid to even consider as a husband now, and Louisa was concerned. Mr. Vogel had been patient and attentive, but the slow and delicate courting had gone on long enough. Despite his age which was twice Ingrid's, he was a successful business man with an excellent income, a sterling reputation, a healthy bank account, a lovely and well-maintained Fifth Avenue townhouse, and many respected social contacts. Louisa knew these facts. Her lawyers had checked into them. Once Ingrid and Hilda left for the appointment, Louisa ordered tea to be readied. She sat in the front parlor and watched the tall grandfather clock. When she heard the front doorbell, she smoothed out her skirt, sat up straighter, and prepared to greet Fredrick Vogel. As he entered the parlor, she smiled and nodded. To herself she thought: *At last.*

***

Sunday evening supper was over. The conversation had been entertaining and light, and Fredrick talked continually, telling humorous story after humorous story, his bright banter belying his nervousness. Only Louisa noted it and knew the reason for it. As the plates were being removed, she adjusted herself and spoke.

"I believe you will need to excuse me from additional society. I am exceedingly tired tonight and need to retire. Ingrid, I am sure you can entertain Mr. Vogel in the front parlor with coffee and sweets. Mr. Vogel, thank you for a pleasant evening. You are always good company and your stories are a delight. Please come again soon." Fredrick stood up, moving to the back of Louisa's chair, helping to ease her out of it, offering her his arm.

Ingrid kissed her grandmother good-night and left to arrange for the coffee as Fredrick walked Louisa Winthrop to the bottom of the staircase. She removed her arm from his, placed her foot on the first step and turned to him. "Mr. Vogel, I wish you luck. However, I believe you will be successful. We will speak together soon. Good night." She walked up to her bedroom suite.

Fredrick turned to go into the front parlor where Ingrid was directing the maid as to where to place the coffee set, cups, and tiered plate filled with delicate cookies and elegant sweets. She smiled as Fredrick entered, and they sat down on the settee facing each other. Ingrid poured coffee into one of the cups, adding the amount of cream she knew Fredrick liked and handed it to him. She poured and arranged her own cup, and they both took a sip. Fredrick placed his cup and saucer back on the small serving table and looked down at his clenched hands. There were some moments of hesitation until Fredrick looked up and began to speak.

"Miss Winthrop, I have a question to ask you, but before I do, I have some things to say. It's important you understand me. I am older than you and have had experiences you may not know about. I want to be honest with you. You know me as a bachelor, but you should be aware that I was not always unmarried. In my youth, almost two decades ago, I had a wife. We were married briefly before I lost her in a terrible accident."

Ingrid felt the hair on her arms stand up. Something important was being narrated. She said to him, "I am so sorry, Mr. Vogel. I was unaware," and she placed her cup and saucer next to his.

Fredrick nodded, looking away for a second. Then he continued. "We were on a wedding trip in Europe. Edith loved travel by rail, and we toured that way through France and into Switzerland. Our plan was to go to Germany and then England before returning home."

Ingrid's breath quickened. She placed a hand on her heart. This sounded like a familiar story, a sad story.

He continued. "There was a terrible accident, a railway disaster involving the train, and many of the passengers lost their lives."

Ingrid's hand against her chest could feel the alerted fluttering there. An invisible diaphanous ribbon, not unlike a spider's silken webbing, was slowly reaching out, joining their heart centers. There was a recognition. An understanding. A sensibility. This was a sign. A connection.

"Edith and I escaped, or so I thought we did. But she sustained internal injuries and soon after, when I thought we were safe, she was rushed to a hospital and died there. She is buried in Switzerland. We were married barely a year."

Later, much later, months later, Ingrid would share with him her parents' catastrophic end, a scenario familiar to him. They would marvel at the circumstance, the serendipity, the fated events which linked their destinies. They would wonder at the connecting threads, the fibers which created a pattern, which drew them together, which assembled their individual singularities into a rendered doubleness, into a comprehensive, detailed pattern. But on this night, with the warmth of an early spring whispering into the draperies, moving them gingerly, the coffee in the cups growing tepid, the sweets on the daintily hand-painted tiered stand remaining untouched, Ingrid said nothing.

"I want you to know about my previous marriage before I ask you a question," and Fredrick looked downward once again, drawing in a breath. He looked up at her preparing to continue, his hazel eyes connecting to her chestnut-colored ones.

Ingrid did not allow him to finish. She reached over and took both of his hands in both of hers and answered the unasked question.

"Yes, Fredrick. Yes, I will marry you."

***

Upstairs in her bedroom suite, seated in front of the fireplace where she had insisted Hilda light a fire despite the evening's genial warmth, Louisa pulled the handsomely embroidered throw to her and sighed. She was sure the situation in the front parlor was going to be happily decided, and as she stared into the flames, she murmured to herself, "At last…"

***

Ingrid resigned from the Manhattan Opera Company before the 1909 fall season went into rehearsal. She was sad to do so, but understood that a genteel wife in 1909 could have only one position: that of genteel wife. She was nervous and a bit fearful to speak to Oscar Hammerstein, so Fredrick went with her. Of course, Fredrick had already spoken with Oscar, explaining why his fiancée would not be part of the upcoming season, and while Oscar was unhappy at losing the talented singer ("*Ach du Lieber Gott!* I knew it!"), he was pleased his friend was happy. So pleased, he insisted upon hosting the wedding luncheon at *Barbetta,* his favorite restaurant, one that catered to the theater crowd, one which served the Italian cuisine he had come to adore, one which was decorated in eighteenth-century antiques and would open the dining hall early specifically because he asked them to, one which would disconcert and agitate Ingrid's grandmother, Louisa Winthrop. But Oscar sent an exceedingly effusive letter with an exceedingly effusive spray of late summer flowers, an act which both charmed and aggravated Louisa. This was followed up by a personal visit, and the wedding luncheon was settled.

However, the wedding ceremony was Louisa's purview. It was held in the front parlor of the Saint Thomas Episcopal Church in Manhattan, a nod to the bride's parentage. There were not many guests at the late morning service, but afterwards, Barbetta's dining room was filled with the men and women of the Manhattan Opera Company as the bride and groom and the other wedding attendees entered. Oscar Hammerstein's gestures were never trivial or inconsequential, and the array of dishes from the Piemonte region of Italy, the personal attention from Sebastiano Maroglio, the restaurant's proprietor, the splendor of the service, the vigilance of the waiters, and the majesty of the venue overwhelmed Louisa Winthrop, creating in her a dizziness she blamed on the glass of imported champagne sipped after Mr. Hammerstein gave a long and involved toast to the newly-wed couple. And, later, when she assessed and analyzed the luncheon with the group of friends who attended, the group of friends who were unable to attend appeared quite jealous. Louisa was certain of this. She was selfishly gratified.

***

While Ingrid was not exactly sure what to expect from married life and intimacy, she was pleased to discover it suited her. Fredrick was delighted. After a month of organizing their lives, settling in the Fifth Avenue townhouse, interpreting the Andersons' position in the house, completing the circuit of expected social visits and obligations to friends and neighbors, spending time with Louisa Winthrop to ensure her that she would not be forgotten, the planned wedding trip commenced. Europe was not the destination this time. Chicago was. The almost twenty-hour trip by railroad from New York's Grand Central Terminal to Chicago's LaSalle Street Station was noteworthy. The dining car, the sleeping compartment, the movement of the train itself enthralled Ingrid, and once her husband relaxed with the assurance that there would be no repeat of the adversities included with his first wedding trip, therapeutic for Fredrick. He had traveled to Chicago on the railroad before, but not with a wife, and this trip becalmed him. As they sat in the dining car sipping their breakfast coffee, readying to depart the train in a couple hours, Fredrick and Ingrid talked about what their three-week visit would include.

"…and I did order the tickets for Orchestra Hall on Saturday. I believe they will be playing Beethoven's *Ninth*, isn't that correct?"

"It is," answered Ingrid. "and I am looking forward to that as well as the special Monet exhibit at the Art Institute. Is the Blackstone Hotel close to these buildings? Will we be able to walk to them?"

"As long as the fall weather holds, we will. But other places such as the Field Museum will require a conveyance of sorts. I have arranged for a carriage when we need it. I believe you will find walking along the Chicago streets an interesting opportunity. There are numerous shops for us to enter, and Mrs. Reason, Julius's wife, has offered to take you shopping at Marshall Field's Department Store. She said the two of you will enjoy the lunch provided in their Walnut Room. I think that is planned for Thursday of this week," and Fredrick waved away the waiter who offered additional coffee. "There is something I haven't yet told you about this trip."

Ingrid looked at him. "I am aware that you will need to spend a few days at the Steinway Hall's showroom. That isn't a problem if you are referring to that. I am perfectly capable of finding things to do. Perhaps Mrs. Reason will want to visit the Garfield Park Conservatory with me. I understand it houses the largest collection of plants in the world."

Fredrick nodded. "No, there is something else. A number of years ago, I bought a parcel of land, about one-hundred acres. It is outside of Chicago about sixty or so miles, and I have arranged for us to visit it. In fact, I have hired a driver and a Model T automobile to motor us to Bonneville. I want you to see the town and the land and the Victorian house which is on the property. The house needs expansion, and I would like to include a library to accommodate my book collection, but I want you to see it and have a say-so about the renovation. I might add additional outbuildings and possibly a greenhouse. Anyway, I thought the automobile trip would be an adventure for us both although it will be lengthy. Close to four hours one way, but we'll stay overnight at the better hotel in town. Just don't expect service and luxury as you will find at the Blackstone."

"You bought farm land! Why?"

"As an investment, I suppose. And also, as a future home for us. Should we have children," and Fredrick's cheeks reddened, "it would be a lovely place to take them for the summer. The fresh country air will be beneficial. Bonneville is only twelve or so miles from Stone City which is large and has a railway station which runs from the LaSalle Street Station. It is possible to take the train there and travel by automobile to the house. The roads to the towns are constantly being improved, and Bonneville seems to be friendly. The place is growing and expanding with new stores and businesses, and while I'm not sure I have any talent or know-how to retire as a farmer, it's wise to own some land. At least someone once advised me to do that," and here he stumbled a bit. He hadn't told Ingrid everything. "There is a real possibility that within a short amount of time, I will be asked to transfer to Chicago to take over the Steinway Hall there. Julius Reason is going to retire."

Ingrid nodded. "Aha! So, this trip is to help prepare me for that move. Fredrick, I don't know if I can leave my grandmother right away. She is not in good health, and I am her only living relative. Did you consider that?"

"Yes, I did. I told Mr. Stetson that I was not interested in accepting the position immediately. He understands, and Julius will be there for a while yet. Don't worry for now. Let's enjoy our time here. I do want you to like this city."

Ingrid reached over and squeezed her husband's hand. "Now tell me more about Bonneville. What businesses are there, and what does this house look like?"

***

The following summer the Vogels took another trip to Chicago, spending a week at the newly renovated Bonneville house. While in Chicago, they actively researched neighborhoods, looking to purchase a residence. Fredrick spent time at Steinway Hall while Ingrid shopped with her housekeeper, Mrs. Anderson. The women walked along State Street searching through the stores, purchasing various items to be sent to the Bonneville house. The Vogels were away for most of June. Upon their return to New York in late summer, Ingrid discovered her grandmother's increasing frailty. She was confined to her bedroom suite and doctors came and went, but there was little to do when the woman was both in poor health and elderly. Nature would take its course. Louisa was seventy-three years old.

Louisa Winthrop lasted through the rest of that year. In the spring of 1912, as the news about the *Titanic* tragedy filled the New York papers, Ingrid sat by the bedside of her grandmother. One cloudy day, as Ingrid held the hand of her grandmother watching her sleep, Louisa's hand grew limp and cold, and the woman found her way into the Episcopalian afterlife where, as she just recently had claimed to Ingrid, she was determined to find her husband and her son. She neglected to mention Eliza, Ingrid's mother. The funeral was exactly as she planned it. In fact, Louisa had planned it all. Months before her frailness and age overcame her, the lawyers for the family were called to her bedside and a revised will bestowed upon the granddaughter she had come to regard a daughter…everything. There was an exceedingly large amount of…everything.

Weeks later, Fredrick and Ingrid met with the lawyers in the front parlor of their Fifth Avenue townhouse. When, after a few hours of surprising revelations, of notifications about bank accounts, of a listing of property and jewelry owned, the lawyers left. The Vogels were somewhat breathless. They sat back in their chairs and looked at each other. Fredrick was the first to speak.

"Ingrid, I am astonished. I had no idea your grandmother held the wealth she did. You, my dear, are a rich woman. Richer, by far, than your husband. Many times richer," and he smiled.

"I am astonished too. Grandmother never spoke about money or holdings or what my father's and grandfather's business brought to her. It was not a discussion we ever had. She considered it gauche to bring up the subject. Well, now, I suppose that new baby grand piano we saw at the Chicago showroom could be sent to the house in Bonneville," and she grinned. And it was.

There was no reason to remain in New York. Both Fredrick and Ingrid were sad to leave the city, but a new adventure was welcomed. Changes happened: Julius Reason retired from the Chicago Steinway Company; Fredrick took his place; the Fifth Avenue townhouse was sold. It was decided to retain Louisa's large brownstone, now Ingrid's, and the lawyers leased the place to a refined and respectable family. Furniture and belongings were streamlined. Some items were separated and stored; others were reorganized and moved. Goodbyes said, farewell parties attended, businesses wrapped up, finances transferred, and the Vogels set off for Chicago. For a month, they stayed in a suite at the Blackstone Hotel as the spacious two-floor, eight-room Morrison Place townhouse on North Lake Shore Drive was repainted, redecorated, and readied for their next move. Time was taken up with the projects, but by late fall of 1912, the new residence was the site of their Thanksgiving feast, and the Bonneville house was fully renovated. Ingrid and Fredrick moved into their new Chicago space, the one they would share with their help, the Andersons, and it was there, after Ingrid had ignored the monthly calendar kept in her top bureau drawer because she was so involved in the moving, she discovered she was pregnant.

***

By 1890, there were about half a million Swedish immigrants living in the United States. In 1900 when New York housed 42,708 of them, two: Margareta Nilsson, called "Greta", and Lars Anderson, married. There was a ten-year age difference between them, but their discovered connections drew them to each other, and they decided that *Fate,* as they learned from the Norse myths they were both told by their elders, ruled life. Martin Luther may have denounced the concept and the Lutheran ministers may have agreed from their pulpits, but the Swedish immigrants knew better. Hadn't Fate in the form of joblessness and landlessness chased them from their homeland onto the ships which docked at various ports in the United States? Didn't Fate offer a wide variety of jobs in this large and continually expanding country? Weren't Greta and Lars fated to meet again as adults and marry? After all, they had come over on the same ship (the *Elder),* and in the same year (1884), and even though Greta was only a few months old and Lars was ten, and their families didn't know each other then, hadn't they both, years later, wound up in New York City working at the same grand house: Greta as assistant housemaid and cook and Lars as apprentice gardener and handy-man? Fate had decreed their marriage. There was no doubt about that.

They were grateful when Fate had brought them to Fredrick Vogel who hired them and trusted them and moved them with him and his new wife to Chicago, the city that housed thousands of Swedish immigrants. More than in New York. Swedish communities, Swedish churches, Swedish newspapers, Swedish social organizations dotted the city, and wasn't Fate responsible for it all? Greta thought so. So did Lars. They did not mind the move from New York. And while Fate had not seen fit to bless them with children, they assumed future Vogel children would be part of their lives. So, when Ingrid called out to Mrs. Anderson on that snowy morning in December, yelling for her help, hysterical because of the blood seeping from between her legs and onto the bed linens, scared because of the pain she was enduring, she was not the only frenzied and distraught woman in the Morrison Place townhouse. Mrs. Anderson silently cursed Fate as she sanitized and settled and soothed Ingrid. Then, as the empty woman cried herself to sleep in the large freshly made bed, Mrs. Anderson sent her husband for a doctor first and Mr. Vogel next, and shed her own tears while she worked at trying to repair the stained linens and reduce the dark crimson color.

Doctor Davies completed his examination, assuring Ingrid that she simply needed to rest and, in a week or so, she would be perfectly fine. She was young and healthy and these things did happen. Often. She should not worry. It was a little thing and not meant to be. The next time would be successful. Many young women suffered through these times. He was sure he was being calming and consolatory. Mrs. Anderson listened at the doorway as he said these things and saw him reach into his bag to remove a small brown glass vial. He placed it on the bedside table and spoke to Ingrid.

"Mrs. Vogel, I am leaving you something for pain and sleep. Three or four drops in a glass of water should help. Don't take it more than three times a day, and a bit of honey will help mask the bitterness. Do you understand?" Ingrid nodded. The doctor turned to Mrs. Anderson and said, "Let me know if more is needed. Can you do that?"

Mrs. Anderson nodded her head saying, "Yes Sir," and after the doctor gathered his bag and put on his outerwear, he was led to the door. She stood outside in the cold air, a light snow falling, examining the streets, watching for the carriage which would contain both husbands, but nothing was seen. She returned to the bedroom to check on Ingrid who lay in the bed staring up at the high ceiling, no longer crying, although grief was obvious on her face. Mrs. Anderson walked over to the table where the vial had been left and picked it up.

"Mrs. Vogel, I'm not telling you what to do, or trying to contradict the doctor's advice, but this is poison. Don't take it. If you are in pain, I have a number of herbs and flowers I can use as tisanes to help you, and I know they will not harm you. Are you in pain now?"

Ingrid looked at the woman and sighed. "Not too much. Is my husband back?"

"Not yet, but soon, I am sure. There is snow on the streets and that is holding up the traffic. Can I bring you something to drink which I know will ease you? And what do you want to do about this?" Mrs. Anderson held the vial up to the light where a dark liquid could be seen, handling it as if she were gripping a monstrous creature.

"Get rid of it, I guess. Do you have something for me?"

"Yes, I'll bring up some strong black tea. That will help to stop the bleeding. Later I'll brew some lemon balm so you can sleep. Is there anything else you need right now?"

Ingrid shook her head and closed her eyes. Mrs. Anderson left the bedroom leaving the door ajar. She went down the stairs to complete her tasks and soon, heard the front door opening and a quick and heavy tread enter. *Good,* she thought, *the two of them can grieve together.* She went to her own room and took out a small case where she kept her supply of botanical medicants.

***

It did not take an entire week. On the fifth morning, Ingrid walked down the steps into the kitchen where Mrs. Anderson was stirring a pot of oats and finishing cooking the stewed prunes. She turned when she heard the footsteps and inquired, "Mrs. Vogel, are you well enough to be downstairs? I was going to bring breakfast up to you. If you sit in the dining room, I'll bring it right out. Is there anything else you need?"

Ingrid pulled out a kitchen chair and gingerly moved onto it. She sighed. "I am fine, Mrs. Anderson, and what I need is company. Fredrick had to leave early yesterday and today and will not be home until very late tonight again. I need to not be alone with my thoughts. I am feeling better. At least physically. What I need is to sit here with you, share that breakfast, and talk. Can we do that? Am I interrupting other things you were going to do?"

Mrs. Anderson stopped her stirring and remained still for a few seconds before lifting off the oats and setting the pot to the side. "If that is what you want to do, that is what we will do. Let me serve this up and I will sit with you. I have already eaten, but I can do with another cup of tea," and she did those things.

The two sat across from each other sipping and chewing for a few minutes. Ingrid swallowed some of the oats, pushed away the rest of the bowl, ate a couple bites of prunes, and stopped. "I know I need to eat. I don't seem to have an appetite. But this tea is good, and it does seem to help with the…" she stopped. There was a delicacy in mentioning bodily fluids at the table, even a kitchen table, and she didn't know how or if she should continue.

"That is what it's meant to do, and I am glad you are healing. Will you go back to your bedroom in a while and rest?"

Ingrid smiled and shook her head. "I feel like doing something useful, so I am going to go to the library and begin to sort through those boxes of books. Mr. Vogel has quite a collection although he rarely reads them. I'm the reader. He said I should decide which books to keep here and which to send to Bonneville. The library there is much larger than the small office library here, and I need to make some decisions. I can do that while seated in the chair, and when I get tired, I'll stop. Perhaps, we can eat lunch together here. Would you mind?"

"Mrs. Vogel, if you don't mind, then I don't either. I have chicken soup simmering, and I believe that will be beneficial for you.

For both of us. In this weather the soup will be warming and comforting. Would you like more tea?"

"Actually, yes. Another cup and I'll go to those books."

Both cups were refilled, the soup simmering on the stove was checked and stirred, and Mrs. Anderson sat down once again.

Ingrid looked at her housekeeper and cook and smiled. "You know, we have lived in the same house since Mr. Vogel and I married, but I don't really know much about you. Your first name is *Margaret*, and is that what you are called?"

"*Margareta*, but I am known as *Greta*."

"Tell me about yourself. How old were you when you came to this country? Where did you meet Mr. Anderson? For whom did you work before Mr. Vogel? Do you mind if I ask these questions?"

"No, I don't," and Mrs. Anderson told the story of the ship she traveled when she was just a baby, the apprenticeships which taught her the skills she owned, the meeting with Lars, the discovery of the connections they had, and the workings of Fate in it all. After the third cup of tea, she stopped and the women sat still, mulling over the account.

"So, you believe in Fate?"

Mrs. Anderson nodded. "Yes, of course. How else can you explain how Lars and I met again after all those years? I remember my mother telling us stories about the three Norms, the Norse gods of Fate, and saying *Det blir som det blir*."

"And that means?"

"*Whatever is going to happen will happen*, is I guess the closest I can explain it," replied Mrs. Anderson.

Ingrid thought through this and nodded. "I believe your mother was right. I think about my own meeting with my husband, and the connections, the attachments we share," and she sighed once again. "One day I'll tell you about it all. But for now, thank you for the company, Mrs. Anderson. I should get to those books; there are quite a few to sift through. I look forward to having lunch with you here. It's warm and consoling," and she got up from the chair and pushed it in.

Mrs. Anderson stood as Ingrid walked through the kitchen. At the doorway, she stopped and turned around to ask, "Would you mind if, when we are alone, I call you by your given name?"

Mrs. Anderson hesitated. There was no suggestion that she could call Mrs. Vogel, *Ingrid*, that there would be an exchange of familiarity, that they would become equals. Ingrid never considered doing that. Her grandmother always called the cook, *Cook*, and all the other servants by their first names. It was just the way it was done. She didn't know that in future years, she and Mrs. Anderson, who were only five years apart in age, would speak to each other using their given names. At least when they were alone, they would. A formal designation would be used when others were around. The line between *Mistress* and *Servant* would eventually blur until the two women melded into a relationship, a friendship, akin to a sisterhood. But not at this time. Not right now.

Ah well, Mrs. Anderson thought, *Det blir som det blir!*

"That would be fine, Mrs. Vogel."

"Good. Thank you. I'll see you for lunch, Greta," and as Mrs. Vogel left for the library, Greta Anderson watched.

***

No further doctor visits were necessary. At least not for the happiest of reasons. Everything appeared to be routine and standard. There were some months when Ingrid waited impatiently to find out whether she could impart exciting news to Fredrick, could begin to plan for a nursery, could shop for tiny shoes and sweet-colored outfits, but she was unable to do those things. Eventually she decided, *I suppose that whatever is going to happen, will happen,* and determined to stay busy with life.

Ingrid remained occupied and active. Daily, she began to run through the vocal exercises just as Madame Duff-Ross had taught her, and she practiced the Czerny finger exercises on the Steinway piano in the parlor. She met women in her neighborhood and went to luncheons and teas with them. Music and theater continued as interests, and the Vogels held season tickets to the Chicago Symphony. The Central Music Hall located in the Steinway Hall Building produced Shakespearean plays that the Vogels attended, and Ingrid would reread the text of the chosen play before performances. The Studebaker Hall and Erlanger Theater often saw the couple seated in front row seats. Museum openings were attended. Evening performances at the Chicago Grand Opera were

Ingrid's favorite nights, and only sometimes, did she wish to be back on the stage. The Vogels did not lack for a cultural and social life. Their activities kept their bodies occupied and their minds devoid of sorrowful thoughts. Most of the time.

Then there was the traveling. Fredrick's position with the Steinway Company required him to return to New York City two or three times each year, and during one of those times, Ingrid would accompany him. Upon arrival in New York City, rooms were obtained at the Knickerbocker Hotel, but when the new Biltmore Hotel, right across from the Grand Central Terminal, was finished, they stayed there in the amazingly tall (twenty-three stories!) building, looked out the window of their room, astounded at the changes they noted in the city they once knew so well. The Vogels visited old friends and always saw a Broadway show. Dinner with Oscar Hammerstein was a pleasant requirement. The opera house in which Ingrid had her debut had closed in 1910, but neither that nor the legal troubles which dogged Oscar Hammerstein, stunted his creativity and entrepreneurship. The Vogels enjoyed a Vaudeville show at Hammerstein's Victoria Theater, meeting their friend afterwards for a late dinner at Barbetta where they had celebrated their wedding. The ten days spent in their old hometown passed in a flash of activity, and on the train ride back to Chicago, after a light dinner in the dining car, the Vogels were anxious to catch up on needed sleep. They would awake to coffee and pastries, anxious to return to their Lake Shore Drive home. In Chicago.

Chicago was a friendlier town than New York City. It was less pompous, more plain; less egotistical, more accommodating; less affected, more sincere. Oh, there were bouts of flashiness and outrageousness as the city expanded and grew into an adult, but it was all done with good humor, a wink, and an attitude which never disappeared. The downtown area's muddy streets, filled with horse droppings and carriage ruts, slowly gave way to concrete which became crossed with Model T tire tracks. The city streets were systemized and organized on a grid which made traveling from growing neighborhood to growing neighborhood uncomplicated, once the method was understood. Horsecars gave way to streetcars, and the influx of automobiles interfered with streetcar tracks. But residents took it all in stride, and the Vogels learned to adjust to the tenor and progress of the town. In fact, Fredrick was so taken with the automobiles he viewed at the 1913 Chicago Automobile Show that he ordered his first one: the Ford Model T. Both he and Lars Anderson learned to drive it, discovered which hardware stores sold the gasoline needed to fill it, and taught themselves to make necessary minor repairs on it. Driving on the Chicago streets was a risk which teetered at the edge of foolhardiness, but both Fredrick and Lars delighted in the challenge. And once she convinced her husband she was fully capable of maneuvering the contraption, Ingrid, too, learned to drive the Model T. And later, in Bonneville, she would impart the skill to Greta. Bonneville would be the site of many things shared by the two women.

Once the house in Bonneville was nearly completed, the Vogels took an early springtime trip to it. Fredrick and Lars evaluated the Model T, filled the tank with gasoline, checked the tires, and carefully and securely tied on the multitude of boxes and trunks which contained necessities for the new home. They left on the almost four-hour trip to open and make ready the house before Ingrid and Greta joined them a few days later. The women traveled to the LaSalle Street Station, taking the Rock Island train to Stone City in a fraction of the time it took to travel by automobile. They were met at the station by Lars in the Model T and made their way to the newly renovated house where they would stay for two weeks. Roads had been much improved, and the trip from Stone City to Bonneville took only over an hour. The Model T chugged through the streets of the expanding city and the women examined the town, noting the shops available to them. As the automobile turned onto the gravel drive, Fredrick waved to them from the wrap-around porch.

"Hello!" he yelled and walked down to the automobile to help the women out and kiss Ingrid. "Was the train trip easier than a four-hour automobile drive?"

"Yes, it was," and Ingrid removed her hat and smiled up at him, "but we are both tired and thirsty. Let us go in and get something to drink. Then I want to see how the house is coming along,"

They entered the house as Lars worked to bring the luggage and packages in. Greta had a sip of tea and went out to help her husband because his arthritis was aggravating him and managing physical tasks were becoming challenging. Once the cases and boxes were piled along the side of the front parlor, the Andersons went into the back of the house to view the three-room suite which was theirs. Then the couples met at the back of the house to look over the additional buildings. The stable/ garage was the one space ready and in use. The horse and wagon were on one side with a space for the Model T on the other. A large shed lacked only the gardening equipment and carpenter's tools which were due to be delivered by week's end. A greenhouse was partly built and would be completed during the summer although it would not be useful until the following year. In the fall, Lars would plant daffodil and crocus bulbs along the sides of the house where they would brighten the area during the following spring.

As they stood together in the sunlight, Fredrick pointed to the wooded area to the south, talking about his plans to, someday, start a crop of sorts. "I'm not sure what would do well there, but I thought I'd talk to some of the farmers I've met and get their ideas. Of course, it won't happen for a time yet. Not until I'm retired from Steinway, and that will be in the future. Anyway, there has been progress here. There is a long fence which needs repairing, and some other woodwork needs to be completed, but I thought that could get done eventually. What do you think?"

Everyone nodded in agreement, and Ingrid added, "It will probably take the remainder of the time we are here to finish the inside and put things away. I can work in the library and get the books put away, and tomorrow, Greta can go into town to pick up supplies for the kitchen. Will that work Greta?"

Greta nodded. "Once I get into the kitchen, I'll make a list of what is needed. Lars will be able to drive me tomorrow after lunch," and the plans were made. The Bonneville house was being organized.

***

Fredrick and Ingrid created a schedule for staying at their houses in Chicago and Bonneville. Each spring, once the snow melted and the roads cleared, the Andersons would take off in Fredrick's automobile for Bonneville. They would spend a week there cleaning and readying the place. Greta had no difficulty hiring young women who were ready to assist in cleaning the house, and Lars had no trouble finding boys to help clear the yard of fallen winter branches and complete the tasks his intensifying arthritis would no longer allow him to do. The compensation the temporary workers received was generous, and they were grateful for it. During the readying of the Bonneville house, the Vogels traveled to New York City for their annual visit; afterwards, they returned to Bonneville. Most of the summer months were spent away from Chicago's noise and congestion and in the fresh country air touted by Fredrick. Additional visits were made during the fall apple season and just before the holidays rolled in. Once or twice, when the weather remained cooperative, the Vogels and Andersons remained in Bonneville celebrating the Thanksgiving feast together before closing up for the winter and journeying back to the city on Lake Michigan.

Fredrick did not spend all that time in the country although he would have liked to. He looked forward to retiring there, but his work was at the Chicago Steinway Hall and occasionally the one in New York City. Friday afternoons, he would leave Chicago's Steinway Hall, travel to the LaSalle Street Station, take the Rock Island train to Stone City, and meet Lars at the station there. They would travel to Bonneville in his updated, larger, and more spacious Model T Touring car. The trip would not take as long because the newer car was faster and more powerful, and the country roads were continually being improved. Modernity was approaching. Fredrick would enjoy being in their country house until early Monday morning when Lars would return him to Stone City and the Rock Island for his journey back to Chicago, to his job. Ingrid looked forward to the weekend visits, but she learned to enjoy her time with Greta and Lars.

It was during that first summer the two women began their friendship. At first, without any committee meetings or luncheons and teas or State Street shopping to occupy her time, Ingrid felt lost. She would read, go for short walks along the property, practice her music in the side room which housed the Steinway. But that did not take up much of the day. She enjoyed being out in nature, and when she saw Lars in the stable/garage taking care of the horse or polishing the Model T, she would wander there and watch him for a while, making small talk and asking him questions. Lars answered them and was polite but maintained a distance from her, one suited to an older servant, and Ingrid soon learned to simply greet him and move on. The same thing happened when Ingrid visited the greenhouse, walking among the flowers and plants Lars lovingly cared for. Ingrid moved inside, into the kitchen, where Greta always seemed busy, cleaning and washing and baking. It was easier to speak with Greta, perhaps because they were closer in age, and Ingrid would stand or pull up a chair in which to sit and watch her at work. One day, as Greta was measuring and sifting and kneading the bread she was making, she glanced over to Ingrid who was intensely watching. She paused her work and spoke to her.

"Would you like to help make these loaves?"

Ingrid looked at her and realized that this was a task about which she was totally ignorant, and she didn't want to be. She nodded.

"What should I do?"

"First, go into the drawer over there," and Greta pointed with a flour-covered finger, "get out an apron and put it on. Then wash your hands. I'll show you how to knead the dough so it comes together."

They worked together, Greta teaching her anxious student, and soon the bread was ready for raising. As the pans were covered with a cloth, they washed up and Greta made a pot of tea for them to share. They sat and talked, mostly about the baking process, and Ingrid asked if Greta would teach her to bake. And maybe cook. Greta agreed, and a comfort developed. When the bread was oven-ready, Ingrid was shown how to place it into the oven. While they waited, the lesson on making strawberry jam began. Ingrid was fascinated with the entire process. There was a pride in the creation of the foodstuffs that Ingrid had never felt, and she was anxious to taste the bread once it was done. Greta showed her how to test for doneness and cautioned her that the oven was very hot. But burning one's hand or fingers is a rite of passage, and that day, Ingrid allowed her fingers to get too close to the bread pan as she was removing it from the oven.

"OW!" she yelled as she slammed the pan down and grabbed her finger with her other hand.

Without considering what she was saying, Greta looked at her and commanded, "Oh, Ingrid! Quick, put your hand into that pan with the cold water and keep it there." She reached over to the bottle of white vinegar and poured some into the water saying, "Just keep your hand there, and I'll bring out something to help you. I know how that hurts," and she rummaged through the far cabinet where the honey was kept and brought it to Ingrid. Greta carefully lifted the burned hand from the water, placed it on a clean cotton towel allowing it to dry, and spread honey on it.

"There. Is the sting going away? This isn't such a bad burn. It won't blister, but just rest there and I'll finish up here," and Greta worked at finishing the dishes and clearing away the baking equipment.

"How did you know to do this?" asked Ingrid.

Greta laughed. "Burned myself plenty. You learn what in the kitchen will do double duty for cooking and healing. How are you feeling?"

"Better," and Ingrid smiled. "And I'll be more careful next time. I have never taken anything from a hot oven before."

Greta questioned her. "So, do you want to continue cooking and baking lessons? This hasn't scared you away?"

"No, it has not. I'll just be more careful. For now, I'll just watch as you finish that jam."

It wasn't until later that evening as Ingrid thought back to the incident that she remembered Greta had called her by her given name. She realized she not only hadn't minded, but found it companiable. And when they were in the kitchen next, it seemed absolutely natural for Greta to begin her cooking lessons with, "Now, Ingrid, when you measure this…"

The two women exchanged skills. Ingrid never became as expert a baker or cook as Greta, but she enjoyed her successes and had the good humor to laugh at her failures. In return, when Greta mentioned that she enjoyed listening to Ingrid play the piano and wished she could, Ingrid began to teach her, encouraging her to practice on the Steinway. Greta could sew buttons, repair tears, hem skirts but never had time to learn the finer skill of embroidery, a skill Ingrid possessed and imparted to her. Greta taught Ingrid some Swedish, and Ingrid replied in French. Greta took Ingrid to the General Store to purchase groceries and canned goods, something Ingrid had never done. Or needed to do. Survival skills exchanged for social skills. But the most fun they had together was when Ingrid taught Greta to drive the Model T. There were a few mishaps. Once, Greta lost control on the country road and Lars was unhappy when he had to come with the horse and wagon to drag the automobile out of the corn field. He was further aggravated when Greta mistakenly made a sharp right turn onto the lawn, destroying the patch of begonias he had just moved from the greenhouse and transplanted artistically along the front walk. Greta looked properly crestfallen and ashamed at these incidents, apologizing to her husband. Later, when she and Ingrid were by themselves in the music room, they muffled their snorting laughter as they reviewed the events.

Without discussing or planning to do so, the cooking, embroidering, piano-practicing, grocery shopping, were activities done only in Bonneville. Ingrid did no baking in Chicago. Greta didn't continue her embroidery there either. While there, they reverted to the roles of *Mistress* and *Servant,* using familiar first names only when they were in the Chicago kitchen together and no one else was around. And those times were rare. Back in Chicago, Ingrid was occupied with her committees and luncheons. Concerts and dinners took up the Vogels' evenings. Greta cooked and cleaned, and once in a while, on the evenings she and Lars were alone in the townhouse, she dusted the Steinway and moved her fingers up and down the keys, trying to remember her Bonneville lessons. There were two separate worlds. The women understood their connections to each other and honored the distinct expectations of the contrasting spaces.

***

Perhaps because of its relative nearness to Chicago, electricity came to the Bonneville main town along with better roads and highway access by late 1913. In early 1914, as Fredrick was completing the updating and renovation of the country house, he ensured that it was part of the electric expansion. He was assisted by the building of additional houses across and down the country road from the Vogel's place, although the acreage belonging to them was allowed, for the most part, to remain empty. And would remain so for years to come. While telephones were placed in most of the shops and businesses in the town, there were few in private homes. Bonneville's mayor had one installed as did the doctor and the funeral director and the chief of police, for they maintained they needed to have quick access to each other, although how quickly the switchboard, run by Mabel McHenry, actually was, remained in doubt. Some of the town's private citizens also included the invention in their homes, but the majority of the Bonneville population waited until the exorbitant price of two dollars a month could be reduced. The Vogels did not have an issue with the cost nor with the additional *toll call cost* to connect with a party outside of the town. Fredrick would telephone Ingrid at least once a week when she was in Bonneville and he was in Chicago. She was always glad to hear his voice. And Mabel McHenry, who made sure the call was put through, was also.

The year 1914 not only saw electricity brought to Bonneville, it saw the start of a European war. In the early years, many people agreed with President Wilson, that the United States should continue to be "impartial in thought as well as in action". As long as the war stayed over there, it was a distant noise and could be contained. For German-Americans like Fredrick Vogel, the less said about it, the better. Keep working, support the country's impartiality, and hope it all ends quickly. And pray for the relatives living in Europe, in areas of conflict, to continue to stay alive. When the subject came up at a dinner or a social gathering, Fredrick would nod faintly in agreement with whatever prevailing opinion was expressed. Often, if the comments got heated and unpleasant, he would claim to see Ingrid motioning to him and excuse himself from the group. "Gentlemen, I see my wife wants me. Please excuse me. No domestic war needed!" He would leave the group chuckling, and find his wife. They would say farewells to whomever the hosts were, pleading an early business meeting or a minor headache. The war in Europe was not just civically concerning, it was socially uncomfortable.

***

The time spent in Bonneville slowly increased. Being in the country was more serene, and Fredrick relished his time there. As he traveled the Rock Island on a late Friday afternoon, soon to be met by Lars, happy to be traveling towards Ingrid, glad to be away from the Chicago commotion, he breathed easier, and his heartrate slowed. There would be a delicious dinner waiting for him, a long soak in the claw-footed bathtub after dinner, and an ease in sharing the bed with Ingrid, the woman for whom he gladly gave up his bachelorhood. Ingrid was delighted to see him, to share what news she had, to entertain him by describing her activities. She and the Andersons had attended the country fair on Wednesday, the opening day. There was the Wild West show which was both exciting and frightening, the acrobats who astounded them, the constant noise and the variety of music. Plans were made for a Saturday visit when Chicago politicians, Roger Sullivan and William Mason, would expound upon their achievements, when a ballgame with two of the best local teams would be held, where there would be exhibits of farm animals, farm machinery, farm implements. It would be entertaining and different, and the war in Europe would appear even more distant. The Vogels treasured their country residence.

But Chicago, too, was their home where they were involved in social activities and community events. Ingrid was active in an Art Institute women's group and when the 1913 Armory Show moved from New York to Chicago, she and Fredrick acted as one of the sets of hosts who greeted visitors on opening night. The Vogels were patrons of the newly built Wabash YMCA, and were honored at its opening. Operas, plays, and musical events of all sorts were held at the Auditorium Theater with Ingrid and Fredrick attending often. During 1914, whispers of the European war were almost drowned out by the yells and cheers at the ballgames held at Weeghman Park on Chicago's North side. Ingrid did attend a couple games with Fredrick, and she did admire the loveliness of the ballpark (soon to be renamed *Wrigley Field*), but mostly she left the sporting events to her husband. The Eastland Disaster that occurred in 1915, shocked and horrified Chicago, taking attention away from the European war for a time. When a benefit was held at the Auditorium Theater in August of that year, Ingrid and Fredrick traveled in from Bonneville to be part of the massive group of attendees, offering both condolences and cash to help the families. In January of 1916, the Vogels attended the operas *Faust* and *Cleopatra* at the Auditorium, while in April, they were present as Sarah Bernhardt gave yet another farewell performance. There was plenty to keep the Vogels occupied, to keep them from addressing the sadder issues of a war that seemed to get closer and closer, and the continued lack of tiny feet running through the houses they owned.

In the spring of 1916, on a temperate, soft evening, during the first long week spent in Bonneville, Fredrick suggested something to his wife. They were seated together on the hanging porch swing, watching the sky grow dusky, content to be with each other, comfortable after a delicious meal topped off by a rather decent sponge cake made by Ingrid. Fredrick pulled Ingrid close to him, leaned down to kiss the top of her burnt-umber hair and said, "I thought we might travel to Europe next year."

Ingrid turned to him with a quizzical look asking, "Europe? During a war? You know that Americans have been warned against travel! How could we?"

"I know what is being said, but there are plenty of rumors around, and I've discussed it with lots of people who say that it will all be decided soon. It will be over. This has gone on for two years now, and America has stayed out of it, despite the mess about the *Lusitania.* I'm not talking about this year, but next year. Specifically next fall. In 1917, the entire thing will be done and we will be able to travel. After all, this fall we celebrate our seventh wedding anniversary and next year our eighth. We should do something exciting and different to mark that, don't you think?"

Ingrid was silent for a minute, thinking it over. "Well, if you are sure the war will be done and we will be able to travel, of course, I'd love to go to Europe. It will give me a chance to use my French and German, and I should probably start to review the languages. Where will we travel?"

"Certainly to Germany. You know, I will need to visit the Steinway factory, but I would also like to go to Berlin. Once the war is given a chance to subside, we'll be safe there. Then, perhaps Switzerland? I thought you might want to visit your parents' graves. That could be arranged. Then France and England on the way home. What do you think?"

"It sounds wonderful. Thank you for thinking about my parents. I would like to see where they are resting," and Ingrid thought of something but wasn't sure whether she should suggest it. She waited for a time, staring off into the sky which was filling up with small beams of light. She took a breath and asked, "Would you want to visit Edith's grave? I wouldn't mind. I know you had a life before we met."

Fredrick leaned over and kissed her cheek. "Perhaps. That entire time seems so distant. I'm not sure, but will think about it. Anyway, we have lots of time to plan. I won't even contact any ship lines before this fall, and we'll wait out this war. I'm looking forward to the world being at peace again. Look, was that a shooting star?"

They sat outside until the night breezes chased them inside and upstairs where they got ready for bed. They lay on the cozy mattress which was settled on the wood-carved antique bedframe Fredrick bought years ago from Germany and discussed the possible trip until their voices faded away and became gentle constant breathing. There were the highest of hopes for peace and travel and excitement in the coming year, in 1917. But the plans they discussed while lying on the bed in the Bonneville house would be nullified. Capricious Fate would intervene.

***

He was going to travel to Bonneville later in the afternoon and remain for a week. Their seventh wedding anniversary was on Sunday, and Ingrid was going to make an entire dinner for them on Saturday night. She would do all the cooking and baking. She had been planning it all summer, and Greta would guide her in the preparation of the roasted chicken, mashed potatoes and gravy, fresh green beans, and home-made dinner rolls. A three-layered iced cake would be served for dessert, and the perfect wine from the supply in the house's cellar would be poured. Ingrid was planning a lovely table setting and would arrange the flowers she would gather from the greenhouse. She was anxious to show off her newly learned skills.

Fredrick was anxious to celebrate with his wife, but he hadn't felt well for a week. Actually, he hadn't felt well for longer than that, probably since more than two weeks ago, when he had needed to remain in Chicago and organize and host several weekend meetings and performances orchestrated by the Steinway Company. But he continued to get ready, packing his valise, making sure the gold and emerald bracelet he would give to Ingrid that weekend was carefully hidden in the side zippered pocket. He finished dressing, checked once more around the house, ensuring everything was locked and safe, and went down the stairs where the taxi cab he had called was waiting. It was early fall, and the weather was stuck in late summer, and despite the morning warmth, he felt chilled. There were times it seemed difficult to take a deep breath.

He didn't want to ruin this weekend or the following week and hoped he would feel better if he ate breakfast. He had the driver drop him off at the corner restaurant, the one just a few steps from Steinway Hall, and he went in. He hadn't eaten much the past couple of days. He was tired and had no appetite, and last night he had been unable to keep down the dinner he had ordered to be sent from his favorite restaurant. His stomach was better this morning, but it was empty. For a while, a couple weeks at least, his heart had been racing, but he just assumed it was due to the weather, to his workload, to the general aggravation of living in a busy city. He ordered eggs and toast and coffee, but the coffee did not taste right. He called the waiter over and asked for tea. He drank most of a cup and ate a piece of dry toast, but just pushed the eggs around on the plate. He was sure they would reappear if he tried to swallow them.

He left a decent tip; after all, it wasn't the waiter's fault he couldn't eat, and walked around the corner to his building. When he got to his office, he placed the valise, which seemed heavier since he left the apartment, in the corner and looked over his schedule for the day. There were three meetings to attend, one right after the other, and they would take him up to noon. He had a driver ordered for one o'clock and he would take the one-fifty Rock Island to Stone City where Lars would be waiting for him in the new touring car which he was anxious to drive. He thought that once he was at the house, a short nap would refresh him, and he would feel better. He continued his day, going to the meetings, glad they were all in the building, and turned down the offer, actually two offers, for lunch. He felt warm and somewhat damp. Then he felt cold, and asked his secretary to bring him some hot tea and find some toast. He sat in his office sipping and eating and staring out the window until it was time to travel.

The trip to Stone City was miserable. Fredrick tried to rest, laying his head back against the seat in an attempt to get some sleep, but he vacillated between chills and fever, and his thoughts were scattered. When he saw Lars and the automobile, he felt relieved. He handed his valise to Lars who placed it in the back seat and started to get into the passenger side. Fredrick stopped him.

"Not feeling well, Lars, and I don't think I'll drive. Here, get in and drive us back," and Fredrick climbed into the passenger seat, rolled down the window and allowed some fresh air to cross his sweaty face which he periodically wiped with his handkerchief.

The ride was grueling. Fredrick was hoping to keep breakfast and lunch down, and even though the roads had been smoothed out and the journey was not as lengthy as it used to be, he suffered. There was something wrong. He could feel his heartbeat quicken. There was little conversation in the car, and Lars knew there was a problem. Fredrick usually talked all the way to the house, wanting to know how things were, how Ingrid was, what was new in the town, but nothing was asked or said during this trip. Trying to avoid bumps in the road, he drove a bit faster, getting the car up to almost its top speed of thirty-five miles per hour. When Lars pulled up to the house, he got out, pulled the valise from the back seat and went around to the passenger door to help Fredrick. He leaned the unsteady man against the car and turned and yelled for his wife. When he turned back, Fredrick was doubled over, covering the marigolds planted along the walk with the partly digested meals of tea and toast. He groaned, and Lars placed his arm around the man, pulling him to his side, helping him into the house, a feat for Lars who was ignoring both his arthritis and the split front step which had not yet been repaired. As they entered the house, Ingrid and Greta came rushing over, their happy greetings turning to worried questions. Fredrick was placed into the nearest chair and Greta rushed to get a cool cloth, a warm cloth, some towels, unsure exactly what would be needed to make the man more comfortable.

Fredrick was taken, slowly, upstairs to the bedroom suite. The bedroom was large and had an attached room meant for a sitting area. At one point, the Vogels thought it would make a perfect nursery being so close to the actual bedroom and connected by a large door. But since there had been no need for that, they began to call it a "dressing room", storing items in the mammoth wardrobe which was there, allowing another, smaller bed to take up space, putting a small side table and two chairs in one corner. A large window allowed in light and air, and it was to this room Fredrick insisted on being taken. "I don't want you to get what I have, Ingrid, and the dressing room is comfortable enough," he murmured as he was helped into the space.

Lars assisted Fredrick as his outer clothes were removed and given to Greta to clean, and nightwear was placed on him. Ingrid assisted and arranged the pillows so he was comfortable. She opened the window to allow a bit of air into the stale, unused room, pulled one of the side chairs over to his bedside, emptied the side table of the knick-knacks which decorated it. Room was exposed for whatever cups or bowls or sickroom implements were going to be needed. She placed his valise into the wardrobe, closed the curtains, allowing just a small bit of light into the room, thanked Lars and told him to go downstairs and rest. Greta was in the kitchen creating a tray of various drinks, hot and cold, to bring up to Fredrick should he want something. She was also searching through the small case in which she kept her herbs and medicines, searching for something to reduce his fever. Once Fredrick seemed settled, Ingrid spoke to him.

"I'm going to call Doctor Marshall. I think he should take a look at you. Perhaps there is something he can give you to help."

Fredrick shook his head slightly but stopped because the headache that was forming was simply another pain to endure. "No, Ingrid. Wait until morning. Let me see if I can get over this on my own. Really, I just need to rest. I'm exhausted from work, but glad to be here and sorry to ruin the dinner you have planned. Please do whatever you were going to do for it. By tomorrow night, I'll be up and about. I'm sure of it. So sorry."

Ingrid soothed back his hair, all gray now, and felt the heat from his forehead. She reached over to the pan of tepid water Greta had left, took a cloth from it, and after wringing it out, carefully wiped his face. "I will only wait until morning, and if there is no change, Doctor Marshall will be called. Here, give me your hands to wash," and as she took his hands which were shaking, Greta came in with the tray.

"Here we go. I have some ginger tea for you. It will help reduce your fever and settle your stomach," and she placed the tray on the cleared side table, and Ingrid spooned the tea into the mouth of her sick husband.

***

Ingrid stayed by Fredrick's bedside all night. He urged her to go to bed, but after a while, he just stopped talking. His breathing was getting heavier and Ingrid thought it sounded labored, as if he were breathing through water. Greta appeared every few hours, attempting to take over whatever nursing needed to be done, but Ingrid refused to leave. She stayed in the chair, and before morning, fell asleep against the back of it while Greta covered her with a light coverlet before leaving. When the sunlight came in, Ingrid stirred and then sat up. Fredrick was breathing in a strained manner, and she went to the top of the stairs and called for Greta who hurried up the stairs.

"Here, help me raise his back and head with these pillows," and Greta pointed to them, "because he will breathe easier." Fredrick still felt feverish and clammy, as they carefully moved him. He groaned as they placed the pillows behind him but never opened his eyes. Ingrid stood for a moment and then turned to Greta.

"Please stay here. I know it's early, but I'm going to telephone Doctor Marshall. I hope Mabel is close to her switchboard so she can put the call through. I'll be right back."

Ingrid did not come right back. Mabel eventually heard the ringing and worked her switchboard magic, but the Marshall telephone rang and rang until a sleepy Mrs. Marshall finally answered. When the doctor came to the phone, he explained that his automobile had a flat tire, and it needed repairing before he could travel out to the house. Ingrid told him to get ready and Lars would be sent out to pick him up. Then she had to get Lars up and out, and as she explained all this to Greta, she began to cry.

"Ingrid, stop. The doctor will be here soon, and Fredrick doesn't need to wake and see you in tears." She reached into her pocket and pulled out a handkerchief and handed it to her. "I am here. Go and clean up and change your clothes. Comb your hair. You don't want your husband to see you in such a state. Go now, before the doctor comes. I won't leave," and Greta took her place on the chair which Ingrid had pushed as close to the bed as possible.

When the women heard the car drive up to the house, Greta went downstairs to open the door for the doctor who went directly upstairs. As he examined Fredrick, he asked Ingrid a number of questions to which she had no answers. How long had he been feeling unwell? Had he been around anyone who was ill? What had he eaten yesterday and how much? Had any medications been given other than tea? Did this come on suddenly or had he been feeling ill for a while? Did his heart usually race in this manner? He listened to his lungs and his heart, tapping and causing Fredrick to cough and open his eyes.

"Good morning, Fredrick. Can you tell me what pains you have? What did you eat yesterday? How long have you felt unwell?" and the doctor continued his poking and prodding while Fredrick attempted to answer coherently.

Doctor Marshall reached into his bag and pulled out the same kind of small brown vial Greta had disposed of years ago. Years ago, when there had been another illness, a loss. Ingrid glanced over to Greta who was standing by the doorway. She lightly shrugged her shoulders. The doctor looked around for a glass and asked, "Is there some fresh water? Please fill this up about a third of the way," and Ingrid followed directions, willing to do anything to ensure her husband's health. If this poison would do that, she would allow it. She was frightened. She was desperate. The doctor placed three drops of the reddish-brown liquid into the glass, swirled it around, and managed to get most of it into Fredrick's mouth. He wiped the dribbled liquid off Fredrick's chin with a towel and took the vial, placing it on the table next to the remains of the cold ginger tea. Poison and curative.

Fredrick closed his eyes and the doctor helped him to lay back against the pillows. He replaced everything in his bag, turned to Greta and said, "I need to speak with Mrs. Vogel for a minute. Would you say here with Mr. Vogel?" He led Ingrid out by the elbow into the hallway while Greta stood by the door of the bedroom, positioning herself so she could both view Fredrick and hear the conversation.

"Mrs. Vogel, I believe your husband has the *grippe*. I know that crowded large cities such as Chicago have been dealing with an outbreak in recent months, and it is possible your husband has been ill for a while. When did you last see him?"

"He was busy last weekend with some special programs and meetings at work and was unable to travel here, so this is the first I have seen him in two weeks. Will he be all right?"

Doctor Marshall hated this part of his job. He never knew whether it was kinder to encourage optimism or tell the truth. He waffled, and spoke somewhere in between the two options. "He is a very sick man. I believe from what I can gather that he has not felt well for a time. To be honest, the disease has advanced and I detect both dropsy and pneumonia in him. His lungs are filling with some liquid, and his fever is high. There is some medicine I will send back with Lars. Use it. It should reduce his fever. It's called *antifebrin*, and while I'll write out the directions for its use, you should administer it in boiled water every thirty minutes through today and see if that helps. Continue to make him comfortable. I have left a small bottle of morphine for your use. It will ease him and allow sleep, so use it. Encourage him to take broths and teas, and he may rest easier on his left side. The right lung seems to be worse. Keep him clean and comfortable and I will stop in tomorrow after church to check on him. Do you have any disinfectant in the house?"

"I will ask Greta, but I am sure we do. Why?"

"Wash down as many things as he has touched with it. Chlorine or charcoal will do. I believe the pharmacy in town has carbolic which Lars can pick up. The disease could be contagious, but it is advanced, and that stage may have passed. You should all wash your hands carefully and often. If you and Greta are going to nurse him, mask your mouths and noses. I don't mean to scare you with these precautions, but follow them and you should be safe as long as you are careful."

Ingrid could barely breathe with fear. She nodded her head and walked down the stairs with the doctor who asked for a place he could wash up. Lars was given instructions, and he readied the car to take Doctor Marshall home. When he returned with the additional medicine from the doctor and the carbolic from the pharmacy, Greta was cleaning everything she could with the chlorine she found, and she had a mask covering her mouth and nose. She told him to go and wash up, clean the automobile thoroughly, then change his clothes. Ingrid was upstairs wiping down whatever she could as she watched Fredrick sleep. Her heart was beating as quickly as was his, although for different reasons.

It was a long day and longer night. Greta and Ingrid took turns watching Fredrick and trying to sleep. Greta had a pot of broth on the stove and both women would drink it to keep up their strength, since there was no time to prepare actual meals. It was decided that Lars, being much older than either of the women, should stay downstairs and away from any possible infection. Fredrick would wake periodically, but for most of the time, he moved around restlessly. A couple times, he seemed to be wide awake and would speak quietly and coherently to Ingrid.

"I'm so sorry, Ingrid. I've spoiled this entire weekend for us. I guess it was good I planned to stay for the week. Don't think I could travel back to Chicago like this."

Ingrid pulled down her mask so he could see her smile at him. "Fredrick, just work at getting well. We will celebrate once you are, and I'll make the dinner I planned for you. Now please take a bit more broth and then rest," and Ingrid would attempt to get him to swallow the liquid before she wiped his face and hands once again. He would lay back on the pillows which were propped up and fall in and out of a sleep. But the fever remained, and a terrible coughing started, and Ingrid did not want Greta to take her nursing turn when the time came. Greta had to force her to rest.

"If you get sick, how can I care for you both?" she whispered. "Go now, Ingrid. Lay down and rest and when you get up, eat some of the sandwich I left for you. Go on, now," and reluctantly, Ingrid left.

Doctor Marshall did drive himself to the house on Sunday, after church, his automobile repaired. When he examined Fredrick, noting that the fever remained and his coughing was worsened, he became sure about what the outcome would be. He could not bear to tell Ingrid, however, and when she asked, answered, "He's doing as well as possible. May I use your telephone to inform my wife that I am going to remain here for a time?" He went downstairs to the library where the telephone was located and called home to inform his wife that he would not be home for Sunday dinner. And probably not until tomorrow. Unless there was a medical emergency in town, he would stay at the Vogels until the worse had happened. Recovery was not expected.

The day dragged on. The night was worse. The doctor stayed through an additional day and into the second night. Ingrid was insistent upon remaining in the sickroom, refusing to rest, refusing to leave, and Doctor Marshall became stern with her saying, "You need to sleep for a few hours. I'll wake you if needed. Greta is also here, and we can care for him. Now, go rest."

Ingrid lay down, but she heard every cough and moan. After an hour, she returned to the dressing room, declining to leave Fredrick's side again. The doctor nodded and sat her down in the chair. He patted her shoulder and said, "I'm going to get some coffee. Greta went down to make some, and I'll be back soon. If he should wake, see if you can give him another dose of the morphine. I'll mix it and leave it here on the table. Call out if you need help with something. I'll return shortly," and he prepared the solution and went down the stairs to find Greta.

Fredrick moaned and coughed, and Ingrid rose to rearrange the pillows beneath his neck and shoulders. His breathing was loud and labored, but when she cradled his head to shift it to one side, he opened his eyes and looked at her. She smiled as she moved to sit on the side of the bed, placed her hand on the contours of his cheek, and said to him, "Fredrick, I am here. Can I make you more comfortable?"

Fredrick struggled to sit up, and when he did, he leaned into Ingrid, resting his head on her shoulder. She placed her arms around him holding him gently, holding him as she would have held a child, had there been one. She tenderly rocked back and forth with him, not willing to lay him back down, not wanting to let him go, and as she rocked him, he spoke. His voice was faint and feeble; his mouth next to her ear. She heard each word.

"Ingrid, my love, I am sorry for ruining the party. I am sorry for being sick. I am sorry for not giving you a child. You should have one. You would be a wonderful mother. You are…" His voice faded, and he became limp.

"Shh," said Ingrid to him. "You will get well, and we will try again. We are connected, Fredrick, you and I. Always. Always," and she waited to hear an answer. One did not come.

There was a sudden release of a long final moan, guttural in essence. Fredrick slumped in her arms, but Ingrid held him tightly. She listened for any sound: a moan, a breath, a heartbeat. A horrific hush perpetuated until the noise of her own voice happened, and she shrieked his name louder and louder and louder. When Doctor Marshall and Greta came rushing up the stairs and into the dressing room, it took both of them to pry Ingrid's arms from around the slack body of her husband who was moved back onto the waiting pillows. As Greta cradled the hysterical woman in her arms, the doctor carefully and gently closed the eyes of Fredrick Vogel so that his wife, his twenty-seven-year-old widow, would not observe his glazed hazel eyes peering into an unfamiliar nothingness.

Five

Interim: 1917-1921

Ingrid had been sitting on the stone bench for most of an hour and was beginning to realize she was uncomfortable. She glanced over her left shoulder and saw Greta walking towards her, so she moved over, making room on the small bench for her. Greta came over, saw the space, and squeezed in next to her. They were silent for a time until Greta remarked, "That man did a good job with the marker. It's nicely done, Ingrid."

Ingrid sighed. Then she nodded in agreement. "I wanted something to be carved into it using his German language, but because of the hostile feelings about Germany and this war, I used French instead. Yes, I think it looks dignified. I suppose I should have come down to see it sooner, but I just wasn't ready."

"I know you weren't. And we can stay here as long as you want to. I finished shopping, and it's all in the car which is parked by the general store. There's no hurry."

"I'm done here for today. I just needed some time to be alone with him. We can go back to the house now. I suppose Lars will be wondering where we are for so long," and Ingrid wiped her eyes again and stood up.

Greta stood up too and waited while Ingrid walked to the stone, running her fingers along the carved words which proclaimed:

Votre amour a éclaire mon chemin
Votre mémoire sera toujours avec moi
Fredrick Vogel
1863-1916
Beloved

They walked back to the automobile and Ingrid climbed into the passenger side while Greta started it. They took off through the main street of Bonneville, heading towards the house to which they had arrived only the day before and which had been closed for almost a year.

After last fall, after Fredrick's death and burial in the town's cemetery, Ingrid returned to Chicago where she had remained until the following summer threatened to journey into autumn.

***

Fredrick's burial had been sparsely attended, for he was not well known in town. Ingrid, after the doctor had sedated her allowing her to sleep for most of a day, was able to make some decisions. She decided that her husband should stay in Bonneville, the town in which he had wanted to retire. "He loved being here," she explained through sobs to Mr. Martin, the town's undertaker, "and I want him to remain here." Mr. Martin was considerate towards the young widow, discovering through carefully worded questions that there would be no funeral, and only Ingrid and the Andersons would be invited to view the deceased in his casket before the burial which would take place in two days. At the cemetery, Ingrid and the Andersons stood with Doctor Marshall, Mr. Martin, and Oliver Martin, son and apprentice to his father, while Pastor Riordan, minister of the Methodist church Ingrid and Fredrick sometimes attended, led the brief service for the burial of the dead. It was shortened because rain was falling, and the only umbrella available was held by Doctor Marshall over the bowed heads of Ingrid and Greta. Afterwards, Ingrid thanked everyone. She headed back to the house with the Andersons, Lars doing the driving.

One week later, necessary tasks were completed: the house was cleaned and shuttered, the rented horse and buggy returned to Harold Jones, the neighboring farmer who had agreed to watch the house. The furniture was covered, windows and doors securely locked, and the Bonneville sheriff was informed they would be gone. The car, loaded with cases, bags, and people, left for Chicago. Once there, Ingrid busied herself alerting friends and acquaintances, neighbors and Chicago newspapers about Fredrick's death. She contacted the Steinway Company to explain that Fredrick would no longer be available to work or travel back and forth between Chicago and New York. He was on a much longer journey. She wrote to Oscar Hammerstein, living in New York, unhappily married to his third wife, arguing with the courts and his daughters over money, and informed him about his friend's death. Oscar sent a lengthy letter in return, mourning Fredrick, praising him, assuring Ingrid that they both would be forever in his thoughts. He hoped that Ingrid would soon visit New York where they would have a wonderful meal at Barbetta's Restaurant, discuss old times, and raise a glass or two of the good Italian wine to Fredrick's memory. That did not happen. Oscar Hammerstein was ill, and just a couple years later went on his own dark and solitary journey. There were letters to old friends in New York and newer associates in Chicago, meetings set up with lawyers to discuss the legalities of death and its financial obligations, long evenings when attempts were made to alleviate loneliness by sitting in the kitchen, sipping valerian tea which Greta assured her would reduce her anxiety. Ingrid grew silent, lost weight, found life almost intolerable without Fredrick.

Death has its requirements, and Ingrid completed them. She contacted a memorial mason in Stone City to create the tombstone she envisioned for Fredrick's grave. Then she contacted him again to ask for a stone bench to be set at the foot of his grave. She answered letters of condolence. She set herself the tasks of learning how to monitor and organize the budget, of grappling with banking and checking concerns, of managing payments to various people, all Fredrick's former responsibilities. She was the widow and in charge, was responsible for making decisions and creating a life for herself, but it was all done in a fog she could not shake. She would rise each morning after a few hours stressed sleep, make the immediate decisions which were needed, travel fuzzily through one day and then another, drink and eat part of whatever Greta put in front of her, and somehow remained upright. She continued to plod along through the remainder of 1916 and into 1917, ignoring the holidays, refusing the few invitations she received, speaking softly, not smiling.

The world would not stop for her despite her sorrow. Woodrow Wilson, was reelected in November, the Suffragist movement continued to fight for women's rights, the war in Europe with descriptions of the battles of Somme and Verdun were announced in screaming newspaper headlines along with dozens of additional important and unimportant events. Tensions mounted because the United States' neutrality in world affairs was shaky. Then, in April of 1917, just a couple weeks after President Wilson gave up the stance on neutrality and shifted the United States into a wartime perspective, Ingrid Vogel turned twenty-eight years old. She felt much older. But that was not the only change of which she became aware.

Chicago had become firmly patriotic, encouraging a constant air of loyalty which bordered on zealousness. Language, newly created, abounded in the streets, the shops, the schools, the parks, the newspapers. English now required additional knowledge of words and phrases such as: *Doughboy, Victory garden, war bonds, Huns, Hello Girls, trench coats.* Some Chicago area German immigrants continued to convey pride in their former homeland, but they were easily and rapidly shouted down. Newspapers' political cartoons warned them against it. Immigrant schoolchildren were harassed. Friendships ended. Expressed anger about their heritage frightened many into metamorphosis. Mrs. Schmidt, housekeeper to a wealthy family, became *Mrs. Smith*; Mr. Kock who worked at the butcher shop would be known as *Mr. Cook*; the Bruckner family informed their children's school that they were now the *Brooks family*. And comments were made to Greta and to Lars about the fact that they worked for a woman whose last name, *Vogel*, was undoubtedly Germanic.

A warm June morning, another sleepless night for Ingrid, found her quietly entering the kitchen where she overheard a conversation between Greta and Lars. Greta had gone out on an early morning mission attempting to find fresh eggs, and was met with sharp remarks about the "German woman" for whom she worked. It wasn't the first time. Greta stood up for Ingrid again, but after the conversation escalated into a nasty shouting match, she returned eggless. Lars was listening to and consoling her, and suddenly he looked up to see the "German woman" standing just at the doorway listening. He shushed his wife who turned. All of them were quiet. Ingrid pulled out a chair and sat down and looked at them both.

"So, people are talking about Fredrick and me," commenting, not questioning.

Greta sat down in the chair across from her, noticing the dark circles under Ingrid's eyes, knowing that without eggs she could not make the coffee cake she had planned to, the one Ingrid did like and could be encouraged to eat, and she nodded.

"Just ignore it, Ingrid," and Greta attempted to brush aside the remarks made, hoping she had not heard all the conversation, "the woman sold old eggs anyway. There are other places to get the things, and I'll try someone else tomorrow. Tea?"

Ingrid sighed and nodded. She knew things were being said. She hadn't received any recent information about friendly gatherings or meetings for her committees, and was fairly certain it was not just because she was in mourning. There had been a few snubs she opted to ignore, not caring about them, considering the sources, but in the recess of her mind, she questioned the explanations. Now she was sure she knew them. Greta brought her tea, then opened the window to encourage an early morning breeze. Lars left to take care of his daily tasks while Greta sat down with her own cup. For a time, the women were quiet.

Ingrid sipped, held the warm cup, then looked up. "Greta, it's time to leave Chicago. At least for a while. I know the Bonneville house has been empty since last September. It needs to be aired out. Perhaps the weather will not be so warm there. Anyway, I've heard from Stone City, and Fredrick's marker is in place. I want to check on it and spend some time there to be close to him. I have a few business issues to take care of here, and we need to close this house down. Clothes and supplies need to be packed, but I'm sure that it will take a short time. What do you think?"

"I think that's a good plan. Do you want Lars and me to go down and get the house set up, cleaned, and organized for you? You could take the Rock Island once everything is done here, and Lars can pick you up from the station."

"No. We'll go together in the car. In fact, we should all share the driving. You need more practice, and Lars has been driving me around the city. I need practice too. When you see Lars, let him know about the plan. He can get the car ready, and you and I can work in here packing and organizing."

Greta cocked her head to one side and said, "There is no need for you to work at the house tasks. I'll hire one of the young girls from my church to help."

"Go on and hire someone to help, but there *is* a need for me to work with you, to stay busy, Greta. That has been one of the problems. I need to work, and I don't mind doing it. Although," and here Ingrid smiled for the first time in ten months, "I'm sure Grandmother Louisa would disapprove."

Greta laughed. It was good to see Ingrid excited about something. Even if it was only packing clothes and covering furniture. She was right, Greta decided. They needed to leave the city for a time. It would be good for everyone. Wholesome country air to breathe, fresh farm eggs to buy. Neither Greta nor Ingrid realized that this decision would turn their lives around. That in time, they would end up living in Bonneville, visiting Chicago only a few weeks a year. And when they would eventually come back to Chicago, their lives will have been completely transformed.

***

They left Chicago. The new automobile, the 1916 Dodge Brothers Closed Car which Fredrick ordered just months before his death, was packed to overflowing with the cases and bags and packages Ingrid and Greta thought necessary. They left during the last week of June, 1917, just as the weather was becoming unbearable. July would have the most one-hundred-degree days anyone could remember, and the breeze that worked its way through the car, traveling about twenty-five miles per hour, was appreciated. The trip took less than three hours with quick stops to change drivers and stretch legs. And once Ingrid drove up the side driveway to the house, there was a collective and audible sigh from all.

"Finally," said Greta, "I'm hungry and thirsty, and I'm sure you are too. Let's leave the unpacking until we rest and eat. Lars, those two top boxes contain the food and water. It you can take one, I'll get the other."

Ingrid climbed out of the car with the keys to the house, opened the door, and they all entered. Food boxes were placed on the kitchen table, and Greta began to wipe and clean the kitchen furniture and get the food ready. Lars went around to open windows and check that the water, the telephone, the electricity were all in working order. Ingrid helped in the kitchen, and once they washed up, they ate the sandwiches and fruit Greta had packed that morning, discussing what must be done.

"We won't get it all done today, and I'll need to hire some of the girls from the town to help, but we can get the bedrooms organized and set up for tonight, and there is enough food so we won't starve," and Ingrid took another bite of her sandwich. "Lars, could you drive over and let Mr. Jones know we are here and ask if perhaps he has some fresh milk and eggs for us? That would help. Greta, I need to make a few telephone calls to town and then can help you with the bedrooms. Let's take stock of what we need and make a list so it can be picked up in town tomorrow. I want to go to the cemetery and perhaps you can shop while I do that. What do you think?"

They both nodded, and Lars spoke. "I'll ask Harold Jones to get the horse and wagon ready for me to pick up tomorrow. In the morning, before you drive to town, you can drop me off there and I'll drive the wagon back. I'd like to see what condition the greenhouse is in. Think it's a little late to plant much. Maybe I can get some autumn vegetables and plants in, but there will be cleaning to do."

Plans were made and the remainder of the day was a busy one. Once the windows upstairs were opened, the fresh breezes cleared up the musty house smell, and Greta and Ingrid worked together in the bedrooms. Lars came back with the milk, eggs, and some of the season's last strawberries. Mrs. Jones had just baked bread and sent a fresh loaf with him. A dinner of sandwiches, coffee and strawberries was eaten, and the three of them sat on the front porch talking about nothing of importance, but relishing the air, the country air Fredrick had claimed would be beneficial to them. The sunset covered the sky with a blazing orange which they all admired, mentioning such a sight would rarely be seen in Chicago. They went inside. Lars closed up the downstairs windows and locked the doors while Greta and Ingrid bid each other good night. The next day would find Ingrid seated in the Bonneville Cemetery on the stone bench in front of Fredrick's grave, thinking about him, mourning his absence, and wondering what her future would be like.

***

The Chicago heat followed them to Bonneville, but the open spaces, clear azure sky, and lack of traffic and congestion kept it from being too oppressive. They worked at the tasks needed to reopen a home not lived in for almost a year. Teen-aged girls wanting to earn extra money were hired to assist Greta, and their younger brothers came along to pull the weeds, mow the expansive lawn, and work with Lars who was a kind taskmaster. Ingrid began to help with the cleaning, but Greta told her to allow the young girls to do it. "I'll teach them what to do. Go on now and be the lady of the house," and Ingrid just grinned. Greta was pleased when she saw a smile.

Sleeping through the night remained a problem for Ingrid. She often woke early, even before Greta was up, and went into the library to sit in the semi-darkness at the large desk or in the leather club chair in the corner. Sometimes she sat in the chair, looking around at the tall mahogany bookcases filled with collected volumes and thought about the times Fredrick would be at his desk working. They would talk, or she would read and he would work, and the memories of those times created a lump in her throat which would soon dissolve through her eyes. She would wipe the tears and pull the coverlet from the back of the chair to wrap around her. Sometimes she would put her head back against the leather and sleep a brief time, or she would stare out the east-facing window and watch the sun rise. When she heard Greta in the kitchen, she would go there and they would sit and drink some morning coffee or tea before Ingrid went upstairs to dress, then drive the car to the cemetery.

For the first month or so, as long as the weather cooperated,

Ingrid visited Fredrick daily. She sat on the stone bench, reread the inscription on the tombstone and spoke to her husband under her breath. At first, the cemetery's caretaker, Mr. Jenson, didn't know the early morning visitor, but he soon became acquainted with her and would wave as he made his early morning rounds. Ingrid would offer a slight smile and a soft wave and continue her discussion with Fredrick. When early fall weather came and leaves began to turn, she visited twice a week, then once a week, then twice a month, then once in a while. She felt guilty, thinking her wifely duties were neglected. While wiping tears from her face, she confessed this to Greta who countered with comfort and common sense.

"Ah, Ingrid, *Det blir som det blir*. You have your husband always in your heart. Grief never goes away but it lessens. Besides, the weather is changing, and you should not catch a morning chill sitting on the cold bench. Allow Mr. Vogel to rest. You should also. Come, I made a coffee cake you like. Let's have a piece."

The months were sad ones. Ingrid was silent much of the time. She stood at a window, staring at the distance, not hearing when Greta asked a question. One morning, as the sky clouded over and threatened snow, she sat with the Andersons in the kitchen, cozy with breakfast smells, and they sipped their second cups of coffee silently. Ingrid took a last sip and sighed. She looked at Lars first and then Greta.

"I need to talk about something because it involves you. I am thinking about remaining here, in Bonneville, over the winter, but will not do that if you are not both in agreement. I don't want to return to Chicago right now, but if you do, we will. We need to agree about this. Thanksgiving will be here at month's end, and while the weather holds, we either need to pack up and return or prepare to stay. I don't know what the winter will be like here, and I'm unsure if we are ready for it. Lars, what is your opinion?"

Lars squinched his mouth to one side and thought. "When Mr. Vogel took over this house, he did plan for spending winters here, and a coal furnace was installed. There is a small supply of coal there, and a coal stoker which works, but with the war and the coal shortage and the problems in getting any delivered this late in the year, I'm not sure how long it will last or how warm the house will be. There are wood-burning fireplaces in most rooms, and the kitchen stove is warm, but the furnace hasn't been used much. I can check it out and ask in town about the possibility of coal, but we shouldn't put that off any longer."

"That would be a good idea. What else could we do?"

Greta chimed in, "If we are staying here, we need winter clothes, and they are all in Chicago."

Ingrid nodded. "I thought of that. If we are going to stay, I think that you and I, Greta, should drive to Chicago and pack the car with needed things. Lars, would you object to being here by yourself for a week or so while we are gone?"

"I can manage fine. If I can hire some of the young boys around here to help cut and stack wood and clean out and ready the fireplaces and furnace, I believe we can be ready before the winter sets in. Greta, make sure you get my high boots stored way in the back of our closet. One other thing. The price of coal is high. I believe it runs about ten dollars per ton."

"Alright," said Ingrid, "whatever you can get, order it. If we are going to stay here, we should leave for Chicago in a day or so. Lars, please make sure the car is in shape for the trip, and Greta can prepare some food for you while we are gone. I'll telephone a few people I think can help us. Are we agreed about doing this?"

Greta looked over at Lars and they smiled at each other. Then she said, "I'm one for an adventure. Should we plan on leaving the day after tomorrow? We'll be back before Thanksgiving. Ingrid, can we make plans to telephone Lars just to check on him?"

"Absolutely. We'll make a schedule," and Ingrid, excited to have a plan, grateful to have the Andersons agree, happy to stay closer to Fredrick, smiled once again.

***

That first winter of 1917 was the coldest one they would spend in Bonneville. Lars got the furnace going with the help of Harold Jones, and there was plenty of wood stacked up at the back so that once the winter arrived, at least the fireplaces kept rooms warm. Ingrid and Greta made it to Chicago and drove back before snow fell. The car was packed with their stored clothing as well as newly bought winter clothing, extra blankets, shovels, available foodstuffs, anything the women thought might be useful through the winter. They all wore extra clothing that winter. Sweaters and shawls were left on all the chairs, ready to add to their outfits any time the pitiless winter wind shook the windows or drafts crept in, penetrating exposed skins. There were grins and pointing as the two women saw how each other dressed. Greta said they looked like scarecrows wrapped in old clothes to scare off hungry birds. But they survived the winter, learning what they would need to do in the future to remain warm in the three-story house. Lars, who was unused to shoveling the needed coal into the stoker, would rub his aching arms and knees. Greta made him drink a concoction of rose hips and ginger tea to combat his arthritis and rubbed his sore hands and knees with an oil of wintergreen solution she created using ingredients from the small case beneath her bed. She attempted to keep them all well by dosing Lars and Ingrid and herself with a spoonful of warmed honey daily. She kept a large pot of water boiling on the stove, filling the air with a comfortable steam, creating needed warmth in the kitchen where they spent most evenings. Only a slight cold kept Ingrid in bed one week and Lars another, and Greta, who did not get sick, commented that they must have skipped their daily dose of honey. In the spirit of the western pioneers Ingrid jokingly compared them to, they managed to make it through the winter.

The new year of 1918 was celebrated with a shared bottle of sparkling wine, and they began looking forward to the spring, planning what needed to be done. Lars was going to plant a vegetable garden and Greta wanted certain herbs grown. Ingrid listened to them and began to organize a list of needed supplies and added *coal* to the top of the list. There were some trips into town when supplies ran low, but the war and the necessity of feeding millions of soldiers meant that supplies were limited. Even when cash was available, one could not purchase what was not in stock. They did without things, just as the rest of the population of Bonneville, and the country, did.

Food substitutions were suggested, although rationing was not mandated in the United States as it was in Europe. Americans were asked to forego white sugar which was difficult to obtain and use molasses, honey, or maple syrup instead. Wheat was difficult to find. *The kitchen is the KEY to VICTORY! Eat less bread* recommended a U.S. Food Administration poster which was hung up in plain sight at the Bonneville General Store. White bread and biscuits were rarely made for dinner tables, but rye flour, cornmeal, and oat flour were acceptable substitutes, claimed newspapers where recipes for alternate breads were printed. Using different ingredients was not only important to the war effort, but helped create a healthy, wholesome loaf called "War Bread". Mashed potato biscuits became, if not popular, tolerated. Additional items: tea, coffee, beef, butter, was mostly absent from tables; soldiers needed those supplies. *Feeding the Soldiers helps in Fighting the War.* Even when the war ended at the end of 1918, foods were limited, but the citizenry of Bonneville did their duty, and accepted Meatless Tuesdays and whole wheat bread and bean soup and cornstarch pudding, and considered it a small price to pay to prove their patriotism.

***

A trip was taken in the spring of 1918. First, Ingrid was worried about the Chicago townhouse being vacant for so long and wanted to check on it. They could count on Harold Jones in Bonneville to keep an eye on the old Victorian house, but there was no one in Chicago to check on the Morrison place. Second, they all believed it might be easier to find needed provisions in Chicago. Over the years, Bonneville had expanded, adding more main street stores, additional homes, a new park, all demands of a growing population, but it was still miles from Chicago and considered a small town. Supplies were limited. Third, Ingrid had decided to do something with Fredrick's wardrobe, with his clothing. The thought of his suits and coats and shirts hanging in the closets saddened her.

"Greta, I think there are some things in his closets which can help the war effort, especially the woolen items. Also, if Lars can use any of the clothes, he should have them. Other than that, do you think there are men in your church who might want some things, or are there charities who could use them? I hate to see them wasted, and I know Fredrick would want his clothes to be of use. He was always so careful with his wardrobe."

"I'm sure there will be a use for his things, and I'll be glad to help with it," and Greta was pleased that Ingrid had decided to do this. It meant her grief was lessening. Cleaning and sorting were healthy steps.

Once the snow melted and the sun was out, the car was readied and packed, the house cleaned and shuttered, and they left, sharing the driving responsibilities once again. During their three weeks in Chicago, they all noticed changes which had taken place. Streets were filled with automobiles, and because traffic lights would not be installed for a couple years, policemen were stationed on every other corner to direct traffic. Grand buildings, tall ones with modern architecture continued to be constructed, sports teams maintained their rivalries and probably as a diversion from war, ballpark seats were filled. The cross streets of State and Madison remained the busiest pedestrian and vehicle intersection in the state, and expansion of the city continued to the south and the west and the north. The Morrison Place townhouses remained the same although Lars had a difficult time finding a convenient street parking place due to the influx of additional cars. Some of the townhouses had changed hands, bringing unfamiliar neighbors to the area. New neighbors, an older couple, Mr. and Mrs. Ricci, had moved next door to the Vogel house, and Greta introduced herself to their housekeeper who agreed to keep her eye on the house when Ingrid and the Andersons were not in town.

The war effort continued. Prominently displayed throughout the neighborhoods on store fronts, backs, and sides, wooden posts, and streetcars, were war posters of all sorts. *I Want YOU* claimed a bearded Uncle Sam, *For The US Army. CORN: the FOOD of the Nation* encouraged families to accept an alternate food, and *FIGHT or Buy LIBERTY BONDS* gave people a choice in supporting the war effort. Tiny rumbles about a new and deadly type of influenza were heard, and by September, Chicago along with the rest of the country would be fighting another war with the Spanish Flu. The United States would end one war by burying 117,466 soldiers and the other by burying 675,000 victims.

Ingrid and Greta and Lars would return to Bonneville by summer's start in 1918. They stayed there, fearing another trip to Chicago because of the expansive influenza epidemic. The news from Chicago was frightening, and while a couple dozen people in Bonneville contracted what was thought to be the Spanish flu, only a few actually died. Ingrid and Greta thought it best to make do with the supplies they had, so trips into town were limited. Their first winter in Bonneville taught them how to prepare, so the second winter was easier to withstand. Lars' vegetable garden ("Victory Garden? Nonsense!" uttered Greta, "Just common sense to grow things.") flourished, and Ingrid was introduced to the skill of canning vegetables and fruits. Greta continued her treatment of Lars and established a schedule of preventative medicines for all of them. She created home remedies and teas from the herbs she grew in the garden or foraged from the wooded areas. "Better me than the doctor," she told Lars who often balked at the teas and elderflower tincture forced on him. But, because Greta's remedies seemed to help them all to avoid major illnesses and survive the minor ones, both Lars and Ingrid swallowed her doses and were grateful for them. They remained healthy through the winter and into the spring of the following year.

By the time another Chicago trip was taken, almost a year had passed. Close attention was given to reports about Chicago area influenza outbreaks. It was only when Ingrid wrote to Henrietta Reason and heard back from her that Chicago was fairly safe to visit, that a trip was planned. Using masks and keeping distances helped to reduce fear in Greta, but she packed a goodly supply of her teas and doses and tinctures to continue her ministrations. From then on, trips were planned twice a year, sometimes three times, if the summer weather in Chicago wasn't too miserably warm. Ingrid considered selling the Chicago house but decided that a periodic trip to the city she had come to enjoy was good for all of them. Besides, she still owned Grandmother Louisa's house in New York City, and who knows…perhaps one day she would be able to visit there again.

World events did not place too much of a role in the lives of the *Bonneville Three*, a name Ingrid and Greta jokingly called themselves, but in 1919, when the war officially ended, they celebrated with a shared bottle of wine. "Better drink up," said Greta, "because that new Eighteenth Amendment will have us all in jail in a year." There were snickers because the dozens of bottles of wine and spirits in the Bonneville basement were safe. Lars was more attentive to the shocking sports world catastrophe in Chicago. He talked about the White Sox and the shame of the 1919 World Series until Greta told him to hush up about it. He left to go to town where he knew there would be a gathering at the barbershop, where serious talk about serious topics such as sports, could be reviewed by serious men. Anyway, he needed a haircut.

A late summer trip in 1920 was important for two reasons. The Nineteenth Amendment had been ratified, and Greta and Ingrid were anxious to register so they could vote in the fall election. The Chicago League of Women Voters actively encouraged registration, and since the *Bonneville Three* considered their main home in Chicago, this was where they would cast their votes. Another, shorter trip was taken in the early autumn so the actual November 2nd voting could take place. "Not sure why Greta needs to vote," groused Lars, "she always told me who I was to vote for anyway." Greta hushed him again. The voting done, a brief shopping trip completed, an expedition was taken to the car dealership to exchange the old Ford for the new 1920 Nash Touring Car Ingrid had ordered earlier in the spring. Cars were being manufactured again because war supplies were no longer needed. Their trip back to Bonneville was more comfortable and faster because the new machine was more comfortable and faster. While the drivers never approached the fifty miles an hour the salesman claimed it could go, Lars did speak loudly to Greta when she pushed it over forty. She shushed him again, but did slow down.

The winter of 1920 was the easiest winter for *the Bonneville Three*. There was no snow in November and only a trace in December with a scant two inches coming the day after Christmas. January and February of 1921 were the same, and there was plenty of coal in the basement of the house. This had been a concern for Lars. The previous year, a coal workers' strike was worrisome, and once it had been settled, he told Ingrid that additional coal should be ordered just in case, so it was. The weather continued cold and there were winds which managed to blow down and destroy some of the back fencing, but Lars said that if that was the worse that happened, they should consider themselves lucky. Mostly, they did.

Luck, thought Greta, had nothing to do with the gradual change she observed in Ingrid. Time did. And over time she observed a lessening of the hulking grief which had wrapped itself around Ingrid, threatening to consume her. There were demanding and agonizing days during the first grieving year when Ingrid would not say more than a word or two. She would sit in the chair in the library, holding a book in her lap, and never turn a page. There was no music in the house either. Ingrid's fingers never touched the piano; her voice never given to song. The few times she spoke it was raspy with the sobbing she had done, thinking she could not be heard. When, months later, one evening before the darkness fell, Greta heard soft tones coming from the music room's piano, and she was relieved. *She is healing*, she thought to herself, and when Lars peeked his head around the kitchen door and started to say something, she held up her finger for silence, and they stood there, listening to the restorative sounds which, to Greta's mind, indicated recovery and rejuvenation. A few days later, Ingrid opened the book of *Schubert Lieder,* the songs she learned when she began to study voice, and quietly at first, began to sing again. When, during the spring of 1919 Greta suggested to Ingrid that she offer voice lessons to some of the girls who would periodically be hired to help with the cleaning, Ingrid shook her head. But she thought about it, and agreed to teach two of the older girls who sang in the church choir. They were grateful for the lessons and did their best for a couple years. As they aged and became busier with life, the lessons ended, but they were grateful to Ingrid and thanked her profusely. On the few occasions Ingrid attended Sunday service, she heard the girls singing, their voices clear and pleasing, and she felt pride in both the girls and in herself.

The one-time Greta thought she would lose her again to the spiritless sorrow which now and again glared out through Ingrid's eyes was the summer of 1918, the time after they had returned from cleaning and sorting through Fredrick's wardrobe. That task had been difficult, and more than once, Ingrid broke down into sobs as she touched and folded Fredrick's suits and shirts, sometimes holding an item to her face, thinking she would be able to smell his scent. But she soldiered through it, and once everything was sorted and offered to needy and worthy causes, she felt better. So good, that she said to Greta on the trip back to Bonneville, "I need to do the same with whatever is in the wardrobe in the dressing room. It's time. Next week, let's sort through the items. There's not much there, but there is no need to keep things around if they can be of use somewhere else. I'll feel better once it's done."

That's what they did on an overcast day which promised rain. Lars was resting on a chair in the Andersons' rooms because his joints were responding to the coming dampness, and the house was still. It was afternoon, and Ingrid had helped Greta cut up the dinner vegetables, and the finished bread was cooling.

"Let's get the dressing room wardrobe done, Greta. Either tomorrow or the next day, once the rain is gone, Lars can go to town and drop off the items at the parsonage. I told Pastor Riordan that this week I would have some things for him. Are you ready?"

They walked up the stairs and entered the bedroom. The dressing room door was closed because Ingrid did not need to use the room. She sometimes considered shutting it off completely, telling Lars to nail two-by-fours over the door, for there were sharp memories connected with the room. She accepted these thoughts for what they were: repulsive remembrances. She would overcome them. Greta went to the window and cracked it open, allowing fresh air to kiss the mustiness. She drew a chair close to the wardrobe so items could be folded and placed on it. They began to pull out the clothes. There weren't many, just as Ingrid said, and the task did not take long. Then Ingrid spied the valise stashed in the corner and pulled it out.

"I forgot that Fredrick sometimes brought additional things with him. Let's see what there is," and she opened it up and began to pull out some shirts, a pair of folded pants, some miscellaneous socks and underwear, and at the side, in a zippered pocket, she felt something hard. She opened it up and pulled out a velvet case. She held it and looked at Greta, and her eyes immediately filled with wetness. Moving to the chair and sitting on top of the clothing, she opened the case and stared at what was inside. Swallowing hard and reaching into the case, she removed the gold and emerald bracelet which Fredrick had purchased for her. The one he was going to give her at the anniversary party they never had. Ingrid's hands shook as she held the jewels.

Neither of the women spoke for at least a minute until Ingrid said, "We were walking on Michigan Avenue some years ago and were looking at the shops. There was a jeweler, Horwitz, I think, and this bracelet was there. I said to Fredrick that one day when he could, when he thought I deserved it, he should give it to me. He laughed and said I deserved it then and always, and he would surprise me one day. He was going to do that. Then he…"

She stopped talking and began to sob. Greta allowed her to cry for a time before attempting to console her because sadness needs to escape. It was a long time before Ingrid could gather herself, could control the despondency she felt. Suddenly, as if it felt her heartache, the sky shook and rain poured down. Greta ran over to shut the window, to prevent the skytears from entering. Then she said to Ingrid, "Come down to the kitchen. I'll make tea, and later will come up for these things. Lars can take them tomorrow. We've done enough for today."

They went to the kitchen, Ingrid still clutching the bracelet and the box. Greta prepared the tea and came to the table. They sat and looked at the jewels. "It's wonderful," said Greta. "It's a wonderful gift."

Ingrid nodded, "I don't think I can wear it," and didn't explain why, but Greta, understanding, just nodded.

Ingrid put it back into the velvet box and closed it. When she went up to her bedroom, she opened her top dresser drawer, putting the box next to her other jewelry. She was right. She would never wear the gold and emerald bracelet, but one day, in the future, it would be of great use.

***

The winter of 1920 eased into the early spring of 1921, and Ingrid celebrated her thirty-second birthday by baking her own cake. She had asked Greta if she wanted to continue the piano lessons, and Greta countered with offering to continue baking lessons. They agreed, and now, Ingrid was excited to make the pineapple-upside-down-cake as her contribution to the dinner. Pineapple in cans had recently been stocked in the Bonneville General Store. None of them had tasted the exotic fruit, and Ingrid was anxious that the cake would be a success. It was. They loved the dessert, and Greta and Lars sang "Happy Birthday" to Ingrid as she smiled. It was a pleasant evening and they moved to the porch.

"Are you sure you won't go with us the see the picture show, Ingrid?" Greta and Lars were planning to attend the Bonneville Movie

Palace, an enterprise which had been in the making for almost two years. It had opened just a month ago, and almost everyone in Bonneville had been to see at least one moving picture show. Charlie Chaplin's *The Kid* was currently playing, and Lars was excited to go. Greta was not that interested in it although she did wonder what it would be like. A number of invitations had been given to Ingrid, but they were declined. She would have gone, but thought it would be good for the Andersons to get away by themselves. That rarely happened.

"Thank you, but go and enjoy it. You can tell me the story afterwards. Maybe in a month or two I'll get out and see something with you. You should go and have a good time."

"Well, we aren't going until Friday night, so if you change your mind, you are still welcome."

They sat on the porch, talking about unimportant things. Lars was anxious to get one of those new Westinghouse radios which were all the rage. The hardware store had an order in for some, but they hadn't been delivered yet. Perhaps by summer they would be available.

Greta mentioned that she thought the ticket price for the moving picture show was outrageous. "Really, fifteen cents each? Why that Mr. Owens must be a rich man by now, and the place has only been opened for a month or so."

Ingrid said she read about the awful things that were happening in Chicago. "I read that people are calling this time the *Roaring Twenties*, and Chicago is just rampant with gangsters. Did you see the article in the *Stone City Times* about how all the young girls are cutting their hair into something called a *Bob*? I'll leave the paper on the table for you. I'm almost afraid to travel there next month. I hope we'll be safe."

The talk continued and the night grew chilled and soon they went inside where they sat at the table and each had another piece of the pineapple birthday cake. As they sat and nibbled at the sweet and talked, Greta looked at Ingrid. *Thirty-two*, she thought. *She looks ten years younger. Too bad she never remarried. She might have had a child. She would have been a great mother.* But Greta kept her thoughts to herself.

***

They were safe in Chicago. There were two trips. One in May and another in early autumn. Supplies were gathered for the winter, shopping on State Street was accomplished, and Ingrid surprised the Andersons by treating them to the fabulous Chicago Theatre which has just opened. It was spectacular and sat almost four-thousand people. They saw Rudolph Valentino in *The Four Horsemen of the Apocalypse,* listened to the fifty-piece orchestra, and enjoyed a stage show afterwards. Even Ingrid was astounded. All the way back to Bonneville, they discussed the amazing sights and wondered at the money which must have been spent to create a place called, *The Wonder Theatre of the World.*

"Well," commented Greta for the third time, "Mr. Owens certainly has something to work up to. I can't wait to see Marion Owens and tell her about this." Lars and Ingrid laughed.

The fall was the usual loveliness in the country. Greta and Ingrid hauled baskets of apples into the kitchen to make applesauce and to can some for use in winter pies. Cabbage and kale, cauliflower and corn were harvested and prepared for winter eating. Winter draperies were cleaned and hung, and heavy blankets were brought out and hung outside to rid them of the mothball odor. Lars kept busy as he monitored the boys he had hired to cut and stack wood for the fireplaces. He made a repair to the broken chair which belonged to the set he and Greta used, but he was unable to do many other repairs due to the cooler weather aggravating his arthritis. "Time for the rose hips and wintergreen," said Greta and she began to prepare those solutions. They worked to get the house ready for the cold. Ingrid helped where she could, even though Greta said she had everything under her control. Most afternoons Ingrid went to the library to read and write letters. By now, the three of them knew what the winter could be like, and they prepared for it.

One night Lars remarked to Ingrid that there were things which needed to be repaired. Two of the dining room chairs were broken, one of the old bedframes upstairs was loose, the fence in the back which had fallen down during one of the wind storms should be repaired. There was still a broken stair on the front porch, a baluster was broken and a post down. He wasn't able to make the repairs, and some of them required someone who knew woodworking.

"When I go into town for a haircut in a couple days, I'll mention the repairs. Somebody must know someone who can do them. I'll mention it at the hardware and the barber shop and maybe the post office."

Ingrid nodded. "Thanks, Lars. That will be fine. I'm sure someone will be able to help."

***

The late October day was cool but not cold. It was mid-morning. Ingrid was in the library finishing up some letters and then planning to read. On one of the trips back to Chicago, she had gathered Fredrick's beautiful set of Shakespeare plays, all individually bound in their own brown tooled leather coverings, and brought them back with her. They were placed on the mahogany book shelves, and she had pulled one to read. The *Sonnets of Shakespeare* was the volume she had on the desk, waiting to be opened as soon as she finished the letters. Lars was in the back kitchen tinkering with something, and Greta was in the front of the house. She was cleaning and trimming the large fern that was placed in the window, considering what she could put in the soil to ensure its continued growth as the cold months approached. A movement caught her eye and she peeked out the window and watched as someone came up the front walk, up the steps, and stood at the door. He turned his head, and she got a close and careful look at his features. Her hand went to her heart and she took in a deep, shocked breath. She was stunned at what she was seeing.

She stood still, gazing at the person in front of the door, trying to calm her rapidly beating heart. She watched as he reached for the door knocker, hesitated for a brief second, then moved it. Greta, the fern and its condition forgotten, did not move.

Fate, in the guise of a ghost, slammed the front door knocker three times against the sturdy oak door and stood there, waiting for an answer.

Six

Thomas Allerton

April, 1922

As I lay on the bed watching the mid-morning sun sprinkle spring light throughout the room, I wondered what Greta would say when I told her. I was fairly certain she knew. She was the one who soaked and washed my monthly rags, and there had been none to soak and wash for two months now. I wondered what she would say; what she would recommend. I wondered what her reaction would be when I told her that I intended to do nothing to stop this process.
I welcomed it.

Late October, 1921

Greta stood in front of me babbling about something, and when I finally looked up and listened to her, she still made little sense. I held up my hand to stop her and asked, "Greta, what are you saying? Who is at the door? Go and answer it."

"That's what I'm trying to tell you. I don't believe in ghosts, and you never saw your Fredrick when he was younger and wore a beard, but I swear he is standing at the door!"

My head suddenly began to ache. "Stop! Take a breath and be sensible. Fredrick is gone. Why would you even say that? What are you thinking?"

She looked at me and then down at the floor. "I was just startled. There is a man at the front door and I thought for a second…"

I closed my eyes and sucked in the air. Letting it out in a sigh, I looked at her and once again we heard someone knocking.

"Do you need me to answer that?"

"No, I will. Sorry to upset you, Ingrid."

"It's probably just one of those traveling salesmen or a preacher selling Bibles. They often work their way up and down this road."

Greta nodded and turned to go to the front. When she was gone, I listened to hear what was being said, and while I could hear her clearly, the words spoken by the man at the door were muffled.

"We don't want to buy nothin' and already been Jesus-saved," is what I heard, and I smiled at the usual answer she had perfected. Something was mumbled, and soon Greta appeared before me at the library doorway. I looked up at her and waited.

"The man says he's a good carpenter and can fix those fences in back. He said the front porch needs to be repaired and he can do it. Then he asked to speak to you. Do you want to see him?"

"I don't need to see him if you think he's responsible and can do the job."

Greta shrugged. "No one else has showed up, and he apparently heard from the town about the fences. But he's not smart enough to know he shouldn't come to the front door as a workman. What should I tell him?"

I thought for a minute and then said, "Tell him he can fix the porch. There's plenty of work to be done in and around this house, but I'll need to inspect the porch once it's finished before giving him more jobs. If it's acceptable, I'll give him five dollars. What do you think?"

"Hmph! Seems like a lot to me, but you're the boss," and Greta turned to go.

I called her back. "Greta, what are you making for Lars' dinner tonight?"

"Making the pork chops and cabbage he likes. I know we don't like that, and I have some beefsteak and potatoes for us. Why?"

"Tell the man he can have a meal too, if you have enough."

"There's plenty, and he can eat what Lars is getting." She left.

I waited to hear her end of the conversation, and after she closed the door and walked past the library, she poked her head in to say, "He don't have tools, and I told him to meet Lars at the shed. Some workman. Hope this isn't a mistake," and she gave me a sideways look which indicated she thought it was. I just shook my head and finished the letter I had started. I thought that when the man was working, I would peek at him and see what startled Greta. I had not known Fredrick when he was younger, and when we met, he was clean-shaven and remained so. I was curious about this man's looks.

I continued the work with letters and bills in the library, and eventually heard hammering and knocking on the porch, so I knew the work was being done. I peered out of the doorway and heard Greta in the back, so I quietly entered the front parlor which was next to the porch. I didn't want the man to catch me looking at him, so I was careful as I stood behind and to the side of the winter draperies and looked out. His back was turned to me, and he had removed his jacket. He was muscular and tall, about Fredrick's height, and his hair was dark just as my husband's was when I first met him. I waited until he turned around and tried to get a look at his face, but I was worried he would see me, so I walked back to the staircase and went to the second floor. The small front bedroom looked down on the porch, and I was certain he would not look up. I stood watching him work for a time. Once he stopped working and put down the tools and stretched out his back, I saw his face. There was a catch in my throat, and I thought Greta was right. He could be a young Fredrick.

I wish I could have seen a youthful Fredrick. Greta had once described his younger self as *just like the Norse god, Baldur, the son of Odin.* I didn't understand the comparison and she explained, "Baldur was the handsomest of the gods. He wore a beard and his eyes flashed and he was so beautiful that light poured from him. The difference is he had golden hair, and your husband's is dark. But they are both kind and wise, so I think you are lucky in your choice. Your husband is older, but he is just as handsome and kind as he was when he was younger."

I thought about this as I looked down at the man tightening the loose screws and railings, and wondered about his story. How did he come to be here in Bonneville? Who was he? I watched as he walked around, checking the wood rails and repairing what should have been repaired years ago. Whoever this was, I was grateful he had shown up. I hadn't been sure the entire front porch would last through another winter under the weight of snow. As he disappeared along the side of the house, I thought I should stop snooping and continue my own work.

Later that afternoon, as I relaxed in the back parlor with the book I was reading, Greta came in to speak to me.

"Well, he's finished. He ate his meal. Ate a lot, if you ask me, and now he says he can paint the porch. Says there's paint in the shed and he can come back tomorrow to do it. What should I tell him?"

"I did examine the porch, and it all seems sturdy to me. He even repaired that broken step. What does Lars think?"

Greta shrugged. "Lars said the job is well done. I think he's just glad it's all fixed. Should I tell him to come back or not?"

I considered. "Tell him I would like to speak with him," and Greta left. I continued to hold the book, but stood up, waiting for him to enter.

I heard Greta's step and when she entered, she cleared her throat and spoke, "Mrs. Vogel, here's that workman." And she left.

He stood at the doorway. He was tall, Fredrick's height, and I was startled by his youth and benumbed by his familiar aspect. We stared at each other for a few seconds and I said, "I'm sorry, but I don't know your name."

"Thomas, Ma'am. Thomas Allerton."

I nodded and placed my book on the nearby table. "You have done a fine job, Thomas Allerton. I inspected your work just now and am pleased with it. Mrs. Anderson informs me that you would be willing to paint the porch, and that would be fine. While the weather holds and before the snow sets in, I would like to have it done. Could you return tomorrow?"

"Yes, I will be here."

"Fine. Then tomorrow's pay will be the same. Please see Mrs. Anderson on your way out. She'll have your money. And, Mr. Allerton, do you do other repairs? There are some things around the house needing repairs, and I could probably keep you busy for a week or so."

He looked at me. For some strange reason there was a tingling on my neck, but I decided to ignore it, and he said, "Yes, Ma'am. I'm a carpenter and furniture maker and can help. Thank you for the work, Mrs. Vogel."

I took up the book I had laid down as he walked away, but I could not concentrate on the reading of it.

***

Mr. Allerton came every morning, walking in from town, and staying until the afternoon light faded. I made sure he was fed a decent lunch, and despite Greta's reluctance, she appreciated his appetite and was privately pleased when he praised her cooking. He and I did not have much to do with each other at first. Sometimes we would pass each other on the stairs or outside, and there was a polite deference on his part. A few times when he was working on a table or tightening chair legs in the same room I was in, we spoke politely to each other but I remained guarded. He was expert at his duties, and once or twice I told him so. He worked around the house and the property fixing and repairing the items which needed to be fixed and repaired. The back fence had been in tatters for years and many of the pickets needed replacing. Some of the furniture Fredrick had imported from Europe needed adjustments, and I was worried about the old wood, but he showed me what he had done to create the sturdiness which had been original to the century-old pieces.

The weather edged towards winter, and one afternoon just before the Thanksgiving feast day there was a sudden snowstorm. Greta had been preparing much more food than the three of us would consume, but she enjoyed doing it, and there would be leftovers for days so she did not have to do much cooking through the weekend. I went to her on Wednesday as the snow piled up and said, "Greta, there is so much food here. Make a large package for Mr. Allerton to take with him and remind him that he won't be expected until Monday due to the holiday."

Greta sighed and said, "Fine, Ingrid, but the pies won't be done before he leaves. I suppose I can send some of those molasses cookies I made the other day," and she looked perturbed.

"Perfect. Thanks, Greta," and I reached out to squeeze her shoulder with additional gratitude. I wasn't sure why she didn't seem to like Mr. Allerton. He was courteous and friendly. He was diligent and hard-working. I thought that it might have had something to do with his resemblance to Fredrick. Or my actions. Although that was not until later.

***

The snow continued through most of the weekend. Greta and Lars and I celebrated the Thanksgiving feast together in the dining room, and I helped with the serving and the cleaning. Afterwards, we all enjoyed playing rounds of checkers with the loser (that was me) having to finish the dishes. Lars was feeling the effects of the wetness on his knees, so Greta and I pitched in to clear off the snow on the front and back steps of the house. As I shoveled the snow from the steps, I thought Grandmother Louisa would be shocked if she knew the manual labor I engaged in, but it invigorated me, and I was content to be part of the small family the three of us had created. When the sun came out on Sunday, some of the snow melted, and we were glad, but on early Monday it had started once again.

I was awake early that Monday, and I looked out at the snow which fell gently and thought that walking in it would be a miserable task. As I readied myself for the day, I glanced out of the bedroom window, and saw a figure trudging slowly towards the house. It was Mr. Allerton coming to work. An idea came into my head, and I decided I would carry through with it. I went to the kitchen to pour myself some coffee before sitting at the head of the long table. I waited.

"Ingrid, can I serve you breakfast?" asked Greta when she saw me there.

"No, thank you. Mr. Allerton is on his way, and I would like to speak to him, so once he is here, have him come in."

Greta gave me a strange look, but I ignored it. Soon the back door (Greta had been sure to inform Mr. Allerton that he was to use the correct entrance.) was opened. I heard Greta tell him to wipe his boots with the rag she handed him and then to go into the kitchen. When he entered, he was surprised to see me.

"Mr. Allerton, please sit down. I wish to speak to you. Mrs. Anderson, please bring him some coffee, and I will have another cup."

He sat down. I thanked Greta when she brought the coffee, and watched as he sipped the hotness.

"Where do you stay at night, Mr. Allerton?"

"I have a room in the small hotel in town."

"What is your story? Where are you from, and why are you traveling around? You are obviously talented and skilled, and could easily find a job in one of the larger towns."

Mr. Allerton looked down and then up at me. I could see his eyes which were a shade of hazel. "I was married and my wife and newborn son died earlier this year. There was nothing left for me in that town, and I needed to leave, so I have been traveling and picking up a job here and there. I could, and at some time, probably will settle down somewhere, but for now, I'm happy with the way I'm living."

I took a swallow of my coffee and looked down at the cup for a few seconds before speaking. I knew that what I was going to suggest would be viewed as unusual at best, but I was determined to at least ask and spoke clearly as I suggested it.

"Winter has come, and winters here are bleak and stark. I would like to make a proposal. There are many bedrooms in this large house. The Andersons live in the back where there is a three-room suite for them. Would you consider moving here for the winter and accept staying in one of the third-floor rooms? That would save you the cold walk twice a day, and it would make it more convenient for you to complete the work. Besides, I am thinking of adding a new side table to the dining room and a small bookcase in the front parlor, and you being here would make accomplishing that easier. I fully understand if you would prefer not to."

He looked at me and then smiled. "Yes, Mrs. Vogel, that would be acceptable to me."

"Fine. Then tomorrow when you arrive for work, bring your things, and Mrs. Anderson will show you to your room." I got up from the table, and he also rose. I started to leave, but turned to ask one more thing, "Mr. Allerton, how old are you?"

He wiped his hands on his pants and answered. "I'm eighteen."

"Eighteen," I repeated. I left the room.

Thomas Allerton moved in.

***

The inside repairs continued through the weeks. The side table and bookcase took longer because Mr. Allerton did the majority of the work in the outbuilding, and it was extremely cold there, so there were times he just could not work outside. Eventually it was all done, and I was pleased with the work. It remained cold and snowy and a freeze set in, but I was reluctant to make the man move back to town. Greta would periodically ask when he was to leave, and I didn't understand why she disliked him because Mr. Allerton was polite and helpful. He noticed that Lars had trouble with his knees in the cold, and Mr. Allerton offered to carry in the fireplace wood, to shovel the coal, to move and place things for him. He repaired the old rocker Lars could no longer rock on, and tightened and repaired all the legs of the Anderson's table and chairs. The snow on the front and back steps was kept shoveled and swept, and while Lars and Mr. Allerton rarely spoke and did not form a friendship that I was aware of, Lars appreciated the help. Small items were repaired and fixed and tightened. Things which needed to be done were done, but Greta went around with a scowl on her face when he was around. I decided to just ignore her. Perhaps she thought he was taking advantage of the offer I made, but I never felt that. Somehow it was comforting having him around although we rarely spoke.

One morning I was in the library reading and Greta brought my coffee to me. "Has Mr. Allerton come down yet?"

"No."

"When he does, please send him in here. Thanks, Greta." And I dismissed her look.

When he softly knocked on the library door, I looked up from my book and motioned for him to come in. No repairs had been needed in the library, so he had not been in the room, and when he entered, he stopped and stared at the books which surrounded us. I knew he read. Greta had told me about the few books which were kept on the dresser in his third-floor room. I smiled as I spoke to him.

"My husband was a collector of fine books," I explained, "although he wasn't much of a reader. I am, and from what Mrs. Anderson tells me, you have a few books of your own. Do you enjoy reading, Mr. Allerton?"

"I do. I own three books which I reread. They were given to me by a teacher when I was younger. This is amazing," and he slowly walked up and down the mahogany bookcases and looked at the titles.

"Mr. Allerton, I am inviting you to take and read whatever you want. These books are wasting away here, for lack of use. I often spend afternoons and early evenings reading and would enjoy your company. It is good to read and discuss, and I know that, for now, there are few further repairs needed. The winter is here, and the fireplace in the back parlor is kept lit and warms the room. I hope you will join me there later with a book you have chosen."

He reached for one of the volumes of Shakespeare and pulled out *Much Ado About Nothing.*

"Ah, you read Shakespeare. Have you read many plays?"

"Only two. I have a copy of *The Tempest* and have read *Julius Caesar*, but I would like to read this, if you don't mind."

"Please, Mr. Allerton. This library is open for your use. I haven't read that play in a while, so when you are finished, I'll reread it, and we might discuss it."

And so, the reading started.

***

We met together twice a day: the early afternoons and the evenings. We eased into a comfortableness, sitting and reading silently, although periodically we would read aloud to each other. We discussed Shakespeare's plays, and sometimes I would suggest he read a novel or an essay which we then talked about. He had a scholar's mind, and I was entertained by his comments. We laughed often, and slowly an unusual sort of friendship developed. Perhaps not a friendship. I didn't know what to call it. I still don't.

He was in the habit of eating in the kitchen by himself, but I thought that was unnecessary once we became familiar. One evening, I approached him and made a suggestion.

"Mr. Allerton, it is silly for us to be apart at mealtime when we spend so much of the day together. Please have your meals with me in the dining room. We can continue our discussions. There is no reason for us to be so formal."

That is what we did. At first, he seemed to be uncomfortable but soon he relaxed, and as we ate, we continued our discussions. I encouraged him to talk about himself. I questioned him about his background, and he told me his story. When he was two years old, his mother died and he went to live with his Aunt Jennifer until his father brought him back to the farm and taught him to work in the woodshop. He loved his schooling and excelled at it but was filled with sorrow when his father told him it was time to end it. He spoke about his mother he didn't remember, about his twin brother who died at their birth. He expressed shame at leaving his father when he was dying, and told me about his travels and experiences on the road. I teared up, as he did, when talking about his dead wife, Ava, who did not survive the birth of their baby. Neither did his son. His father-in-law, Mr. Turner, became a father-figure to him, but his mother-in-law despised him and wanted him gone. He made me laugh with his adventures in the same way Fredrick used to, and as I listened to him, he seemed older than his actual eighteen years.

The Christmas season came and it was a quiet time. The Andersons and I decided years ago that gift exchanging was not something we wanted to do, and we usually celebrated the day by going to church, if the weather permitted, and later, sharing a quiet simple meal. That year, snow continued, so we stayed at home. Mr. Allerton commented that he would spend the day relaxing and reading, so we both did that. But the New Year's Eve of 1921 was a late night filled with game playing and joke telling, and the Andersons joined in. Greta, to my surprise, was friendly to Thomas that evening. Perhaps it was due to the wine. We celebrated and brought in the new year of 1922. Although Prohibition was the law of the land, all of us drank many glasses of a wonderful sparkling wine from the cellar. Fredrick had made sure there would always be good wine available, and drinking it made me remember the times we enjoyed it together. Despite the fun and festivities, at least once I excused myself to weep and wipe my eyes. I missed my husband. Mr. Allerton had not had wine before, and I explained he should sip it slowly, but he became silly with the enjoyment. The next morning, he said he could not eat breakfast because he was sure he was coming down with a horrible disease. I just laughed and asked Mrs. Anderson to bring him black coffee and dry toast. He was better by that evening.

We settled into the winter and when weather permitted, we dressed warmly as possible and went for walks along the wooded areas. We would examine the paths, and Mr. Allerton would name the various trees and point out the animal tracks we found. Periodically we would see a deer in the distance and stand to watch as it stared back at the humans who were in its territory. The trees would sometimes drop their heavy loads of snow on our heads, and we would laugh as we shook it off. The days passed. The evenings were spent in front of the warmth of the fireplace, and I was happy enough to sometimes play the piano and sing. I told Mr. Allerton about my musical training and singing at the opera, and one night when I was feeling especially unreserved, I recounted the lovely flower bouquets I would find in the dressing room and the introduction to Fredrick made by my grandmother. I didn't mean to allow any tears to fall, but when they did, Mr. Allerton reached over and put his hand on top of mine. I was startled by the touch and sorry when he removed his hand. I looked into his face and for a second, I saw the face of my husband, my youthful husband. It stunned and shook me, and there was another feeling which surprised me. I excused myself early that evening, and when I went to bed, I lay awake for most of the night. Brazen thoughts ran through my mind, and in the darkness, I felt myself blush.

***

There were no improper words spoken or unseemly actions taken towards me from Mr. Allerton. And I made none towards him. Some mornings I awoke, disturbed by the dreams I had, dreams which were unfocused and undefined, but unsettling none the less, and on those mornings, I waited up in my bedroom until I was sure Mr. Allerton had eaten breakfast and was otherwise engaged. Then I would travel downstairs to the kitchen and sip morning coffee and greet Greta, encouraging small talk with her, trying to clear my mind. Some days I asked Greta to tell Mr. Allerton that I would not meet him for the reading session, but he was to continue on his own. I spent those days in the dressing room just off my bedroom, reading or attempting to read a book, staring out the window, looking at the place my husband had spent his last days. Those were sad times, melancholy hours, and I just needed to be alone. After a day or so, I continued my usual meetings and walks with Mr. Allerton who never questioned where I had been and was always cheerful and offered comments, often humorous ones, about the reading he had done. Being with him was restoring. It was almost as if Fredrick was with me again.

We sat at dinner and were comfortable with each other. We walked outside when weather permitted and pointed out the beauty we saw in nature. We relaxed in the parlor and read, or sat in the music room where I played the piano and sang and enjoyed a growing companionship. And that was all it was meant to be. I didn't consider what would happen in the spring when the snow was melted and the need for furniture repairing was gone. It was the end of January, and the coziness of a companionship, different from the friendship I had with Greta and Lars, calmed and stilled my sometimes-strained soul.

Mr. Allerton and I were in the parlor one very cold evening while the snow was moving in a swirl outside. I had just finished reading a passage out loud to him, one that I found particularly descriptive, and we spoke about the author's choice of words. There was a quiet moment when he looked at me, noticing I had pulled my winter shawl up around my neck because the fire was fading. He did not ask, but walked over to where an extra blanket was thrown across a chair, brought it over, and spread it across my lap. It was the sort of gesture Fredrick would have made. The hairs on my arms stood up, but I ignored them. I looked up to smile my thanks. He said, "It's particularly chilly tonight. Do you want me to add more wood to the fire before I go to bed?"

I shook my head *no* and answered I was going to stay up to complete the reading of the chapter and would then retire. He said another good-night and left. I listened as he walked up the stairs to the second floor and then to the third, but I did not continue to read. I stared at the fire and allowed my hands to clutch the blanket he had laid on my lap. My heart beat quickly, and I needed to sort out what I was feeling, what I was thinking, what I was considering. I listened for sounds in the house, but there were few noises. Greta and Lars had gone to bed earlier, and the fire in the parlor was almost out. I waited until the embers were done, and after covering them with the cooled ash, I walked upstairs to my bedroom.

The room was chilly but not cold. I washed my face and put on my nightdress. I unwound my hair and brushed through it mindlessly. Standing by the window, I looked out over the snow-filled space, into the darkness, then pulling the winter draperies closed, I climbed into my bed. The entire house was still, but I was wide awake. I lay in the bed and tried to get comfortable, turning one way and another but was unable to find rest. Finally, I sat up. Pushing the covers to the side, I walked to the bedroom door and opened it. My eyes focused, and I looked into the dark and over to the staircase which led to the third-floor. I stared at it for some time, perhaps as long as fifteen minutes before I walked over and began to climb it, placing one bare foot and then the other carefully and gently down on each step until I was at the top. The third floor contained three small rooms meant for servants, but they had never been used. Mr. Allerton…Thomas…was in the largest of the rooms, the one to my right, the one which was above the dressing room which was attached to my bedroom. I am uncertain how long I stood there before walking over, I gently pushed open his door, and quietly shut it behind me. I remained there giving myself time to think, but honestly, no thoughts came. Except for one. I walked over to the bed where he was sleeping, breathing softly. I pulled back the covers and lowered myself next to him. He still slept, and in the night light I could just see the side of his face, its contours under his beard, so similar to Fredrick's. I reached over and placed my hand against his cheek, feeling the soft hairs, and he turned to me and slowly his eyes, those hazel eyes, opened. Then they opened wider and he started to say something, but I placed my finger against his lips, shook my head and said "Shh!". That was the only time that night anything was said.

***

An hour later, perhaps two, I left and went back to my own bed. I fell asleep immediately and woke up with the first light. I readied myself for the day and spent some time seated at my dressing table staring into the mirror and wondering what was wrong with me. What did I do and why? How would I face this day? Face Thomas Allerton? What would he say or do? I decided to pretend nothing had happened and hoped he would take the hint and do the same. It was the only thing to do, and I went downstairs where Greta was setting the table for breakfast.

"Good morning, Greta. Is coffee ready?"

"Sure is. Lars isn't well today, Ingrid. That arthritis is acting up with the cold and snow. I'm going to make a new batch of the wintergreen salve today and rub his knees with it. Hope it helps."

"I hope so too, Greta," and then he came into the dining room and I turned my head and added, "Good morning, Mr. Allerton. I trust you slept well. Mrs. Anderson, please bring breakfast now."

We sat at the table drinking coffee and eating breakfast and speaking of nothing important. Apparently, he was sensitive to ignoring what had transpired the previous night, and the day progressed in a normal fashion. Nothing was said; nothing was suggested; no knowing looks were exchanged. We read together, walked outside, met in the music room that evening where I sang and played the piano, and then we bid each other good night and went our separate ways. And an hour or so after I prepared for my bed, after I had washed my face and brushed my hair, after I crawled under my own covers and lay with my eyes open to the darkness, after I listened to the stillness in the house, I once again left my singular bed and climbed the stairs to the third floor. I opened his door, closing it behind me and this time, before I crawled into bed next to him, I slipped my nightdress off and let it fall to the floor. Again, we did not speak.

I never stayed the night. One time he held me back as I prepared to leave and whispered "Stay" into my hair. I whispered back "No," and left. I could not remain. Some nights, I never climbed the stairs. I relied on my own whims and wants; I was completely selfish, doing what I wished; and in the darkness, for a short time, I could close my eyes and pretend, could make-believe, could fantasize I was with Fredrick, my husband, my love. I did not consider any consequences. I had no hopes. I lived in two separate worlds. One was the daylight sphere, filled with sunlight, and books, and conversations, and normality. The other was a dream universe, filled with sensual actions, carnal deeds, fleshy engagements, maneuvers not allowed to be considered during daylight. I became two people.

I never spoke of my nightly activities to Greta, but she knew of them. She never said anything to me except one time and I understood the veiled comment for what it was. It happened in the beginning of March. Spring was peeking around the corner making Greta anxious to start deep cleaning, and she decided that the crystal we never used needed washing and polishing. It was stored in a dining room cabinet which was tall, reaching almost to the ceiling, and we needed a small ladder to get the pieces on the upper shelves. I helped her as we began to remove the glassware, placing it all on the dining room table to be cleaned. Mr. Allerton walked by and saw us starting to gingerly move the pieces, and he came in saying, "Wait, allow me to do that. I can reach those things for you," and he proceeded to do so. He handed the glassware to us and when the cabinet was emptied, told us to call him when we were finished. He would put the things back. That is what happened. When it was finished, I thanked him for his thoughtfulness and assistance, and he smiled, and I watched him leave. Greta, who had remained completely quiet while the removing and replacing tasks were done, watched him leave also. Her mouth was contorted in a manner I recognized as controlled anger. Our job completed, she said she needed to do her potato peeling, but before she turned to go to the kitchen, she stopped and looked over her shoulder at me and said, "He may look like your youthful Fredrick, but he is *not* your husband." She emphasized the word *not*. I understood what she meant. I knew to what she was referring. I did not answer her.

***

Snows came, and rains melted it; the months passed and it was possible to know, to feel, the seasons shift. It was early April, some days before my thirty-third birthday, and I knew what the changes I was observing in my body meant. I considered what I should do. I did not end my nightly visits, but I decreased them for a practical reason. He had been married. His wife had a child. He might recognize the symptoms I was observing in my own body and then there would be complications. He needed to leave, and once I decided this, I stopped the visits. Our days proceeded as they had: we walked, we discussed, we shared meals.

I maintained an outward appearance of normalcy, but within, I was torn. I was elated, and I was impassive. I was hopeful, and I was discouraged. A familiar tiredness began to set in, and I wanted to sleep during the afternoons. A few mornings I woke from a restless sleep with an urgent need to rid myself of the previous night's dinner. I barely tolerated the various smells emanating from the kitchen, and my appetite was poor one day, and I was ravenous the next. The day before he would leave, I spent some time in the library alone, and then went to speak to Greta. I told her what to do, what to say, and I gave her the envelope into which I had placed what I thought was an appropriate amount of cash. I also gave her a package I had wrapped in brown paper and tied with twine.

"Make sure Lars gives this to him once he has been taken to town. Offer him a breakfast before he leaves. And Greta, I do not want to see or speak to him should he ask. I am going to sleep in tomorrow, and I'll be down around lunchtime. Do you understand?"

To her credit, Greta gave me no looks which expressed her true feelings. She simply nodded her head and answered, "Yes, Ingrid, I will take care of this." I was grateful for her tact because I was sure she knew my secret.

I wanted to tell him in some way what the months had meant to me, but I could not speak. I tried writing a letter but tore up the many versions of it. There were no words. I sat in the library and looked around at the books. Perhaps there was one which would be suitable for a gift. I pulled out many of them and rejected them all until I saw the one which would do. It was the copy of Shakespeare's sonnets. He had never read it, although we had discussed a number of the plays. I reread many of the sonnets and found one which, if he read it carefully, might explain all my actions. I read and reread number seventy-three and then I took my pen and underlined the last two lines, the couplet which I was positive he would misread. He would study it, and I was sure that he would ponder it, thinking it was meant for him. The lines said:

> *This thou perceiv'st, which makes thy love more strong,*
> *To love that well which thou must leave ere long.*

He was a man, and despite his intelligence and ability to perceive, would consider the lines, and believe he was the mentioned love. That would be acceptable. Perhaps his mistaken belief would mollify the pain I knew I would cause. He would not consider who the real love was who had left me much too soon. He was unaware of his resemblance. I marked the page and wrapped up the book.

***

The last evening we spent together, the night before we would disappear from each other's lives, I tried to maintain a routine. We met in the back parlor and spoke about Shakespeare's characters, a subject we enjoyed discussing. Our conversations had centered around many of the famous men from the plays: Hamlet, Julius Caesar, Macbeth. I asked if there were any of Shakespeare's women characters he thought admirable, and there was some silence before he spoke.

"Some are frighteningly forceful, maybe cruel, like Lady Macbeth and Goneril. A few are sweet and gentle, and remind me of my wife, Ava," and here he stopped for a minute. "But I am taken by the strong individuals such as Viola and Beatrice. I suppose I admire their humor and practicality and the words Shakespeare has them say. I guess Beatrice is the one I remember best partly because *Much Ado About Nothing* was the first play I read here. I'd like to think my Aunt Jennifer might have been like Beatrice. Perhaps my mother was, but I don't remember much about her. Of course, I haven't read all the plays, so I don't know all the characters."

I smiled at what he said, thinking that I would miss these discussions, that this would be the last one we would have, that I knew this. He did not. There was a sudden ache in my chest which had nothing to do with my physical condition. I recognized it for what it was, and after a few more minutes had passed, I stood up to leave.

"Mr. Allerton, it is late, and I am going to go to bed. Feel free to sit a while and read if you wish. Good-night."

He stood up when I did and smiled and said *good-night.* I left. There was no prolonging the farewell. He would discover in the morning that he was to leave. I thought it best to not discuss, to not explain, to not excuse my behavior. I walked up the stairs and closed my bedroom door against the night. I would not sleep. I would lay awake the entire night thinking about the future and what I would do. Should do. When morning came, I remained in my own bed, waiting to hear steps on the staircases, staying perfectly still and soundless, and wondering at the ache in my heart-center which would not dissipate. The pain was similar to one I had felt years ago when I lost my only love. My heart twinged, and it felt as though I was losing him again.

***

I watched him from the third-floor bedroom. I saw him turn to look at the second-floor, looking for me, but as he and Lars traveled in the wagon, the embryonic tree buds hid him from my view. I left that room to go and rest in mine, to attempt to get back some of the sleep I lost. As I passed the space he had occupied for six months, I was drawn to something by the mirror and went to it. I picked it up, walked down the stairs, and when in my own room, placed his comb in the dresser drawer next to the jeweled bracelet Fredrick had bought for me. I lay down but did not sleep long or soundly, and when I turned to see the time, it was almost noon. I needed to talk to Greta.

I walked into the kitchen where she was working. When she heard me, she turned and said, "Have a seat. I'll make us some tea. Lars is going to be gone for a time. The horse needs a new shoe and he was going to take care of that. Do you want some breakfast or lunch?"

"No," I replied, "Some tea is good. I want to talk to you."

Greta finished preparing the tea, set cups and saucers down for us, placed some freshly cut bread and honey on the table, and filled our cups with the steaming liquid. She sat down, and we waited for it to cool before taking sips. She looked at me expectantly. I looked back at her but could not speak, so she did.

She took a breath. "You're going to keep it, aren't you?"

"Yes," I confessed. "I am."

Greta sat back with a sigh. She placed her hands in her lap and neither of us made a sound. Finally, she looked at me and with an additional sigh said, "Well, *det blir som det blir.*"

Seven

The Plan

On the evening of Ingrid's thirty-third birthday, after the dinner was served, the birthday song sung, the cake eaten, the dishes washed, Lars retired to nurse his arthritic knee while Greta and Ingrid sat at the dining table to discuss the Plan.

"Let me explain," began Greta who had put herself in charge of the Plan, "and I know just who to talk to first."

Ingrid leaned her head on her hand and nodded. She was tired. And bloated and achy and teary. Extraordinarily teary, and most of the time she felt there was a fog surrounding her. She had not felt this way before when there had been a similar situation. Of course, she was over a decade older now, and there were additional worries this time. Strangely enough, the one item, the scary item, the horrific item most women in her position worried about, the terrible loss which might occur, which could occur, which had occurred once before, was not on her list of items about which she was concerned. This time, she knew without any doubt that the seed which had been planted would come to full and complete fruition. She intuited this. She was sure of it. Her assuredness about this could not be explained, and she didn't waste time trying to analyze it. She accepted it just as she had accepted Thomas into the household, into the library, into the dining room, into the back parlor, into her nighttime routine. Just as she knew what the changes in her body meant, what the achiness in her breasts signified, what the fogginess from her brain ordained. Just as she knew when it was time for him to leave, to disappear, to wander away with the envelope filled with money and the wrapped book. Ingrid accepted this was providence, destiny, fortune. This was fate.

She listened as Greta talked. She was grateful that Greta, once she understood Ingrid's intention, took over the planning and the preparation for what could be a disreputable and degrading situation. Greta would not allow it to become that. If the herbal preparations Greta kept in her small case under the bed were not wanted, that was acceptable. For all her confidence in telling Lars she could "help" the situation, she wasn't positive the provisions in her case would be successful. Greta knew some of the young Swedish girls in Chicago had relied on the services of certain doctors, but those instances were years ago, and they were not currently living in that city which offered the necessary arrangements. Once Greta, looking into the face of Ingrid, had determined that the distrustful abortifacients would not be wanted, she began to prepare and to plan. As she explained it all, Ingrid sat at the dining table, her celebratory thirty-third birthday cake resting heavily on her stomach, and listened to Greta, allowing her head to nod in agreement with the strategy explained to her. It sounded reasonable and reliable. Anyway, there was no other choice.

***

"Oh yes," Greta explained to Mabel McHenry, Bonneville's telephone switchboard operator, who she happened to run into just as they were both gathering necessary supplies at the general store, "and the poor woman is simply beside herself. So sad," and Greta took up the bag of cornmeal and examined it closely.

"And this is Mrs. Vogel's cousin who is in this sad state? I didn't know she still had relatives in Chicago," replied Mabel, holding her basket partially filled with groceries.

"Well," and Greta replaced the cornmeal that she never intended to purchase, "she is a distant cousin, and while she and Mrs. Vogel were never very close, they did sometimes see each other in Chicago. I know Mrs. Vogel feels awful. Her poor cousin just lost her husband and finds out she is in the family way, and there is no one close to her to help. Parents are gone and no sisters. So, have you tried this kind of coffee?" and a cannister was held up to Mabel's face.

"No, I haven't. I drink tea. So, is your missus going to help her out in some way? Perhaps go back to Chicago to be with her?"

"I have no idea, Mabel, but Mrs. Vogel is so kind-hearted, who knows? Well, I need to get going. I told Lars I would be right out, and he is waiting for me. I'll see you," and Greta paid for the few items in her basket and left.

***

"…and now the poor woman is close to five months along, and the letter Mrs. Vogel read to me was just heartbreaking," and Greta examined the poster advertising the film The Bride's Play as Marion Owens, wife of the owner of the Bonneville Movie Palace, supervised her youngest son as he adjusted and placed it. "Oh, Marion, this film stars that Marion Davies! You have the same name!"

Marion Owens nodded her head, "So Mabel said Mrs. Vogel was thinking about going to Chicago to help her out. Will you be going then? Poor woman; I can't think what I would have done without my own mother, rest her soul, when my four were born. Ben, look at that side. It's crooked. Pay attention!"

"Well, she's thinking about going there. And of course, I would go, and Lars, I am sure would eventually travel there too. But it's all up to Mrs. Vogel. She does feel for her cousin, even though they are distant. I am sure that whatever she decides will be the proper decision. Perhaps I can talk Lars into coming this weekend to see this film. Better get back now. Good-bye, Marion," and Greta walked across the street where Lars was waiting in the automobile for her.

***

Doctor Marshall's wife stood in front of his office, having just delivered lunch to her husband when Greta happened to walk by. They smiled at each other and Greta stopped to hand the loaves of cinnamon bread she had just made to Mrs. Marshall and to say her good-byes.

"…and I'm just trying to use up the pantry supplies before we leave. I know how much you liked the cinnamon bread, so I wanted to drop off these loaves and tell you good-bye for now."

"Marion Owens said the poor woman was close to her sixth month now and she has no one. What a shame! How kind and generous of Ingrid to travel to Chicago and be with her. I assume you will stay with her until the child is born, won't you? I do hope everything goes well. When is the baby due?"

Greta looked puzzled for a second before answering. "I believe sometime in early November, but I am unsure exactly when. Yes, Mrs. Vogel feels a responsibility for the woman although they are not close cousins."

"Will you be back after that?"

"I just can't answer that. I know her cousin has been sickly throughout her time, and with her husband just dying a few months ago, it has been difficult. Mrs. Vogel might stay in Chicago through the winter, but I suppose she will wait to see how everything turns out. Anyway, I wanted to drop this off and wish you Merry Christmas just in case we are not back by then."

Mrs. Marshall laughed. "Yes, Merry Christmas to you also although it does seem like August is a bit early for holiday greetings. Please tell Ingrid to let us know how things turn out. Are you going to travel by automobile?"

"Mrs. Vogel and I are readying the house and packing now, but Lars will be taking us to the train in Stone City in a couple days. It will be a faster trip for us. Lars is going to stay at the house for a time and will be driving up in a week or so. There are things he needs to do just in case we spend the winter in Chicago."

"I hope things turn out well for Mrs. Vogel's cousin and the new baby. Have a safe trip and thank you for the bread. Smells delicious!"

Greta said her good-byes and walked over to the car she drove into town. She needed to get back to the house and continue organizing for the trip. The trip to Chicago where she would settle Ingrid into the townhouse and do what was necessary to plan and prepare for the birth of the baby.

***

Greta took over organizing, coordinating, managing life in Chicago. She found a doctor at Chicago's Lying-In Hospital, made an appointment and accompanied Ingrid there. The doctor pronounced Ingrid healthy and the baby fine. He asked a few questions of Ingrid, was sympathetic about her husband's very recent death, and suggested that a hospital birth would not only be safer and more hygienic but would also provide access to the most modern surgical techniques should they be required. After all, Ingrid was thirty-three, an advanced age for childbearing. Greta hired two Swedish girls to thoroughly clean the entire house, upstairs, downstairs, the small porch and outside steps, the small back area, and the automobile, once Lars drove it back to Chicago. A painter was found to repaint the small unused bedroom next to Ingrid's a soft yellow color, perfect for whichever sex would inhabit it. One wall was covered in a duckling and bunny wallpaper which Greta absolutely adored, and the necessary furniture: a wooden cradle, a baby crib, a baby dresser, and a heavy wooden rocking chair, was set in place. Some tiny white clothing, a workable hue for boy or girl, was obtained, and trappings for an infant including a stack of diapers and necessary small blankets were carefully folded, waiting in readiness. As the expectant mother needed clothing to accommodate her flourishing form, Greta let out the dresses she was able to and ordered additional ones from various Chicago stores. Greta was constantly busy. Ingrid found herself, book in hand, watching Greta move from project to project, following the directions given to her, signing receipts, writing out required checks, not being particularly helpful but also not getting in the way. She was grateful for Greta's commandeering of the entire situation, indifferent to the decisions being made for her, and marginally concerned about her own participation in the birthing portion of this enterprise. Ingrid was disengaged.

Greta noted this, but was too engrossed in her many undertakings to brood about it. In fact, she recommended to Ingrid that Dora Olsson, one of the young hired girls, be kept on for a time because she was a decent cook and housekeeper and Greta, being so preoccupied with necessary tasks, could use the help. Ingrid agreed. Greta suggested that the soon-to-be mother use her embroidery skills to decorate some of the baby bibs. Perhaps a bunny munching on a carrot would be appropriate. And if some sweet ducklings were found waddling across one of the blankets, the sky-blue embroidery floss marking the little pond into which they were headed, why that would be just lovely. Ingrid nodded and resurrected her needles and hoop, but the bunny never got a chance to eat the carrot, and the sky-blue floss never created a watery home for any ducklings. Ingrid was simply uninterested in taking up the needle. She began the projects, but they remained fragmentary. One evening, in an attempt to engage her, Greta began a conversation about baby names. Had Ingrid thought of any? Did she have a preference for a boy's name? A girl's name? She had just brought in a cup of raspberry leaf tea to Ingrid who was entering her ninth month. The tea was supposed to help prepare the body for birth and maybe shorten the mother's time in labor. Ingrid took a sip of the tea which she didn't really like, and shrugged her shoulders.

"Well, if it's a boy," and Ingrid would prefer this outcome although she never voiced it. "it will be *Fredrick*, of course. I haven't thought about a girl's name," and she put down the embroidery hoop which contained an incomplete bunny and picked up her half-read book but just stared at it.

"Might *Louisa*, after your grandmother or *Eliza*, your mother's name be acceptable for a girl? Do you have a favorite female name?" and Greta noted the partial bunny was missing both a tail and an ear. "I suppose you still have time to make up your mind."

Ingrid shrugged and turned the page in the book she was not reading. She did not take any more sips of her tea, and there was no more discussion about baby names.

Greta had no answer for Ingrid's apparent impassivity about the upcoming birth and her entry into the realm of motherhood. She was concerned about it but thought it would resolve itself once the child was here. Safely here. That was another concern and the reason for searching out a doctor and a hospital and not relying on a midwife and a bedroom. If Ingrid wasn't excited about the upcoming delivery, Greta felt enough of that emotion for the both of them. Besides, once the child was born, things would set themselves right and Ingrid would adjust. It would happen. It might take some time.

***

The advertising pictures for the evaporated milk formula showed a genuinely cheerful, almost euphoric mother as she gazed with adoration at the happy infant resting in her arms and feeding from the bottle. The magazine pictures showcasing the Chicago-based Storkline Furniture Company's new baby furniture portrayed a joyous and obviously well-rested woman rocking in the wooden rocking chair with her arms around a cherubic babe. In the background of the glossy ad, on the wall, was the same bunny and duckling wallpaper Greta had chosen for the nursery. When Greta went on a shopping trip to Marshall Field's fourth floor children's department to arrange for additional clothing for the new baby to be sent to the townhouse, she looked at the furry toys: yellow ducks, dozens of softly-browned bears lined up on shelves, even a small light-blue bird-like toy which called to her. But these items were just not yet needed. She walked past some of the larger toys and stopped at a colorfully painted swinging horse, considering that in a year or so, it would fit perfectly into the corner of the yellow painted nursery. She chose a set of Pyrex baby bottles, both four – and eight-ounce sizes, rubber nipples, bottle cleaning brushes. Besides additional bibs (these were decorated) and another blanket, Greta added two baby rattles and a small, softly stuffed lamb she just couldn't resist to the pile. She had been assisted by the clerk, Mrs. Jennings, who walked around with her, collecting the goods and explaining the use of many of them. Once the items were settled, the address of the apartment noted, the amount totaled, and the bill assessed, Greta found her way to the elevators and to the street where Lars would meet her, and they proceeded to the Lying-In Hospital where Ingrid had given birth the previous day.

But the birth was not as glorious and stately as the glossy ads and magazine pictures and the Marshall Field Department Store would have women believe. Even Greta, who had not yet seen either Ingrid or the new baby, was surprised when she learned of the delivery methodology. She had been informed by the doctor that everything went well, that Ingrid was resting, that the baby seemed healthy, and that on the following day, she and Lars would be able to visit the new mother for a brief time. Perhaps they would be able to view the newborn through the nursery window which was on a separate floor. The actual procedure used to help deliver the baby was not explained, but Greta was assured that progressive, advanced approaches had been utilized to protect both the mother's and the baby's health. Greta was impressed with the cleanliness of the newly created hospital and the sterling reputation of Dr. Joseph DeLee, the hospital's chief physician, who insisted upon the hygiene, the handwashing, the mask-wearing of the nurses and doctors. He had also devised what he determined were sound and solid guidelines, created to support and benefit women in delivering their children. The doctors at his hospital used, besides various drugs to dull the pain, Dr. DeLee's own inventions of a forceps and the helpful but painful episiotomy procedure. The smiling woman in the magazine ad seated on the wooden rocking chair obviously had not endured this protocol.

A fourteen-day stay was the recommended amount of time for mothers and their babies to remain in the Lying-In Hospital. However, on her ninth day in the sanitary and sterile but dull room, when Doctor Kaminski came in to check on her condition, to survey the patching job done on her nether parts, to observe her general fitness and constitution, Ingrid told him, she would be leaving to go home.

"Doctor Kaminski, I intend to leave today. I feel fine, and don't need to stay longer. Please arrange things so that I can inform Mrs. Anderson and her husband I will be coming home. I believe the baby is fine, and I appreciate your help, but it is time to leave." Ingrid was in pain, particularly as the doctor continued to examine her, but she was determined not to complain. She wanted to leave the hospital. Complaining would not help.

Dr. Kaminski continued his examination of her before saying anything. The woman, in his estimation, seemed fine physically. She was not eating as much as she should, but that was not unusual. She was attempting to breastfeed the baby, but according to the nurse the patient's milk was not always enough, and when the infant was returned to the general nursery, it was still hungry and needed to be given an additional bottle feeding. He had met with and spoken to Mrs. Anderson, and knew Mrs. Vogel would have help at home, but there was a melancholy air about her which bothered the doctor. Perhaps going home to familiar surroundings was the best thing for her. Some women just did not respond to a hospital setting. He listened to Mrs. Vogel and then nodded.

"Well, you appear healthy and are healing. Let me go to the nursery and check on your baby before a decision is made. There is some paper work to be completed, and I understand you did not name your daughter yet. Is that correct? There are papers to file, and I can send the nurse in with them. If everything checks out, I can approve a discharge tomorrow. Will that be acceptable?"

Ingrid sighed, but tomorrow would be better than another five more days, so she adjusted the way she was sitting, avoided uttering a moan, nodded, and replied, "Yes, thank you Dr. Kaminski. I'll let Mrs. Anderson know I am coming home then. Will I be able to leave in the morning?"

"We can arrange for everything right after breakfast tomorrow. I do want you to eat more and drink plenty of fluids. That is necessary for your milk production. I'll see you in my office in a month, and the nurse will be right in with additional instructions and the necessary papers. I assume you know what you will name your baby?" and he smiled encouragement.

"I do. Thank you," and Ingrid actually smiled back at him, now that things had been settled to her satisfaction. Thirty minutes later, the nurse came in with various forms to be filled out and signed, including the official birth certificate form which, because Ingrid had not named her daughter yet, was the most important one to complete.

"Again, I am so sorry about your husband's passing, but I do need to ask the month of his death for this form," and Nurse Kate waited patiently, pen in hand.

Ingrid swallowed a sob. This was one of the reasons she had hesitated to complete the forms, but she obviously could not tell the truth. Dr. Kaminski and all the nurses had been understanding and considerate to her, knowing that she would have this baby, but the baby's father, would never join in the joyous moment. He would never hold his child, never listen to the burbling baby laughter, never note the first feeble steps or mark moments of advancement. That part was the truth. Ingrid had listened to Greta's advice and allowed the semi-truth to be told: Ingrid's husband had died. That was all that was needed to be confessed. That he had died six years previously, that this child was not his, that the actual father was unaware of his progeny, that Ingrid had no idea who he really was or where he went when he left her Bonneville house, was not necessary information to share. Even the few Chicago neighbors who were acquainted with the Vogel household were not informed of the truth, and they didn't appear to remember Fredrick's death six years previously. This was all part of the Plan, and necessary so that nothing disreputable or degrading would be said about Ingrid Vogel. With this in mind, Ingrid answered, "June. The end of June," and even that was a lie, but she watched as the nurse filled in that the *father was deceased in June 1922*. The nurse pursed her lips and silently sighed with sympathy.

"And now, to a happier question. We have been calling the baby the *Ingrid baby*, because you haven't yet given her a name. I'm excited to know her name. Will it be *Ingrid*?"

"*Beatrice*," said the mother. She will be named Beatrice."

"Let's see. I don't want to misspell it. B-E-A-T-R-I-C-E. Is that correct?"

"Yes."

The nurse wrote the name down carefully. There was another space to complete. "And will you give her a middle name too?"

"Yes. I'll spell it for you.," and Ingrid took a deep breath as she listed the letters. "A-L-L-E-R-T-O-N."

The nurse had a quizzical look on her face, but carefully wrote *Allerton* in the space which demanded a middle name. "So, she is *Beatrice Allerton Vogel*. Lovely! Is the middle name a family name?"

"Yes," replied Ingrid, gauging her comfort with the lie which was only a partial one, "Yes, it is."

***

Ingrid relaxed in her warm Epsom salts bath and adjusted the towel beneath her in an attempt to get comfortable. She leaned back in the water and closed her eyes. Her mind wandered over the events of the last few weeks, but she took a sudden breath and sat up as she remembered that the baby's official birth certificate was not stored in a safe place. She would need to find a place, perhaps in Bonneville. A place where it would not be found and questioned, where Beatrice's middle name would not be known, where it would remain a secret. She berated herself again and wondered why she named the baby in the way she had. Wouldn't *Louisa* or *Eliza* or even *Ingrid* have been a more reasonable choice? A safer choice? It didn't matter now. The deed was done. When Greta asked about the baby's name, she also asked if she had a middle name. For the first time ever, Ingrid lied to her. "No, no middle name. Perhaps I'll let her choose her own in the future," and they smiled at each other. Ingrid's smile hid her guilt.

Taking periodic Epson salt baths had been recommended by Nurse Kate who gave directions to Ingrid before she left the hospital. "Place a rolled-up towel underneath you in the tub, and just allow the warmth to help heal you. Eventually you will recover. Most of the mothers who use this method think it helps. Sitting on a soft towel whenever you sit will also ease you. By the time you visit Dr. Kaminski in a few weeks, you should be feeling much better," and the young nurse smiled at her sage advice. She had not yet had a child.

And at the doctor visit, a few weeks later, he was pleased with Ingrid's physical condition. "Well, Mrs. Vogel, you seem to be progressing nicely. Continue to do whatever it is you are doing," and he asked about her eating habits and noted that she appeared less melancholy than the previous month. Leaving the hospital a bit early was the right move for her.

As she carefully stood up from the bath and began toweling herself off, she heard Greta in the nursery cooing to the baby. It was time for another feeding and Ingrid sighed. She felt like a failure as a mother. Where was the consuming love she was supposed to feel? Why was her baby so unresponsive to her? She was not producing enough milk for the child, and Greta sometimes had to bottle-feed her. What was happening? Was this some kind of punishment because of the baby's questionable parentage? Was it all her fault? She had read about the mother/child bond in novels and poems, viewed museum artwork portraying loving mothers caring for their children, poured over the magazine ads which proved the intimate devotion of maternal love due, apparently in part, to the advertised products. Ingrid slipped on her dress which opened in the front, allowing for nursing, took her time pulling on her stockings and shoes, and stood in front of the bathroom mirror wiping the steam away before she could view her reflection. Her face was thin, her skin appeared sallow, and she thought she looked every one of her thirty-three years. Brushing through her hair, she anchored it at the nape of her neck, and wondered again if she should simply cut it off. Have it styled into one of those *bobs* which seemed to be so popular. Sometimes taking care of herself was an arduous task, and if she wasn't able to do for herself, it was no wonder she had difficulty caring for the baby. Ingrid held back tears, took a deep breath, placed the shawl hanging on the doorknob over her shoulders and went into the yellow painted nursery.

Greta was seated in the rocking chair with Beatrice and was feeding her from the four-ounce Pyrex bottle purchased from the Marshall Field Store. When she saw Ingrid standing at the door, Greta said, "Come here. I'll get up and you sit down. I'll hand Beatrice to you."

Ingrid shook her head slowly and gave a slight smile. "No, don't disturb her. Just continue. Is the coffee ready?"

"Yes, it is, and there are oats on the stove. Once she finishes, she'll take a nap, and I'll be down. Are you sure you don't want to rock her for a bit? She does like that," and Greta smiled down at the infant.

"No. I'll see you in the kitchen. Perhaps I'll try to nurse her when she wakes up," and Ingrid walked down the stairs.

Greta watched her go and listened to her footsteps. She looked at the baby she held, thinking how much she was starting to look like her mother. "Oh, little one, your mother just does not know yet how much she loves you," and the baby, unaware of any heartache, continued to suckle from the Pyrex bottle's nipple.

***

Christmas was the usual quiet affair. Dora was spending the holiday week with her family, and Ingrid, the Andersons, and almost two-month-old Beatrice gathered together for a simple dinner. The adults shared a bottle of wine from the stock Fredrick had stored in the library's closet, and they relaxed while watching Beatrice turn her head towards the noises they would make. Lars mooed, Greta meowed, and Ingrid sang a few notes of an opera aria. Beatrice was starting to pay attention to sounds and noises, and Ingrid was feeling a bit more relaxed around her. The baby continued to breast-feed, but obtained additional nourishment from the formula in the Pyrex bottles. She seemed fairly healthy and mostly content. After the holiday meal was cleared and Beatrice settled in her bed, Greta and Ingrid worked together washing the dishes and talking while Lars went into the front room and adjusted the Westinghouse radio which he had brought with him from Bonneville. The Chicago station KYN usually had something to listen to, and Lars was fascinated by the transmissions. He would spend hours simply listening to the static noise and humming which periodically would erupt in some strange voices or even some music. The women knew he would be occupied for some time.

Greta handed Ingrid the large tureen to wipe. She began the washing of the pans as she spoke. "Ingrid, Lars and I are thinking of joining some friends at the church on New Year's Eve for a service and then a potluck dinner. It would be a late night, but we don't have to attend if you don't want to be alone with the baby. There has always been two of us here over the past weeks, and we can certainly plan to stay here is you are worried. Really, think about it. Whatever you decide will be fine."

Ingrid looked at her and smiled. "I don't need to think about it. Go. You and Lars are stuck here all the time, and I will be fine with Beatrice. Have a good time and don't even consider *not* going."

"Well, it will be a late night. We'll stay until the new year is here and won't be home until after midnight. Are you sure?"

"Of course, I am. You should plan on it."

"If you change your mind, let me know. I can prepare some bottles just in case…" and here Greta stopped. The bottle-and breast-feeding issue was a sensitive one, and she didn't want Ingrid to feel bad about it. At least not any worse than she already did.

Ingrid wiped the pan Greta handed her. "That will work. I am sure Beatrice and I will do just fine," and she smiled although her stomach suddenly clenched at the realization that she would be alone with the child. Her child. Her baby. It would be fine, she assured herself. It would only be a few hours.

***

It had been a warm December, and the snow which remained on the ground had almost disappeared. Lars was outside cleaning the automobile's windows, and Greta was in the kitchen finishing her ground beef, cheese, tomato sauce, and noodle casserole she would take to the church for the potluck dinner. Ingrid was standing and watching. She held Beatrice in her arms.

"There will be plenty of the usual Swedish meatballs, the potato casseroles, the noodle dishes, and I wanted to do something different. I got this recipe from Mrs. Ricci's housekeeper, Christina, who said that Mr. Ricci insists on having this weekly. There is a smaller casserole baking in the oven for you to try. Make sure you eat a goodly amount. You are still too thin, Ingrid," and Greta glanced at the woman standing to her right. Then she reached over and tickled Beatrice under the chin. "Little baby, you are such a sweet one," and she was glad to see Ingrid's smile.

Just before seven o'clock, Greta finished up in the kitchen. She would not be there to make sure that Ingrid ate, and she did not want to give her any excuse not to, so the table was set for one. Ingrid was putting Beatrice to bed and would be downstairs shortly. Although she attempted it, she was unable to nurse Beatrice who was hungry and fussy, so Greta prepared a bottle for the baby and left Ingrid in the nursery to feed and soothe her infant. Greta was just getting on her coat and pulling the scarf around her neck when Ingrid came down to the hallway.

"Is she sleeping?"

"Yes, finally," and Ingrid sighed. "I hope she'll sleep for a while. She seemed fussier tonight, and I can't help but feel it's my fault," and there was another audible sigh.

"Ingrid, we haven't left yet. I can call Lars in from the car and we can just stay here. I don't mind," and Greta tried to sound as sincere as possible.

"Nonsense. Go and enjoy yourselves. We will be fine."

Greta nodded, "Well, we'll return in a few hours. Perhaps Beatrice will sleep until then, and I can do the late-night feeding. Try to get some sleep yourself," and she finished pulling on her hat and gloves and left to join Lars in the car.

As she watched Greta get into the car and Lars drive off, Ingrid thought she wasn't very hungry but should attempt to eat something. She listened at the foot of the stairs but didn't hear any crying, so she went to the kitchen, removed the casserole from the oven where it was warming, and sat at the place set for her. A small serving spoon amount of the dinner casserole was placed on her plate, and she took a tentative bite. She took another and soon, the serving was gone, so she helped herself to another spoonful. *This is not bad,* she thought. *I can see why Mr. Ricci likes it, and I'll tell Greta she did a good job.* She finished the second plate and sat back. The kitchen was warm and she felt good. She put the leftover casserole in the icebox and washed the few dishes. As she dried them, she saw the apple pie Greta had made earlier in the day for the New Year's Day dinner, and thought a small piece would taste good. She cut into it and sat down at the table to eat it. *I haven't eaten this much in a while,* she considered. *Maybe this is a good thing.*

It was almost eight o'clock, and the house remained quiet. Ingrid decided to go upstairs and take a bath. The house was cooling, but a bath would be warming and relaxing. She turned out the lights but left the small hallway light on so neither Greta nor Lars would stumble while entering. She climbed the stairs and went to the nursery and stood at the door hearing no sound except for a light baby breathing. She walked to the bathroom next where she placed a towel and her nightdress on the chair next to the tub which was filling up with warmth. Piling her hair on top of her head so it would remain dry, she eased herself into the water, and gave herself to the pacifying wetness. She soaped up and rinsed off and did not think of much. Once the water began to cool, she lifted the tub's plug, stood up, and toweled off. Nightdress on, hair brushed and braided, she once more walked into the nursery, this time standing next to the crib and looked at the sleeping baby. *Beatrice,* she thought, *is a large name for such a small package. Perhaps I should call you something else,* but nothing came to mind. Ingrid reached into the crib, touched the small arm, and a new wonder at this miracle emerged.

It was just nine o'clock, and normally she would be up for another hour or so, but she felt sleepy and went into her bedroom. She left the door opened so she might hear the baby cry, lay down under the heavy covers, and within a short time was asleep. She slept for some time, but was awaken when a familiar sound penetrated her slumber. Ingrid opened her eyes, then sat up, and grabbing the shawl from the bottom of her bed, threw it over her shoulders as she hurried to Beatrice.

She saw the clock near her bed claimed the eleventh hour. *It is still 1922,* she thought, *not yet the new year.* She entered the nursery, leaned over to pick up the crying infant and realized there was a wetness down the front of her nightdress. Wrapping Beatrice in a blanket, Ingrid sat down on the rocker, still carefully padded with some soft towels, and without analyzing her actions, opened the buttons of her gown, and placed Beatrice close to her bareness. Immediately Beatrice found what she wanted, and began to nurse. Ingrid, still half asleep, watched as her daughter took her nourishment. After a time, after Beatrice was properly burped, she was switched to the other breast and continued. Ingrid, now fully awake, did not realize she was smiling. She reached her free hand to touch Beatrice's, wondering once again at the perfection of the tiny palm and five fingers, and was unprepared when the baby wrapped her miniscule hand around one of Ingrid's fingers, holding on to it as she continued to nurse. An unanticipated emotion washed over Ingrid. Suddenly, everything fell into place. Everything was the way it should be. The poems and novels, the paintings in the museums, the glossy advertisements in the magazines were proving true. Without meaning to, without expecting it, Ingrid's heart and head acknowledged her motherhood. This was her daughter. They were bound, and just as once before, a long time ago, a thin diaphanous ribbon, not unlike a spider's silken webbing, was slowly reaching out, joining their heart centers. There was recognition. An understanding. A sensibility. A connection.

Beatrice finished. Her head fell back and a small bubble of mother's milk was blown from her lips. She was milk-drunk, and Ingrid's face reflected tenderness at the sight. She allowed the baby to enjoy the fullness before another burp, a change of her diaper, and a readjustment into the arms of her mother. She sat back down on the rocker and slowly moved as she cradled her daughter. There were some distant sounds which alerted Ingrid to the fact that it was now a new year. The year 1923 had officially begun out there. But in the nursery, there was no time, no hurry, no quickness or gravity or uproar. Just the stillness which comes with recognition, awareness, fulfillment. Just a mother and her child. That was all. A gentle change settled.

Ingrid did not know or care about the passing time, but eventually she heard a movement downstairs. Greta and Lars had returned. There were quiet whispers and soft steps, and Greta appeared at the doorway. She stood and watched the scene before her, and she understood. Ingrid turned to her and smiled and then whispered, "Did you have a good time?"

"Yes," Greta whispered back. "Everything fine here?"

"Yes," and Ingrid smiled the kind of smile not seen by Greta in a long while. "Bess and I are fine."

"*Bess*?"

Ingrid nodded. "Beatrice is a big name for such a little girl. We are going to call her *Bess*. I think it fits, don't you?"

"It does. Bess," repeated Greta. "Do you want me to take over?"

Ingrid softly shook her head. "No. Go to bed. I know you're tired, and we'll talk in the morning. Sleep in, Greta. I can take care of Bess."

Greta nodded. "Well, good-night then. And Happy New Year, Ingrid. And Happy New Year, Bess."

"Happy New Year, Greta. See you in the morning," and Ingrid watched as Greta turned and disappeared into the darkness.

Noises from the outside world ceased. A small brightness was noticed in the sky just outside the nursery window, and Ingrid stared for a while at the star, then looked down at her daughter. She rocked her slowly for a long while before placing the child in her crib. When she climbed into her own bed, there would barely be time for her head to feel the pillow beneath it before she fell asleep. Neither mother nor daughter woke during the remainder of the night, and when, in the earliest morning, the first day of the new year, Ingrid went to Bess's room, she noted that the star from last night's sky was gone, replaced with a larger and brighter and more pleasant one.

Eight

Bess and Ingrid and Greta in Bonneville

June, 1923

"And, of course, Mrs. Vogel was more than willing to take in the small babe. It was such a kind thing to do. We have all fallen in love with Bess," and Greta smiled.

She was explaining the situation for the third time in two days. This time to Mrs. Marshall because Greta had, the previous day, already run into, purely by coincidence, Marion Owens and Mabel McHenry, telling them the same story, giving them the essential facts, explaining the significant circumstances so that the news would be announced as it was meant to be. Mrs. Vogel's deed was a kind response, an honest action, a fortuitous incident, and there was nothing disreputable or degrading about her adoption of the orphaned baby, whose mother, her recently widowed mother, Mrs. Vogel's cousin, did not survive the birth of the child. Why, Mrs. Vogel even named the baby after the deceased mother. She was *Beatrice* and would be called *Bess*. Greta was richly pleased with the success of her Plan.

"How wonderful for Ingrid. I am sure she is the best of mothers, and I will let Dr. Marshall know there is another little one for him to look after. Please tell Ingrid I will telephone her and plan a visit very soon. I am anxious to see the baby. She is now about six or seven months, correct? What a happy age. Well, I must return home. I told the doctor I would make his favorite fried chicken for dinner. It was good seeing you again, Mrs. Anderson. Give my message to Mrs. Vogel," and Mrs. Marshall turned to walk away, but turned again to Greta and offered, "If any advice is needed about child-raising, I can certainly help Ingrid. Had five of my own, you know," and this time, she crossed the street to go home.

Greta watched her for a few minutes before she placed her shopping basket on the passenger seat and climbed into the automobile. She pulled out carefully and drove back to the house. It was time for lunch, and Lars needed to start packing the car for his journey to Chicago the following day.

***

It was early Friday morning. Greta waved as Lars turned out of the driveway and traveled to Mr. Jones' farmhouse where he would pick up the oldest son, Raymond. Raymond just turned eighteen, had never been farther than Stone City, and was anxious and excited to visit Chicago. Lars was traveling to the Chicago house to pick up the necessary furniture, packed boxes, and various items they could not manage to bring with them earlier in the week because three adults and a baby took up most of the room in the car. He had to leave his Westinghouse table radio in Chicago and was anxious to bring it back to Bonneville and discover what he could manage to hear in the country. Raymond, in exchange for helping to drive back and forth and load the heavy items into the car, would spend the weekend in the city with Lars, looking at the sights, eating in some of the restaurants, and going to a film at the Chicago Theater. They would return on Tuesday, and after Raymond unloaded the car, Lars would drive him home. It was a fair exchange.

Greta walked into the kitchen where Bess, splashing and laughing, was being given a bath in the sink. She watched Ingrid care for the child to whom she had become attached and stood still for a few minutes. As she moved closer to the sink, Bess slapped her hand in the water and splashed it up and towards both her mother and Greta, creating a large wet spot on the front of Greta's dress.

"Oh, oh," she laughed and addressed the baby, "I should have had on an apron like your mother. Well, I suppose this will dry. It's going to be a hot summer day, and I will probably appreciate some cool wetness later on." She took the towel from the counter, opened it up, and took the wet child that Ingrid lifted from the sink. "Are her clothes down here or are they upstairs?" she asked.

Ingrid pointed to the kitchen table. "There they are. I can dress her. I thought I would take her to the music room and let her play the piano for a time. She really likes to do that. When she's old enough, I'll give her lessons," and she held out her arms for the child.

"Did you remember that Mrs. Marshall is coming by this afternoon for tea and to meet Bess? I thought that something with the strawberries from Mrs. Jones would taste good."

Greta nodded. "I can do that. Let me get a yellow cake made before it gets too warm. Take the baby into the music room, and I'll start the baking. I'll put some tea out in the sun for later. Iced tea would be better than hot, don't you think?"

"Yes, that sounds fine. I was surprised to hear from Mrs. Marshall so quickly, but I suppose the town is buzzing with the news of this one," and Ingrid looked down at Bess. "I suppose I better be prepared for a number of questions about my *cousin*. The simplest answers will be best," and a worried look passed over her face.

"Just stick to the story, Ingrid. So far everything has worked out, and soon there will be another set of instances the town will have to gossip about."

"I hope so," and Ingrid held Bess as they went into the music room. As Greta gathered the ingredients for the cake and placed a large jar of cold water and tea outside in the early sun, she heard the piano send tinkling sounds into the air and smiled.

***

Bess played with the small rattle Mrs. Marshall had gifted her, and periodically peeked up at this strange new person but refused to stay in her arms and fussed until Ingrid took her again.

"She is just darling," and Mrs. Marshall chucked Bess under her chin for the third time. "I remember mine at this age. Not yet walking, not yet getting into things. Soon you will have your hands even fuller, Ingrid. Of course, with just the one, it won't be as bad."

"I expect not," answered Ingrid, "Thank you again for the rattle and the lovely blanket. We brought just what we could fit in the car with us, and left much in Chicago. I'll be glad when Mr. Anderson returns with the clothes and blankets and things we didn't have room for."

"He'll return on Monday?"

"They'll be back by Tuesday in the late afternoon. Raymond Jones went with him to help drive and load the car. But we'll be fine until then. Once Bess has her stroller here, I can take her for a walk outside. She liked doing that in Chicago. I'm a bit worried about it fitting into the car with everything else, but Mr. Anderson said it wouldn't be a problem."

"Well, I'm sure it won't," and Mrs. Marshall reached over to brush Bess's hair. "Her hair is coming in nicely. I remember my youngest didn't have much for almost eighteen months. I was beginning to worry about it, but look at her now. She's the one getting married soon. She recently went to that new women's beauty shop in town to have it cut and shaped into one of those new haircuts because she claims it is just too long and thick to deal with," and the doctor's wife squinted her eyes and examined Bess's head. "Her hair color favors yours. There is a bit of reddishness to it too," and she examined Ingrid's locks next.

Ingrid was prepared. "Her mother and I shared the same coloring, a family trait. Both hair and eyes. So, I suppose Bess comes by it honestly," and she brushed her hand over the baby's new head of hair which was exactly the color of her own.

"Hmm, that makes sense. Her eyes look darkish blue, but I know they can change. Did the mother have brown eyes like yours too?"

"Actually, she did. I believe her husband's eyes were hazel. We will just have to wait and see what happens with Bess," and Ingrid thought this was a good time to end this particular topic, so she called out, "Mrs. Anderson! Would you take Bess, please?"

Greta, who was listening as she waited just around the corner, came in. She entered the front parlor ready to rescue the child from Mrs. Marshall's questioning. She reached for Bess who went willingly into her arms, and said, "I'll give her a bottle and then lay her down for a nap, Mrs. Vogel. If you ladies would like to move to the dining room, the table is set with a bit of strawberry cake and iced tea."

"That sounds delightful," said Mrs. Marshall, and as Greta left, she stood up and straightened out her skirt.

"Mrs. Anderson makes a wonderful yellow cake, and Mrs. Jones was kind enough to send us some of her early strawberries."

Ingrid led the way to the dining room where she hoped to steer the conversation to subjects other than the color of Bess's hair and eyes. She would question her guest about the new businesses that were starting in town and ask about the youngest Marshall daughter's upcoming wedding. Perhaps Mrs. Marshall would have some ideas for a fall garden and answer questions about the church's annual ice cream social which was scheduled for the month of August. The list of subjects Ingrid planned to discuss with this woman was designedly lengthy.

Fall, 1925

"…so I am going into town today and order this from McCory's Store. They don't have them in stock, but there is a catalogue and I can put in an order for Bess's third birthday. What do you think?"

Greta looked over Ingrid's shoulder examining the advertisement in the paper which was spread out on the dining room table. The ad was for a Fairy Tricycle and portrayed a little girl, about the size of Bess, wearing a large sunhat and sitting on the tricycle. It looked like a dangerous idea for a not quite three-year old, but Greta just nodded and replied, "I am sure Bess will enjoy this once she is large enough to sit on the thing."

Ingrid glanced at her. She understood what Greta meant. "She will be soon. It will be fine, Greta. I know it will take at least six weeks to get here, so I need to order it now. As long as it is delivered by early November, it will be a wonderful gift for her. Don't worry so much. Bess will learn to ride it, and I'll watch her. Where is Lars? I need to use the car after lunch."

"He's finishing breakfast with Bess in the kitchen. Made them pancakes this morning. Would you like some?"

"No, thanks. Just more coffee. I'm planning on visiting the cemetery once I have ordered the gift, but I won't leave until Bess lays down for her nap. I'll be gone about an hour, but if she is awake before I return, tell her I had to run an errand. She likes to tag along, and I did promise that we would look at the toy section at McCory's this week, but obviously not today. Don't want her disappointed."

"She will be fine," and Greta closed the newspaper, pushing it back to Ingrid, "I think Lars was planning to drive the car to the filling station later. He may want to go along. I'll go and check on their breakfast and tell him you want to see him."

"Thanks, Greta. If Bess is done, send her to me. It's nice enough to go for a morning walk today," and Ingrid set the paper to the side.

Lars and Ingrid took off for town once Bess was asleep. Ingrid got out of the car in front of McCory's Store while Lars traveled down Main Street to the filling station, newly opened a year ago, and doing a lively business. *Tony's Filling Station* claimed the sign with the additional proclamations that it would not only supply gas and oil but would complete *General Auto Repairs, Excellent Tire Repairs and Sales*, and offered the inducement of *Free Air* to the automobiles needing it. Tony's oldest son, Tony Jr., was the attendant who would pump the gallons required by hand, check the tires and oil, and furnish the free air to tires if insufficiency was noted. While this was done, Lars could enter the small building, pay five cents for a cold bottle of Coca-Cola from the cooler in the corner (Although sometimes the bottle wasn't that cold.), and talk to Tony Sr. about a variety of important subjects. The business had begun to advertise: *Car Wash by Hand:50 cents*, and sometimes Lars would wait around and have Tony Jr. complete the task. The filling station became a haunt for Lars, superseding the barber shop.

Tony's Filling Station was not the only change in Bonneville's Main Street business section. Over the years, whether businesses expanded due to the population increase or the increased population demanded new business, the town gained both. Families, moving into new houses being constructed along the mushrooming streets, brought additional children who crowded into the unassuming school. Additional classrooms were opened, and, of necessity, more teachers were hired. They brought families with them, forcing the current ongoing construction of a new school. *McCory's Five and Dime Store* started in the small, empty building on the corner, but within a year opened the second floor where ready-made clothing as well as dry goods were available. *The General Store* turned into the "groceteria", a new self-service store where women would bring their own shopping baskets and search through the canned options for necessary or new foods. A lawyer, Jason Adill, who also helped sell and buy houses and land, set up an office next to the barber shop. Then the barber shop added a separate room, the *Modern Beauty Shop*, where women of the town could come to have their hair *waved* or *bobbed*, if they dared, and many did. Mabel McHenry was put in charge of both the enlarged telephone switchboard and the two supplemental operators. Unfortunately for Mabel, this deprived her from hearing some of the juicier telephone conversations. Even Dr. Marshall found a need to expand his practice, bringing in a young doctor, the son of an old friend, who was anxious to employ the current medical knowledge he worked so hard to attain. New houses, updated businesses, road creations and expansions which took place not only in the town, but also south of the main street and north of the filling station created hammering and sawing and construction noises of all kinds. This cacophonous amplification caused the older, settled citizens of the town to gripe and grumble and grouse about the town changing, the aggravation produced, the upset to their lives in these horrible modern times. It was worrisome and distressful. But the shifts, the sprawls, the adaptions continued because, as once noted, "Change is the only constant in life."

As Lars and Ingrid drove back to the house, they discussed the town's evolution. "Lars, turn here, I want to see where the new school is being built," and they scrutinized it, noting the size.

"Turn down the next street, where the noise is. Let's see what those new houses look like," and they inspected them commenting on the modern layouts.

"Is that a park with swings being built?" and they watched the erection of the structure, each picturing Bess playing on it.

Once their exploration was completed, they traveled home passing the large empty fields once belonging to Fredrick Vogel who had planned to retire as a gentleman farmer. The land now belonged to his widow who had no interest in farming. As she and Lars drove past her acreage, she examined the unused expanse, gazed at the dormant property, and made a decision.

Spring, 1926

The noise bothered Greta. She complained to Ingrid and said, "I know it will not be forever, but truly, do they need to begin that hammering and sawing so early in the morning?"

"Greta, they don't start until eight, and you know we are all up by then. Besides, it will be exciting, once the houses are built, to have neighbors so close. Perhaps there will be some children to play with Bess."

"I suppose. Bess just wants to watch what is happening all the time. Actually, so does Lars. Neither one wants to do much else. In fact, they are both standing at the side of the house now, and breakfast is ready."

"Let me go and get them. I'll bet Bess is out there without a coat, and it's chilly this morning," and Ingrid went out the back door to the side of the house where both Bess and Lars stood watching the construction of the house take place. Bess, who was not wearing a coat, kept hold of Lars' hand, but because of the noise, they did not hear Ingrid call to them. She walked over and motioned for them to follow her. Breakfast was ready.

Jason Adill, Esquire, as his business card read, was delighted to help Ingrid Vogel sell the vacant land adjacent to her house. Part of the land was sold to the neighbor to the south whose farmland bordered on the acres near the wooded area. The land conjoining the area next to Ingrid's house was bought by Woodwine and Smith Construction Company, the organization manufacturing the new houses in the town proper. The company was building the houses next to Ingrid's, and the closest one was almost finished while the three additional houses were in various stages of completion. Across the road from the Vogel house, available land was being prepared for more residences. That land was owned by Harold Jones who, when he heard of the amount of money Ingrid would receive from the sales of her land (Mabel McHenry happened to be at the switchboard for this call.) decided that expanding his faltering farm was not a good idea, so he sold his vacant land to the same company. Some days the construction noise became too much for Greta, and she would angrily slam the windows and doors shut, preferring to eliminate spring breezes and instead wipe the sweat from her forehead as she worked in the kitchen where the windows were also closed.

The money Ingrid obtained from the sale of the land was useful. Of course, she had money, but she kept the books, paid the bills including the mortgage on the Chicago house, and was aware of increasing expenses. While the house in New York City brought in a rental income, it did not totally cover the outlay. Both the New York house and the one in Chicago remained her responsibility. Then there were the fees paid to the New York lawyers, the Chicago lawyers, and Jason Adill who did not charge nearly what the big city lawyers did, but it all added up. Ingrid was aware of the costs in Bonneville: the house, the automobile, food and clothing for four people, the generous salary paid to the Andersons. She continued to support the arts in Chicago although she was rarely able to attend the concerts or plays for which she held season tickets. So, when the check from Woodwine and Smith cleared and the money became available, she decided part of it should be used for the house in Bonneville which hadn't been updated since it was bought by Fredrick.

And updating was necessary. A new driveway and walkway were needed. Rooms were painted and new furniture ordered to replace things which were either worn out or out-of-date or both. The bedroom next to Ingrid's was redecorated and newly furnished for Bess, and the smaller one at the front of the second floor was also given an update. The upstairs bathroom was renovated and brought into the twentieth century. The furnace and kitchen appliances were modernized, and plans were made to purchase a new automobile in the fall. Ingrid contacted the Chicago

Steinway Piano Company, and when the piano tuner she hired came to Stone City on the train, Lars picked him up at the station. He remained in Bonneville for a week, first tuning up the Steinway in Ingrid's music room, then the pianos at the churches in town, and Ingrid paid for it all. The money which remained, was placed into the bank where Ingrid was assured it would be safe. Someone from the New York lawyers' office suggested she invest in the booming stock market, but since she did not understand it, she decided not to. She did, however, take some of the money in actual cash and hide it in her middle dresser drawer towards the back. *I suppose I'm foolish for doing this*, she thought, *but Fredrick always said that it was wise to have some ready cash on hand.* In the coming years, Fredrick's advice would prove to be sound.

Through that year, the building continued, and by the following spring, the once small town of Bonneville was transfigured. The houses were filled with families; Bonneville's new school was opened; additional businesses filled the Main Street; Tony's Filling Station hired two more attendants, and Mabel McHenry no longer worked the telephone switchboard because she was too busy supervising her staff of five operators. The town's population adjusted to the changes and, for the most part, reveled in them. But perhaps the biggest reveler was Bess, for next door to her, in the new house which she and Lars had watched being built, a family moved in. And the oldest daughter of the family, Marjorie, was exactly the same age as Bess. They became friends.

Spring, 1927

"Mama! Mama!" and Bess came running into the kitchen calling for Ingrid who was not there. Greta was.

"What, Bess? Is there something wrong? Do you need something?"

"Where is Mama? I need to ask her something," and Bess danced from one leg to the other in front of Greta.

"She's in the library doing some paperwork. Can I help?"

Bess shook her head and said, "No, I need to talk to Mama," and she hurried to the library.

Ingrid had received some correspondence from the lawyer in New York and was reading through it once again. She had just started to jot down some notes when Bess showed up.

"Mama, I want to know something," and Bess stood next to Ingrid and tapped her on her right arm. "Can I ask you something?"

Ingrid closed the inkwell, placed her pen down. and turned to Bess. There was nothing that was as important as seeing her daughter, and she smiled at the child. It was like looking in a mirror. Bess's eyes had become the same sort of brown as hers, and her hair, currently, unbraided on one side, exactly matched the shade of her mother's. Ingrid began to adjust the unbraided side and brushed some hair back from her daughter's face.

"What is it, Bess? You are certainly in a hurry. Is everything OK? I thought you were playing with Margie in the back."

"I am. But I have a question," and Bess looked up into her mother's face. "What's my name?"

"Your name? Why you know exactly what it is. What do you mean?"

"I mean what is my *whole* name? Margie said she has *two* names. She said her name is Marjorie Alice Miller. My name is Beatrice Vogel, and is Bess my second name? Am I Beatrice Bess Vogel?"

Ingrid took a breath. She hadn't expected this to be a question asked by her five-year-old, but she knew what she would do. She would lie. There was no way the actual name given on Bess's birth certificate would be, could be, known. She smiled and told the same lie to her daughter that she had told to Greta.

"No, *Bess* is just a nickname we call you. It's a form of Beatrice. Just like *Margie* is a shortened name for Marjorie. You don't have a middle name. That's what the name Alice is to Margie: a middle name. You are Beatrice Vogel, but family and friends call you Bess."

Bess bit her lower lip and thought. Then she spoke the eternal question asked to parents. "Why? Why don't I have a middle name? Do you have a middle name?"

"I just never gave you one. And I suppose I didn't because I don't have one either. But you could pick a name you like and we can make that your middle name. Would that be something you would like to do?"

"You mean I can pick any name?"

"Yes. Choose something you like and we can make it yours. Do you want to think about it for a while?"

Bess shook her head. "No, I want to choose something now so I can tell Margie what it is. What should I pick?"

Ingrid thought. "Well, my mother's name was Eliza, and my grandmother's name was Louisa. Do you like those names? Sometimes middle names honor someone in the family. But you can have any name you want."

"No, those aren't right. I don't want those."

Ingrid nodded. "Well, there's names like Mary, Emily, Julia, Sophie. Do you like any of those?"

Bess shook her head.

"*Greta* is a name of someone you know, although her full name is *Margareta*. Would you want that one?"

"But if you called *Greta*, would you be talking to me or to Greta?"

"I suppose I would be referring to Greta and not to you. We would still call you Bess. People aren't usually called by their middle names. What about Amy or Josephine or Violet?"

Bess shook her head. Both of them were quiet for a time, and Bess played with the belt which hung down on Ingrid's dress. Ingrid smiled at the little girl and thought about the joy she brought her. Bess lay her head on her mother's lap and suddenly looked up and smiled.

"I know what to do!"

"What have you decided?"

"I don't have a middle name and you don't either, so we should use each other's names. I will be Beatrice Ingrid Vogel, and you can be Ingrid Beatrice Vogel. Don't you think that is a good idea?"

Ingrid nodded. "I think that's a wonderful idea."

"When we do the reading tonight, can you write the names out so I can copy them? Then I can put the paper in my room."

"Yes, later on we will do that writing together," and just as suddenly as she showed up, Bess turned and bolted from the room.

"Where are you going?"

Bess yelled back, "I have to tell Margie my middle name and tell her I got to pick it," and she rushed through the kitchen, past Greta, and out the back door.

Ingrid laughed to herself at the cleverness of her daughter. She sat and smiled. Through the opened library window, she could hear Bess calling to her friend. Then her smile faded. She thought of something she needed to do. Reaching into the bottom drawer of the large desk, Ingrid pulled out an envelope she had brought with her from Chicago. One which was too easily accessible. She opened it and glanced at the official document: Bess's birth certificate. The one which contained her real and regrettable middle name. The last name of her true father. She had not meant to leave it in a place where it could be found. Not that she didn't trust Greta, but she didn't want her or Bess to wander in, begin to look for something, and run across this.

Ingrid pushed away from the desk, and taking the envelope with her, walked up the stairs to her bedroom. She opened the small middle drawer of her dresser where no one ever looked except for herself, picked up a velvet box containing a gold and emerald bracelet and a comb with some dark hairs attached to it. The envelope containing honesty was folded beneath a lacy doily, and the box and comb placed back on top of both. Even if the drawer was opened by someone other than her, the envelope would remain hidden. She looked at the contents once again, then closed the drawer. The velvet box and the comb resided on top of the doily and the envelope. Sentries. Guardians of the truth.

Late Summer, 1927

Ingrid traveled to New York City in the late summer of 1927. Earlier in the year, the lawyers had contacted her, informing her that the family who had been renting Grandmother Louisa's house wanted to purchase it, and they needed to know if she was interested in selling it. She took some time to think about it. She discussed it with Greta, and eventually decided that it was a good idea. She had not been to New York since she had last traveled there with Fredrick, and she didn't think there would be a reason to go. She had lost touch with the people they had known. Her mentor and voice teacher, Madame Duff-Ross, had died two years ago, and New York City had undergone drastic changes. The lawyers suggested that if she was not going to return, the sale of the house would be a wise decision. Then there was the warehouse containing furniture and trinkets which had been packed up. Did she want them? If not, they could be sent to be auctioned off. She didn't even remember what was packed in the warehouse, and although much of the paperwork could be done by sending it back and forth in the mail, it was recommended she make a personal trip to complete the transactions. So, she planned a trip to New York.

This was a business trip, and she was not taking Bess with her. Greta and Lars would care for her during the days she was gone. Lars would drive her to Stone City where she would take the morning train to Chicago, transfer to the train to New York in the afternoon, and arrive in that city the following morning. She hated to leave Bess, but it was necessary, so hugs were given, and Bess was assured that her mother would return from New York with a special something for her. Tears flowed. And not just from Bess. Ingrid wiped her eyes and waved from the car until she could no longer see Greta and her daughter standing at the front of the driveway. She turned around with a sigh and tried to relax as Lars drove the new Ford Touring Automobile at a brisk thirty-five miles per hour. The car ride was not bumpy because the roads had been newly covered with concrete surfaces and as Lars drove, Ingrid watched the passing countryside.

Stone City and its Union Station loomed ahead. Lars parked the car and pulled out the one large suitcase Ingrid had packed. A waiting porter stood by while Lars and Ingrid spoke briefly. Then the porter followed Ingrid through Union Station to one of the ticket windows standing to the side with other porters guarding other suitcases while Ingrid waited in line. The station was busy, but then it generally was, and Ingrid was lost in her thoughts as the line moved slowly. She was wearing a light coat and a matching hat. It was one of those fashionable new draped hats which came down the side of her face, over the left cheek and partially blocked the sight from her left eye. She had purchased the outfit at McCory's second floor where up-to-date ready-to-wear clothing, hats, and shoes were available. Her burnt-umber hair was caught in a knot at the nape of her neck, and the fashionable hat covered most of it. There were several ticket windows: one to her left and two to her right, and people were lined up at all of them. She moved forward as necessary and looked straight ahead. Perhaps it was for all these reasons she never noticed that to her left, waiting at the line almost directly across from her was someone from her past. Thomas Allerton stood waiting to purchase his own ticket. He, too, was taking the morning train to Chicago. He, too, was standing in the line, waiting, lost in his own sorrowful thoughts. He, too, moved forward as necessary and looked straight ahead. He did not notice that to his right was someone from his past.

Separately, they completed their tasks. Tickets were purchased and they moved on, going their individual ways. Thomas Allerton adjusted the knapsack he wore across his shoulders and turned towards the trains. He would sit in one of the first passenger cars, in coach, because that ticket was what he could afford. Sitting closer to the engine was unpleasant because of the smoke and the dirt and the noise. Ingrid's ticket put her in one of the cars further back from the aggravating smoke, irritating dirt, annoying noise. Those seats were cushy and commodious, meant for restfulness, and Ingrid was used to sitting in relative comfort. She adjusted her hat, pulling the side down a bit and smiled at the porter carrying her suitcase. They turned towards the trains. Thomas was ahead of Ingrid and the following porter by a few feet. There were many people walking the same direction. No one noticed anyone else, and the noise from the trains and the talking and the general tumult echoed throughout the station, allowing for no communication.

Thomas found his coach car, and when allowed to, entered and found a seat. It was not as cushy or commodious as those in the back cars, but he was tired and sad and sat next to a window against which he rested his head. Ingrid was shown to her seat by a conductor who made certain she was comfortable. She eased in and sat next to a window and stared out at the crowd. Thomas rested his hazel eyes, never fully sleeping; Ingrid closed her chestnut ones but remained wide awake. Neither one thought of the other while sitting in the train traveling to Chicago. The trip took just over an hour.

When the train entered Chicago's LaSalle Street Station, Thomas opened his eyes. He waited in line with the other passengers on the coach car and stepped down into the smoke and cinders and dust which surrounded the front train cars. Ingrid was escorted to her train car's entrance and helped down the four steps where another porter would carry her suitcase to the waiting area. She adjusted her draped hat again, and as she turned to speak to the porter, explaining where she wanted to go, she noticed and then ignored the tingly feeling on the nape of her neck, just where her burnt-umber hair was tightly wound in a knot. At just that same instant, Thomas passed the woman speaking to the porter and walked quickly to his destination. A quivering in his stomach occurred, but he ignored it, passing it off as simply nerves. Ingrid turned just as he passed, and they did not notice each other.

The train trip to New York was a lengthy one. After Ingrid checked into her hotel and rested, she used the days to complete her business. She signed necessary papers and made decisions after speaking with the New York lawyers. Grandmother Louisa's house was sold to the renters, and without even checking through them, Ingrid placed all the items in storage up for auction. A bit of shopping was done, and she purchased one of the new Yo-Yo toys and a picture book about New York for Bess. She called long-distance and spoke to both Bess and Greta, and when her obligations were finished, she packed everything up and repeated the train trip home. Thomas did not return to Stone City. He stayed in Chicago. Eventually he created another life for himself, a happier one. Neither one ever knew how physically close they had been at the train station, how a brushed shoulder or turned head or familiar voice may have jarred them into shocked acknowledgment. The tingly feeling and the quivering stomach were ignored.

What if they had seen each other? Thomas no longer had a beard and was older. Would Ingrid have recognized him? *What if* Ingrid had told him about Bess? Would she have had the nerve? Was a train station the place for such a revelation? *What if* Thomas had asked *why?* or Ingrid had told the reason? *What if* Thomas…? *What if* Ingrid…? Tragedies are not the only occurrences with *what ifs*. There are enigmatic serendipities and chances and connections. The future would hail another time, another occurrence when fate would intervene. It would happen. But it would not happen for many years, and the ending would not be romantic or idealistic. It would be seemly. It would be appropriate.

Summer, 1929

It was July, and Ingrid, Bess, and Greta had already been in Chicago for three weeks. Lars had driven them there in June, stayed for a couple nights and returned to Bonneville to care for the house and garden. For the remainder of that summer, he split his time between the two places, but the women and Bess stayed in Chicago because the townhouse was being modernized and redecorated. They needed to be there to view it and approve the changes. Ingrid used the money from the sale of her grandmother's house to pay off the Chicago mortgage and update the things which needed to be updated. She had placed some of the money into the bank, where it would be secure, but she also had ready cash hidden in the Chicago townhouse in the small safe in the library's closet. Fredrick's advice.

While the work was being completed, Ingrid and Bess visited Chicago's Art Institute and the Field Museum; they walked along Lake Michigan; they shopped on State Street; they made a trip to the Chicago Theater. As interesting as the museums were, and as productive as the shopping trip was, they did not compare with the Marx Brothers' movie *The Cocoanuts* which the three of them saw. The film had sound, color, and musical numbers, and while Ingrid was amused, Bess and Greta laughed uproariously at the antics on the screen. For days afterwards, Bess went around the house singing the catchy tune she couldn't get out of her head. After three days of listening to her daughter make up silly words to *The Toreador Song* from the opera *Carmen*, Ingrid sat her down at the piano and played and sang parts of the actual opera for her. She attempted to correct the movie's parody, but Bess continued to walk around singing "He wants his shirt" until even Greta no longer found it funny.

When the Chicago house was completed, the activities were ended, and the car was packed for their return to Bonneville. Fall was approaching. Bess would be entering the primary class, first grade, and was worried about the new venture. On the drive back to Bonneville, she asked all the questions she could think of.

"Will it be hard? Who is my teacher? What will I eat for lunch? Will I know any of the other students? How long do I have to go to school? Will the teacher be nice? Can Margie and I sit together?"

Ingrid talked with her about school and assured her that all the questions would be answered once school began. She was a bit perplexed about the process herself having been tutored until she was ten. Eventually the car's movement and the long drive encouraged Bess to sleep, her head resting in Ingrid's lap. She woke up as Lars pulled up to the house and parked in their driveway, and everyone was glad to get out and stretch. As cases and bags were unloaded by the adults and a late lunch organized, Bess ran to Margie's house to renew their friendship, talk about their summers, and share worries about the coming school year. She was not the only one glad to be home. They all were.

September, 1929

By the end of the first week, Bess's questions were all answered. School was not difficult, in part, because Bess could read, write a bit, and do simple arithmetic. She had been taught by her mother, and Miss Spenser, the primary teacher who was nice, was stymied when it came to teaching Bess who already knew what the other students did not. When Bess and Margie sat together at lunch, they would share the sandwiches, and Greta always packed extra cookies for Margie. After a time, the six-hour day did not seem too long. Bess adjusted. Miss Spenser had a harder time.

November, 1929

Ingrid dealt with financial issues during the late fall of 1929. There was the fallout from the Stock Market Crash. Fredrick had some stocks, and most of that profit was lost. He owned land and buildings in both New York and Chicago, and some of that was sold. Reluctantly, Ingrid did not continue her support for Chicago arts; that money was needed for necessities. The inherited properties from Grandmother Louisa were kept, but Ingrid, needing to ensure that additional cash was available, took another trip to Chicago. She sold some of her grandmother's jewelry, accepting less money than the jewels were worth. She placed the cash in Fredrick's safe.

"It makes me sad to do this," she explained to Greta, "but we can't eat the diamonds or stay warm with the pearls."

Greta snorted her approval at the comment.

May, 1930

School was over for the year, and a community picnic was held at the start of May. Before a baseball game was started, before the picnic lunches were served and eaten, before Margie had fallen and badly skinned her knee and Bess cried with her, a program was offered. Primary, intermediate, and upper grade students sang appropriate songs, and class recitations were given. Bess stood in the first row of the primary group as they recited Eugene Field's poem *The Duel*. Ingrid, Greta, and Lars watched as Bess loudly and carefully recited her assigned line: "And the calico cat replied 'Mee-ow'!" Ingrid and Greta smiled as each other, proud of Bess, and grateful they would not need to hear that line practiced at home again.

November, 1930

No one in Bonneville seemed to understand exactly why the bank would not give them their money. Some of the customers withdrew their savings earlier in the year, but by November, it was difficult to get any of the cash which had so regularly been deposited. During the summer of that year, Greta and Lars went to the bank after Lars had heard some frightening news on his radio, but they were able to withdraw only a small portion of what they had saved. Of course, Lars had kept most of his cash in the old gray sock which was in the back of the bottom drawer, but Greta had put her full trust in Bonneville's bank and her money was kept captive there. Ingrid had the same problem, but she had much more cash which had apparently disappeared. Bonneville's citizens were upset and angry. Small groups gathered at Tony's Filling Station, and the barber shop, and just outside the bank on the corner to talk about the unfairness of it all. Scenes like this were repeated throughout the country.

During the summer of that year, Ingrid took a trip to Chicago to meet with her lawyers and to check on what she could do. Apparently, she could do nothing. She managed to get some cash from her accounts and sold some more of Grandmother Louisa's gemmed necklaces at a fraction of what she knew they were worth. When she returned to Bonneville, she did not have good news for the Andersons. Things were looking downright gloomy.

Bonneville's farmers were suffering. Many of them had borrowed money to expand their farms and couldn't pay it back. The farmer to the south who bought Ingrid's adjacent land owed money and eventually, the bank would foreclose on his home and farm. Prices of corn and beans and even livestock dropped. Farmers could not pay the farmhands who left to try and find jobs elsewhere. Most were unsuccessful, and the crops they left behind rotted in the fields. Harold Jones, Ingrid's neighbor, grew produce for his family, and sold what he could to surrounding families. Lars would travel there twice a week and pay him for the produce which was once given free as a neighborly gesture. Meat, once an ordinary daily table fare, became a special treat. Belts were tightened by all.

Businesses in Bonneville suffered. McCory's remained opened, but stock was moved to the first floor only, and some of the clerks were let go. There were shorter hours too. The Modern Beauty Shop closed, and the women in Bonneville were reduced to allowing their hair to grow. Sometimes a woman would attempt to cut and shape her friend's hair, but it never looked exactly right. Tithing in the churches stopped. One could not give to God what one did not have, and families came first. The small diner which was just opened shut down. Two of the stores selling women's clothing and shoes went out of business. Woodwine and Smith Construction Company never completed the new houses which were just north of Tony's Filling Station, and the hammering and sawing noises which had been constant for years were silenced. The quietness created a melancholy atmosphere, an unexpected and pessimistic feeling which creeped around the corners, seeping into the meager few who wandered the streets of the once vibrant and animated downtown area of Bonneville, Illinois.

Early Fall, 1931

Nine-year old Bess hopped on one foot down the cemetery's pathway, then turned back, hopping on the other foot, while Ingrid sat on the bench at Fredrick's grave. It was a Saturday morning, the anniversary of his death, and Ingrid needed to be near him. Bess had come with her because the shoes she was using to complete her hopping had holes in the bottom and were tight on her growing feet, so after the cemetery visit, Ingrid was going to take her to McCory's to purchase another pair. Shoes were difficult to obtain, and she hoped the pair she planned on getting for her daughter would last throughout the school year which had just started.

Bess completed her hopping and sat down close to her mother, leaning her head against the arm which found its way around the girl's shoulder. They sat quietly for a time, and Ingrid reached up to wipe her tears. Bess watched her.

"Mama, you are so sad when we come here," she observed. "Do you still miss Fredrick?"

"Yes, Bess, I do."

Ingrid had stuck to the Plan instituted by Greta, and Bess was aware that Fredrick was her mother's husband, but not her father. She was aware that her own parents' untimely deaths allowed her to be adopted by Ingrid. Bess, having never known these supposed parents, never missed them, and rarely asked questions about them, but today, her curiosity was moved.

"Mama, do I look like my dead mother"

Ingrid turned to look at her, brushed the loose hair back from her face, and told the truth, "Actually, Bess, you look exactly like your mother."

"Did she have hair the color like me and you?"

"She did. My own mother did too. Hair this color runs in the family."

Bess nodded. She thought this was the case. "And I am named *Beatrice* which was her name, right?"

A small untruth here. "Right."

Bess nodded. "Well, I know that was my mother's name, but you never told me my father's name. What is it?"

Ingrid was still. Her mind was not. Although she knew that at some time this question might occur, she was unprepared. Thoughts and answers and possibilities raced through her brain. She had no reliable lie, so she told the truth.

"Thomas," and she smiled down at her daughter, "Your father's name is Thomas."

"Thomas," Bess repeated, and the name floated into the air.

Spring, 1933

Lars had been well known in the town. He was friendly to those groups who gathered at the barber shop or Tony's Filling Station or the hardware store. Sometimes one of the men he knew would wander out to Ingrid's house and spend time with Lars, listening to his radio and drinking the iced tea or coffee provided by Greta. He was delighted with Bess and guided her as they weeded and planted vegetables in the garden and flowers around the house. Despite his advancing arthritis, he carved small gifts: a whistle, a toy bird, for the child and took as much pride in her achievements as did Greta and Ingrid. Lars had a distinct voice, and on those Sundays he was in church, his baritone was lifted up. He was kind and considerate to everyone he met, and Ingrid had come to depend upon his advice and common sense. Although he was ten years older than his wife and fifteen years older than Ingrid, the age difference was unimportant to the three of them who considered themselves a family. So, it was no surprise that his funeral was well attended, and many of the attendees wiped honest tears away as his casket was lowered into the ground just a couple of cemetery aisles away from Fredrick's resting place in the Bonneville Cemetery.

For months, Ingrid and Bess took turns comforting Greta when they found her seated in a chair weeping. Bess would put her arms around the woman and pat her back. Ingrid would give Greta a clean handkerchief (she kept one with her for just an occasion) and waited with Greta as she wiped her eyes and cheeks. For weeks, sympathetic expressions in the form of a pasta and pea casserole or a version of a Depression cake would be sent to the house informing the reduced family they were not the only ones missing Lars. Weekly, Ingrid and Greta visited the cemetery. First, they would go to Fredrick's grave where they would sit at the bench and speak quietly of the loss. Then they would visit Lars, tearfully standing at the makeshift cross which would eventually be replaced by a carefully rendered stone from the same memorial mason in Stone City who created the one for Fredrick. Ingrid had insisted upon ordering and paying for both the cemetery plot and the stone, quietly selling Grandmother Louisa's diamond Victorian fringe brooch to cover costs. Months were spent in sorrow and mourning and remembrance.

Every morning, no matter how early Ingrid woke, Greta was awake, and in the kitchen making the coffee and oatmeal, preparing Bess's school lunch, planning a simple dinner for that evening. Ingrid would ask her how she had slept and the answer was always "Well enough, and you?" so there was no reason for Ingrid to suspect what was happening. Except for the morning when she awoke very early and could not return to sleep. She decided she would start breakfast and surprise Greta who, because of the lack of kitchen noise, she assumed was still asleep. And she was. Greta was asleep on the floor of the dining room, having made a bed for herself with blankets and pillows. Ingrid was shocked to see her, and when the kitchen light was turned on, Greta sat up and looked around. Ingrid was staring at her from the kitchen doorway.

"Just how long have you been sleeping here like this?"

Sluggishly, Greta arose from the floor and stretched out her back a couple times before answering. "Don't fuss, Ingrid. I am fine. I have not been able to stay in the rooms or sleep in the bed Lars and I shared. This is acceptable, and I am comfortable enough. Let me fold these things up, and I will start breakfast."

Ingrid, taking one of the blankets to fold, repeated: "Greta, how long?"

Greta placed the pillows on top of the blankets and looked at her. Tears clouded her eyes. "I tried to sleep in our rooms but ended up sitting in the kitchen for hours. I just could not be comfortable without him next to me, and one night, after the two of you went to bed, I made myself comfortable on the floor out here and was able to sleep. Really, Ingrid, I am fine here. Give that blanket to me. I keep these folded and downstairs."

"Well, this is not going to continue. Today you are moving. There is no reason for you to stay in those rooms if you are uncomfortable. There is a perfectly fine unused bedroom upstairs next to Bess's. I'll help you move your things up there today. We will all sleep on the second floor and can close off your old rooms. I will not have you sleeping on the floor in this house."

"That is unnecessary. I can…"

But Ingrid was stern. "There is no discussion about this. Bess will be thrilled that we are all together upstairs. Anyway, with the winter coming, closing off those rooms will help keep the heat in the main house. Honestly, Greta, you should have said something. Now, go on and get ready for the day. I will begin the breakfast for us," and Ingrid turned to the kitchen.

"Wait," said Greta, and when Ingrid turned, Greta came to her and placed her arms around her. "Thank you, *min kompis*," she whispered. They stood for a time in the morning sun, wrapped in fading agony and continuing affinity.

Spring, 1934

Ingrid had business in Chicago and would be gone for about a week. She would telephone and let Greta know when to travel to Stone

City to retrieve her from Union Station. She answered no questions about what the business was, and cautioned Bess to listen to Greta, and informed Harold Jones and his wife that the two would be alone in the house for a time. They said they would watch out for Greta and Bess. Then she left. She returned nine days later. As Greta, the suitcase in the back seat and Ingrid in the front, drove back to Bonneville, the business trip was explained.

"…and while Bess has had a reasonable education here, she needs additional years beyond the eighth grade offered in Bonneville. You know what has happened to schools over the past five years, and it's a shame, but that's the way it is throughout the country. Teachers leaving or being fired, classes doubled up, subjects not taught…I need to do something for Bess. She won't like the fact we are moving back to Chicago, but I need to make a determination about her future education, and this is what I have decided."

Greta listened as she drove. Her education had ended at grade six when she was just thirteen, and she began working, so this discussion about additional studying was not something about which she would comment. However, she knew Ingrid was right about one thing. Once Bess found out she would be leaving Bonneville after this school year, she would throw a fit.

"I visited a number of schools and decided on the *Chicago Classical School for Girls*. I was pleased with their curriculum and the expertise of their teachers and sat in a few classes. The Headmistress is a graduate from Smith College, and she has very specific and modern ideas about women's education, and I was impressed. The school is on Lake Shore Drive, near Elm Street, and on decent days Bess can walk there. We will figure out what to do in the bad weather." Ingrid gave a sigh and leaned back against the seat. She wasn't looking forward to breaking this news to her daughter. Bonneville was the home Bess knew.

"Will you tell her today?" and Greta wondered where she could stay while the news was given.

"No, not today. The school term still has a few weeks, and I'll wait. I suspect it will be the leaving of Margie that will be most difficult for her. I thought we would remain in Bonneville until the end of July. That will give us time to plan and pack and make whatever arrangements we need to," and Ingrid turned to Greta with a realization. "Greta, I suppose I should have asked you about this move. I'm sorry I did not. Are you alright with it?"

Greta nodded, "Chicago is home to me too. I still have friends I can see, and I am as familiar with that city as I am with Bonneville," and she reached over and patted Ingrid's hand. "I just don't know how Bess will react."

Nodding slowly and sighing, Ingrid squeezed Greta's hand. "I know. But we will continue to visit Bonneville and spend summers here. Fredrick was right about the fresh air. And the roads are so much better now, and automobiles travel faster and…" Ingrid's sentence trailed off and she sighed.

"It will be fine, Ingrid. Bess will adjust," and Greta hoped she sounded encouraging.

***

The school year was done. Bess and Margie spent the early summer wandering around their back yards, periodically traveling into town, talking about all the things twelve-year-olds discuss. But when Margie's grandmother died, she left with her family for a funeral visit, and Bess was alone for a week. A couple days into her solitude, Ingrid peered out the window and saw her daughter jumping rope up and down the driveway although the sky was darkening and threatening a summer storm. Once the drops began to descend, Bess ran onto the porch, standing to watch as the rain came down progressively harder. Ingrid sighed with her decision. Today would be the day to tell Bess about the move to Chicago and the new school; she had put it off long enough. She walked to the front door and called, "Bess, come on in. You are getting wet. There's something I want to tell you."

Bess replied, "Okay, Mama," and naïve and innocent and happy, she opened the door and came into the house. As the rain turned into a proper thunderstorm, Bess listened while Ingrid delivered the unexpected and unwanted news.

Nine

Bess and Ingrid and Greta in Chicago

1937
Bess

I know I behaved badly, and I'm sorry for it, but moving to Chicago and going to a new school was difficult. I wasn't happy about it, but now, after we have been here a couple years and I am used to it, I regret all the silly crying I did. It was hard to leave Margie. But when she came back from her grandmother's funeral, she told me her whole family had to move to the town where her grandmother had lived. She said it was something to do with money and their house being expensive and her father looking for a new job, and she was sad and crying too. The fact that she was leaving and wouldn't be in Bonneville either, somehow made my move easier. We promised to stay friends forever and write letters weekly. There were letters for a time, but I haven't replied to her last one and that was a few months ago. Greta said that sometimes happens, and not to worry about it, but I feel guilty and should answer her. The problem is that we have such different lives now. She finished grade six and didn't go on because that was all the school in her grandmother's town offered. She's at home with her mother taking care of her younger brothers and helping on the farm there. I am starting grade nine in the fall, and have new friends, and like the school I go to. Honestly, I liked it from the start.

There wasn't anything wrong with the Bonneville school, but it was sometimes boring. I could do most of the schoolwork, and it was simple and done quickly. My primary teacher, Miss Spenser, sometimes got a strange look on her face when I could already do the arithmetic she was explaining. Twice I saw a mistake she made and told her; then Mother had to go and talk to her and Mrs. DeWitt, the head of the school. I was sent to school with extra books so I could read once my work was done. That's not the way it is at school now. All the other girls know just as much as I do, and some are even better at the mathematics classes, so I need to work harder. I don't mind. It's a challenge, and I enjoy figuring out the answers. Mother was right after all. I needed a different school, and in Bonneville, the school only went to grade eight anyway, and this Chicago school goes up to grade twelve.

The *Chicago Classical School for Girls*, called *The Class*, is not large. It's built on a grassy spot, not far from Lake Michigan, and in nice weather, classes are held outside on the grounds. There are two sections: the *Junior Level:* grades seven, eight, and nine, and the *Senior Level*: grades ten, eleven, and twelve. The Junior Level has more girls in it and not all of them stay for Senior Level. Those who do finish the upper grades often go on to college. That is not just encouraged, it's expected. And the school's principal, Miss Sophia Quinn, makes that clear from the start.

Miss Quinn graduated from Smith College, taught Latin at The Class for some years, and became Dean there at a young age. She has been Dean for about a dozen years, and she is admired, respected, and feared. The fear of suspension or expulsion was real, and seventh graders are warned by the Senior Level girls that the embarrassment, humiliation, and indignity of being called to Dean Quinn's office for any infraction would follow us our entire school career. The only student I knew who was called to her office would not discuss what was said to her, but she did not return the following term.

Dean Quinn insists the school's motto and a *Pledge to Knowledge* is said every morning. We stand in our first period class to recite the motto in both Latin (*Ad Scientiam*) and English (*To Knowledge*), and then we make our pledge which is: *Read, Review, React, Respond, Render*. The pledge is followed by all the teachers at the school, and once it's understood, is an easy method for learning in all the classes. For example, in grade seven, we read poetic ballads, reviewed the characteristics of them, considered our personal reaction to ones we read, responded to the teacher's questions about them, then rendered our own example of one. In eighth grade we did the same for the sonnet. We studied math and botany, and history in the same way, and I think we were always surprised at how this method of teaching and learning could be adapted to everything we studied. At least I was surprised.

Dean Quinn requires us to be practical in everything we are taught. Our school uniforms are white blouses, navy skirts, ties indicating the current grade: red (grade 7), orange (grade 8), yellow (grade 9), green (grade 10), blue (grade 11), and violet for grade twelve, all the rainbow colors. Seventh-grade domestic arts class teaches how to use a sewing machine and complete hand-sewing. We read about how to create a skirt, reviewed instructions for both machine use and hand sewing, reacted (civilly, because some were awful) to the practice skirts each of us made, responded to the questions the teacher gave us checking our knowledge, and then rendered a real skirt, which we then wore. We also made our own ties. The blouses are purchased, but each summer we are expected to make two new skirts to fit our growing bodies. If we don't have a sewing machine at home, we can come into the school to use the ones there. Greta has a sewing machine, but it was much more fun to visit the campus during the summer, especially with my new friends. Twin sisters, Delores and Donna, live just two streets away from us, and they are just my age and attend The Class.

I was surprised at many things, especially during that first year. I was surprised to discover that I really enjoyed learning and liked the new school. I was surprised that I quickly became used to Chicago and enjoyed living in the city. I was surprised that I didn't miss Margie as much as I thought I would, and was surprised I didn't feel as guilty as I thought I should. I was surprised every day about something new, but the thing I was most surprised at was the fact that Mother taught voice lessons at The Class.

1937
Ingrid

I know Bess was surprised that I was teaching at her school. I hadn't told her anything about it because she didn't need to know the reason for it. In order to afford the school's cost, I bartered my knowledge and ability. Once I decided that the Classical High School was the best one for Bess, I needed to be able to afford it. I sold additional jewelry belonging to Grandmother Louise even though I knew I was not getting the full price for the pieces. I was lucky she had such a store of it. I found an honest book seller, and he gave me a decent price for some of the beautiful and rare books Fredrick had collected. I didn't want to part with them, but it was necessary. There were six years of an education Bess needed to have. I'm unsure what to do if she wants to continue after that, but I'll deal with that issue in time. I knew I didn't have enough money to cover all six years, so I made an appointment with Dean Quinn and went to barter with her.

Sophia Quinn is an intelligent woman, serious and concerned. I like her, and will always be grateful to her for understanding and accepting my situation. I was not the only one facing economic problems, and other parents bartered their skills for partial tuition payment. Some men work at keeping the lovely campus green in the summer and free of snow in the winter. Some women work as assistants in various classrooms, and most of the clerks have daughters at the school. So, my suggestion of being a voice teacher was met with interest, especially because Dean Quinn, when young, had once seen me (or rather seen the performance I was in) at Oscar's Manhattan Opera House. We walked over to the music department where I accompanied myself on the Steinway and sang an aria for her. It was decided that I would teach some Senior Level girls on Tuesdays and Thursdays, and I would owe only half the required tuition. The deal was made, and I was satisfied. Bess would have the education she deserved, and I looked forward to being productive and useful.

I didn't tell Greta what my new plan was until we had moved to Chicago and were settled. The first couple months were difficult. Bess cried at the move, positive she would hate the new school. I took her there to visit and showed her around the campus, but she remained sullen. However, I could see her eyes widen at the various classrooms filled with individual desks, intriguing scientific equipment: beakers and microscopes and safety goggles, violins placed carefully on wire racks, colorful posters on the classroom walls, and hallway photographs of smiling girls. We visited the school a second time, and she met Dean Quinn. Bess was suitably friendly to her, and when Dean Quinn told us that a set of twins just Bess's age lived close to us and would be attending seventh grade with her, Bess brightened. I made sure to introduce myself to the twins' mother, and after that, Bess seemed to settle. I did not tell her that I was going to be a teacher at her school until a couple days before the school year began. I was worried that she would be angry or embarrassed that her mother would be on campus, but she seemed to be glad I would be close. I suppose it helped that I would not be teaching any of her classmates for a couple years. When the girls move to the Senior Level, they have choices: three years of violin, piano, or voice lessons, and I expect Bess will stick with piano. Maybe the violin.

The first two years at The Class worked out fine. This coming year, I have been asked to return for three days a week because additional students are being added to my roster. The good thing about this is that my additional day of work will take care of more of Bess's tuition. I will need to pay for her books and class fees and extra things which always seem to crop up. My working an additional day will make things easier for all of us because I don't have many of Grandmother Louisa's jewels left. I am trying to save some of Fredrick's library. Those books mean more to me than the jewelry. Greta has taken on a part-time job, and with what she is able to contribute to the household expenses, we manage. Times are still difficult. I am glad that we have each other and don't need much else. There isn't much to be had anyway.

1937
Greta

It was a strange thing, my getting a part-time position, but I wanted to help with the expenses. In spite of all the difficulties, the three of us are glad to have each other. Bess settled down and is now doing well at school, and Ingrid has taken to the teaching. Ingrid thinks that, once the economy improves, she will be able to offer private lessons. Between working next door at Mrs. Ricci's house and my duties at our house, I stay busy.

When we moved back to Chicago two years ago, I was unsure we would be able to afford the household expenses and Bess's school fees, but then Ingrid explained what she had done, that she would be teaching at the school as a way to afford things. This coming school year, she will be gone three days a week which works out since I am at Mrs. Ricci's for three days.

Mrs. Ricci's housekeeper and I were friendly, and once we settled back in Chicago and I had time, I went over to visit Christina. When I went to the back door and knocked, it was Mrs. Ricci who answered. Christina had been called home to St. Louis due to her father's death and her mother's need of her. I was sad she was gone, but grateful when Mrs. Ricci asked if I could be spared to help out in her house with the cleaning and cooking. It seems the Riccis had some of the same money problems most of us had, although they could still afford my help. Mr. Ricci agreed a part-time housekeeper could be hired, and after I spoke to Ingrid about it, I took the job. It has worked out. I am usually home by the time Bess is there, and if I'm not, she knows where I am. Ingrid's day runs longer, but by five o'clock, we are all together and the evenings are ours. On Thursdays Ingrid gives the automobile to me so I can run errands and grocery shop. Some Thursdays, I have time to visit a friend or two from church.

The last couple of times we went to Bonneville to stay at the house there, Bess fussed about going. She has friends here in Chicago, and Margie is gone from there, and the place just isn't the same for her.

Ingrid talks every now and then about trying to sell the Bonneville house and property, but money is hard to come by right now, and she's just not sure she would get a goodly amount. I'm sure she wouldn't, so the house is ours to visit some weekends and summers. There are so many memories connected with that town. Mostly good. Anyway, it's a place to stay. We visit Fredrick and Lars at the cemetery almost daily when we are there. Almost daily.

1939
Bess

I don't mind staying in Bonneville, but the almost daily cemetery visits are too much for me. I miss Lars, of course, but I never knew Fredrick, Mother's husband, and when I was younger, it was boring. I'm seventeen now, and this summer is better because I am busy most mornings at the Bonneville Clinic with Doctor Joseph who took over when Doctor Marshall retired. I'm not getting paid, but I'm fulfilling a summer requirement for The Class, and for once, I'm glad for Dean Quinn's assignment. Senior level girls are expected to serve as volunteers for a job they might like to do because Dean Quinn believes women should be useful in both society and the home. After our experience, we write a report and present it in speech class during the fall session. I don't think I want to be a doctor, but Doctor Joseph's wife is a nurse and I help her at the clinic in the mornings. Mostly there are cuts and bruises and rashes to deal with, but once a little boy broke his arm, and I had to keep his attention while the arm was being set. When he stopped crying and before he left, he hugged me, and I really felt good about helping out, even though I didn't do any medical work. I can use that in my speech.

I'm not sure when I became interested in nursing. It might have been during the Biology class last year which I thought was the best and most informative science class. Then, in Physical Training Class, a first-aid course was given by a Red Cross nurse friend of Dean Quinn who taught the course for two weeks. She really knew a lot about medicine and what to do in an emergency, and while I hope I never need to use what I learned, I'm glad to know I can. When we proved our ability to respond to emergencies and provide basic first-aid, we received a certificate, and I hung it up in my bedroom. The information was practical and useful, and I think that is important. That experience made me feel confident and capable. That will be in my speech too.

I'm looking forward to the fall session which will be my last at The Class. I'd like to continue with school and go to nurse's training, but money is an issue. Mother thinks I don't know the reason she began to teach at the school, but I do, and since I have no money of my own, paying for more schooling will be a problem. I need to figure out a plan and, I suppose, talk to Mother soon. In the meantime, I am enjoying pretending to be a nurse at the Bonneville Clinic.

There are still things I need to do this summer to get ready for my last year. I must make my skirts and violet ties, and I should start on that soon. All the twelfth graders are expected to make at least two red ties which will be given to the new seventh graders. They will eventually make their own, but the first one is given as a welcome gift to them at Convocation. I still have mine. That's a nice tradition. This last year should be fun. Mother was right to send me there, and I don't mind that she is now at the school four days a week. I appreciate her working there because I know it's for my tuition. She likes it, and the girls taking voice lessons like her too.

1939
Ingrid

I know Bess is thinking about going on to school after she graduates this next year, and I'm unsure how to afford it. Few of Grandmother's jewels are left to sell, and I hate to sell more of Fredrick's books, but I suppose I will need to. I have told Greta that she is not to use any more of the money she is earning to pay for our groceries. That is what she has been doing, and I feel guilty because I haven't been able to pay her a decent salary for years now. Just a pittance when I sell some jewelry or receive a small check from the investments which haven't disappeared yet. I know things are slowly improving for everyone, and we came to an agreement about money a while back. Greta said we are a family now, having been together for so many years and suffering through so many problems. She said that Lars was smart in putting most of his money in his sock drawer, and while I never asked her how much it was, I can't think there is too much left. But I'm still not sure about Bess and her plans. I'll wait until she says something to me. I think it might be soon now because the twelfth graders are encouraged to consider what they are going to do to contribute to society. Dean Quinn always meets with each girl individually throughout the year to ascertain her future plans. That will start as soon as the school term does.

I am considering teaching private lessons at home. There have been a few inquiries from some of the girls about continuing their lessons after graduation. One or two have brought notes from their mothers asking about lessons for younger daughters or girls from their churches who seem to have talent. Of course, every mother believes her daughter is talented. I'll need to be selective if I decide to do this. If I am at the school four days a week, I can teach privately some evenings and perhaps Saturday or Monday. I just need to decide what to do.

Our time in Bonneville has been relaxing, but in another week, we must return to Chicago. It's expensive keeping two houses even though there is no mortgage on either one. I was wise to pay off the Chicago house and lucky to update it when I could. Who knew this country's economic problem would last so long? And now there seems to be another war in Europe. Germany is in a shambles, and Spain is figuring out a Civil War. I hope the United States stays out of whatever is happening. I don't want to think there will be another conflict because I remember the last one and don't want Bess to suffer through that. If there is another war, I suppose there will not be any money to pay for private voice lessons. That is a selfish thought, but there is always something to worry about.

December, 1939
Greta

Ingrid does her share of worrying, and while I would like to help out, there is little I can do. She won't allow me to help pay for groceries anymore. We had words about it, and I gave in, but I do have a holiday plan, and she will just need to accept it. About once a month or so, Mrs. Ricci and her husband give a dinner party. Last Friday I was asked to make and help serve a dinner for their friends. I'm always happy to do that because it means extra money. I intend to purchase the makings of a great Christmas feast for us. My gift to them. That's what the money will be used for, and if there is any left, I intend to buy Bess a gift. It's a shame that there is nothing under the tree for her. She is such a good sport about it all. Anyway, we will have a wonderful time, and I'm looking forward to it.

When I was at the Ricci's house last week to clean, I mentioned that a couple of our dining room chairs needed repairs. One had the leg broken off when Bess moved it, and two others have loose joints and we have just put those to the side. I only mentioned it because I noticed that Mrs. Ricci was sitting in an old rocker which had been broken, and I was warned not to move it because it was so wobbly. It belonged to Mr. Ricci's mother and kept as a remembrance. I mentioned to the Missus that I was glad they had it repaired, and then said something about our chairs.

"Mr. Ricci found a great carpenter to repair this, and it didn't take long at all. It was dropped off at his shop on a Monday and by Thursday, it was ready. His card is somewhere around here. I'll find it for you." That was the end of it. So I thought.

As I worked at finishing the dinner last Friday, Mrs. Ricci came in and waved a small piece of paper at me.

"My, it looks delicious and smells wonderful in here, Greta. Let me know when to call the guests to the dining room. Here is the card I told you I'd find. Maybe Ingrid can get those chairs repaired," and she handed me the card which I took and placed into the front pocket of my apron. I finished the dinner and set the food out on the sideboard for the guests to serve themselves. I would get dessert and coffee ready while they ate.

It was a late night. Once everything was cleared up, Mrs. Ricci thanked me, giving me a generous compensation. She told me to wrap up some of the food and take it with me. Food can't be wasted, and we would have leftovers the next day. I walked out of her back door, over to our house and quietly went in. I was tired, but thought hot tea would be good. The house was quiet since Bess and Ingrid were both asleep, so I put the kettle on, trying to be soundless and not disturb them. I laid my coat to the side, stored the leftovers, and sat down on the kitchen chair. I still had my apron on, and when I removed it, there was the stiffness of the card in the pocket. When I took it out, I glanced at it, and then, put on my glasses and reread the card:

Thomas Allerton
Carpenter

Furniture Repairs	Telephone: LU 5-4633
Furniture Making	3219 S. Western Ave Chgo

It couldn't be! I read and reread the card. It was his name. His
trade. How many men could there be like this? When he left all those
years ago, we never heard about him again, never expected to, and
that was fine. Of course he would travel to Chicago. Of course. The
tea kettle began to sing and I quickly turned it off. I no longer wanted
any. My stomach would not hold it. I wondered what I should do, and
I sat and pondered this until my head began to nod. I could not tell
Ingrid. Why should I? There was no reason to, and those chairs could
stay broken forever as far as I was concerned. I decided to do nothing,
but I kept the card. I turned off the kitchen light, walked up the stairs,
and when I got to my bedroom, I placed the card in my bottom dresser
drawer where it would remain. I got ready for bed and while under
the covers, thought and considered. Fate was fearsome, I decided, but
I would keep it at bay. I would work to do that. I would keep quiet. It
was a long time before I fell asleep.

Fall, 1941
Bess

I have been training at the Chicago Nursing Academy for about
two months. The classes are long and difficult, and there is so much
homework to do that I haven't visited Mother and Greta since I started.
The student nurses' dormitory is a busy and crowded place, and some of
us have formed a study group which is what we were told would help us
through this time. Some of the girls are here from as far off as Florida
and Montana, and they are really homesick. Two of them have already
given up and left due to the strangeness of this city and the distance from
their families. I am lucky because my family lives in Chicago, and I can
easily telephone them, so I talk to Mother at least once a week, and in two
weeks, we have a break. I plan on taking the bus to travel home for the
weekend. Riding the bus is something new for me, and even though I live
in Chicago, I had to learn how to travel that way just like the other girls.

I don't know how Mother afforded the tuition. I know how much
it is, but I can't help out by getting a part-time job my first year. We were
told that working at this time would be the surest way to fail, so I am
trying to be really careful with the little bit of money I brought with me.
We, the first-year students, are so busy that there is nothing to spend it
on anyway except for some ice-cream on Saturday afternoons. My study
group takes a break then to travel to the Walgreens two blocks from here
and treat ourselves.

I love the uniform we wear to classes, and when I go home in a couple weeks, I need to bring them home. Greta will wash and iron them for me, and Mother said she will drive me back on Sunday afternoon, so I'll wear a regular dress then. I'm looking forward to Greta's meals that weekend. She told me to let her know what I wanted to eat because she will make it for me. The meals here aren't bad, but they aren't like Greta's cooking.

We have a cape to wear over our uniforms during the cold weather, and Mother said mine was delivered a few days ago, so I'll be bringing that back with me. I still have a difficult time believing I am here. I hope Mother didn't go into debt for the tuition and fees. That worries me, but it also prods me to do my best and study hard. I intend to make both Mother and Greta proud. Three years in training is a long time, and there is so much to learn. I hope I will succeed. I have to.

Fall, 1941
Ingrid

Bess was just bubbling over with information the weekend she was home from school. She talked and talked about her classes and the other girls and the things she has already learned, and I was delighted to see her so immersed in her training. She did grow teary when she had to return, and insisted I park the car and go up to her room in the dormitory to meet some of her new friends. Greta sent sandwiches on her homemade bread along with a large batch of cookies and some of her date-nut loaf, and Bess said she and her friends would have a picnic in her room that evening. It was difficult to leave her, but Thanksgiving is not that far away. Then she'll be home for a few days.

She asked about money, and I didn't lie to her. I told her what I had done. The cost for her first year, which was almost three-hundred dollars, is paid, and the next two years will not be as pricey. Fredrick's last gift to me, the gold and emerald bracelet was sold. I made a visit to Horwitz Jewelers which is where the bracelet came from and spoke to Mr. Horwitz himself. He is a very nice man, completely understanding, and when I explained about selling the bracelet and the reason for it, he gave me an excellent price. I was sad to see it go, but I am positive Fredrick would have understood. There was one small property left in New York, and I sold that too. It was all worth it to give Bess her education. She will be an excellent nurse.

Fall, 1941
Greta

Bess is a dear, and it was such a pleasure to see her for a couple of days, and if she hadn't pulled that chair out from against the wall and attempted to sit on it, I would not have done what I ended up doing. We were sitting down at the dining table, something we rarely did, but I set out a lovely feast the Saturday night she was home and thought it would be a special treat to eat somewhere other than the kitchen table. I pulled out two of the chairs, and Bess, only trying to help, took one of the broken chairs and started to sit on it. I yelled for her to *Wait*! which kept her from falling. Then we moved one of the kitchen chairs into the dining room. That reminded Ingrid that those chairs needed to be repaired, and she said something about finding someone to do that. I remembered the card I had upstairs in my bottom dresser drawer. I had done a good job of not thinking about it. Had that incident not happened, I would have never investigated.

Ingrid was so busy teaching at the school four days each week and giving voice lessons to three or four young girls at home, that she did not mention finding someone again, so I set myself the task to hire a handyman to repair the chairs. I asked my friends at the church and was given a name. I asked Elias to come over and examine the broken chairs. He did; he fixed them; I paid him. Done. There was no way I was going to chance Mrs. Ricci asking Ingrid about the chairs and mention the card she gave me. The next time I cleaned for her, I made sure to tell her that the chairs were repaired by someone I knew. Then the topic was, I hope, dropped. Ingrid discovered the chairs were fixed and tried to pay me back, but I refused the money. I was just glad it was done.

The problem was the card. I tried to forget about it, and I should have thrown it away, but didn't. I knew where his shop was located. It was close to a large park, one with a lagoon and many trees. I had visited it, and Ingrid and I had taken Bess there when she was younger. I kept wondering whether that card named the same person who had been in Bonneville all those years before: twenty years to be exact. I decided to go to the shop, to see for myself. What I would do with the information was unclear, but once I decided, I planned my trip.

Every Thursday, I drove Ingrid to school so I could have the car. I would grocery shop for us and visit my friends from church before I picked her up from school in the late afternoon. The Thursday I decided to carry out my plan, I allowed Ingrid to think nothing would change.

"Greta, when you shop today, would you pick up some toothpaste and Ivory soap? I forgot to put them on the list."

"Of course; anything else?"

"That's all I can think of. Oh, I have a meeting today, so I'll be at work until about 5:30."

"OK, I'll see you then," and as she closed the car door, I took a deep breath. I completed the shopping quickly, put the items away, and left on my mission.

The shop was not difficult to find, but I drove around the block a few times because there didn't seem to be a parking place. I needed to park across the street so I could have a view but not be seen, and when a car pulled out of the spot I had my eyes on, I pulled in. I turned off the car, took a deep breath, and turned my head to examine the building. A law office, a shoe repair shop, and an empty building which had once been a dentist's office was on one side; a hardware store was on the other. The corner building was a Rexall Drug Store, and while there weren't crowds of people on the street, there were enough. I tried to remain unnoticed as I sat in the car and looked out the window. The name: THOMAS ALLERTON, CARPENTER, was spread across the top of the large window, and the telephone number, hours of business, and the phrase "Excellent Work" was in the window corners. Apparently, I thought, this man has no humility.

From my position in the car, I tried to see into the shop. There were some chairs and a small bookcase stored to one side. A bench, used, perhaps, to sit and wait, was against a wall, and a counter with books and papers and a telephone on top separated the front of the store from the back room. No movement was apparent in the shop although lights were on. I thought I should get out and walk across the street and glance into the place for a better look. I peered into the rear-view mirror and pulled my hat down a bit in front. I certainly did not look like I did twenty years ago. My hair was graying, I wore glasses, and that extra ten pounds did me no favors, but really, would he even recognize me? Would I recognize him? I decided to take a chance.

I left the car and crossed the street, walking to the front of the Rexall. I peeked in and saw a lunch counter and wondered if a cup of tea would calm my nerves but decided I shouldn't go in. What if, for some reason, he was in there? I walked along the street, past the hardware store, and then stopped just before I got to the shop. I opened my pocketbook, pretending to look for something, and I pulled out a handkerchief to blow my nose which needed no blowing. That gave me a chance to peek into the place. Someone was moving in the back room, but I couldn't stand there too long, so I slowly walked past the window, the empty building, the shoe repair and the law office. I came to an alleyway and had to make a decision. Just then, from behind me, I heard a man's voice call, "Hello Tom! How are you?" and I panicked. I crossed the alleyway and heard a voice I thought I recognized reply, "Fine, Andrew, and you?"

The conversation was a short one. I walked to the next corner, waited for the traffic light to change and crossed the street. I wasn't sure if he had gone back into the shop, and I could not turn around, so I continued to walk straight to the next street and turned once I was far enough and sure I couldn't be recognized. Then I crossed another street and looked towards the shop. He was inside. I could see a figure moving and standing in back of the counter, so I hurried back to my car. I was breathing hard; my heart was fluttering, and my hands shaking. I took deep breaths and calmed myself down. *Some spy you are*, I scolded myself. I remained in the car, staring across the street, trying to see the man inside the building.

I couldn't tell too much. He seemed the right height and the right coloring, but his face was turned downward and he was busy figuring something out on the paper in front of him. Once I saw him pick up the telephone and speak into it, and the face looked familiar, but I didn't have a clear view. Just then, a small truck pulled in front of the building, blocking my sight. The driver got out and went into the shop. I waited. In a couple minutes, he came out again, followed by the man I recognized. They walked to the back of the truck and the two of them unloaded a small settee. As they worked to get the furniture off the truck and carry it into the shop, I knew this was Thomas Allerton. Even twenty years had not changed his looks much.

His beard was gone, but his face was familiar. There remained a likeness to Fredrick, but there had also been changes. Thomas had grown into his own looks. He would be near forty now, and I thought there were some wrinkles along his eyes, but I was not close enough to determine that truth. This was the person who had lived with us for six months in Bonneville, who had repaired the furniture and built some new pieces, who had kept the furnace coal shoveled and the snow cleared from the walks. This was the man who had enchanted Ingrid, looking like a young Fredrick, taking what she so willingly, so foolishly, gave. This was Bess's father.

I waited until they went into the shop and finished their business. I waited until the man in the pickup truck drove away. I waited until I saw Thomas enter the back room of the shop, and then I pulled out of the parking place and drove home to the townhouse Ingrid and I shared with Bess, Thomas' daughter.

I entered the house. It was early afternoon, but I would not visit any friends today. I had a store of nervous energy and decided to use it to clean. But before I put on my apron, before I went to the kitchen to remove the cleaning supplies and brushes from the cabinet under the sink, I took the card with his name and address from my pocketbook and tore it in half. Then I tore it in half again, and continued tearing the pieces until there were a million paper snowflakes rolling across the dining room table. I gathered them, carried them into the kitchen, and scattered them into the trashcan, never to be reunited. I watched the pieces flutter into the crevices of the garbage, mixing with the apple and potato peelings and old newspapers, and felt my quickened heartbeat slowing down. There was no reason for Bess to become acquainted with this man. There was no reason for Ingrid to become reacquainted with him. I watched the last of the small pieces sink into the trash, and a feeling of relief entered me. I took up my apron, tied it around my waist, and began to groom the already spotless house.

Ten

Acquainted: Chicago

Early Spring, 1943

Tires were first rationed in 1942. That did not bother Greta and Ingrid much, but when, later that year, sugar and coffee became difficult to obtain, that did. Meat, cheese, butter, and canned milk rationing happened in 1943, and coupons were needed for new shoes, rubber footwear, and nylons. The blue stamps covered canned goods such as vegetables, and dried fruits, and the red stamps were for meat, fish, and dairy. Every person was allowed sixty-four red stamps per month, and bacon was not only thirty cents a pound, but seven ration points were required for each pound. Rationing rules seemed complicated, but they were eventually understood, and although consumers were forced to deal with the loss of favorite meats and dishes, there was little grumbling. It was all for the great cause: USA's Patriotic Push. After all, propaganda posters proclaiming: *Food is a weapon…don't waste it, Grow your own; Can your own, Rationing means a fair share for all of us,* were seen everywhere.

"Just like the last war," claimed Greta serving a dinner of what was called *creamed chipped beef on toast.* "We did this before, Ingrid, so we can do it again, I suppose." The beef was actually Spam and the toast was made from the *War Bread* recipe which was popular because flour was also rationed. Carrots were served on the side. Again.

"We are fine, Greta, and you are correct. This happened once before. I just hope it never occurs again in Bess's life. I worry about her getting enough to eat," and Ingrid pictured her daughter wearing her student nurse uniform. The last time she was home, Greta had to take them all in a couple inches and lower all the hems.

"She will be fine. When she comes home for the next visit, I intend to fatten her up. I am planning a roasted beef dinner with all the fixings, and there will be a pie for dessert. I am sending her back with a bunch of ham and cheese sandwiches, sugar cookies, and a few other things. She and her friends can eat well for a couple days anyway," and Greta glanced over at Ingrid who was taking small bites of the dinner.

"I'm not sure where you will get the meat and dairy and flour, but it sounds great. I do want to feed her well. She works so hard."

"Don't worry, I know where to get supplies. Here, Ingrid, eat some of these carrots. I know we have them often, but they are supposed to help our eyes. So how was school today?" and Greta switched topics.

She didn't want Ingrid to question her about where the supplies for the planned feast would come from. Meat and dairy and extras were available, if one knew where to go, who to see, and had a few coins to spare. Greta knew where to go and who to see, and although she worked for the Riccis only two days a week now, she was careful about spending her salary. She squirreled away extra pennies and nickels, spending them at the forbidden marketplaces she had investigated. She was aware which ones offered suspect merchandise and which ones dealt with wholesome products. Greta was shrewd and practiced, and she kept her knowledge confidential because she was sure Ingrid would not approve.

Bess arrived for a brief break looking more tired than her twenty years should have allowed. She did work hard. Many nurses were volunteering in the war effort, and all available student nurses were expected to fill in where they were needed as well as keep up with their classes and studies. Greta wanted her to rest during the few days she was at home and made every attempt to fatten her up. The beef roast was small but delicious; the vegetables were not carrots; the pie had a whipped cream topping. And the ham and cheese sandwiches were thick and made on home-baked white bread. Bess was delighted and ate heartily while Ingrid looked at the bounty and then at Greta who ignored the knowing gaze. Because it was Bess who was being honored with the lavish opulence, the sullied manner of obtaining it all would be disregarded. Ingrid was more knowledgeable than Greta suspected.

"Have another slice of the pie, Bess. I know you don't get this at school," and Greta placed the pie on Bess's plate and then lightly and affectionately rubbed her shoulders. "You are just too bony. While you are here, I intend to spoil you with food."

Bess smiled and took a bite of the second piece before putting her fork down. "Thanks, Greta. This is all so delicious, but I'll finish this later. I intend to take full advantage of your terrific cooking and baking. You are right. There is nothing like this at school. We are so busy that eating on the run and eating whatever there is has become second nature for all of us. I hope you don't mind if I sleep in tomorrow. Our days are full from dawn until night, sometimes late at night, and with the volunteer summer rotations starting next week, I'll need some extra sleep."

"Sleep as long as you'd like, Bess. I have school, but Greta will be here. After dinner tomorrow we can talk more about your summer rotation. Are you sure you need to stay all summer to do it? After the school year is finished, Greta and I will travel to Bonneville for the summer. I had hoped you could come for at least part of it," and Ingrid tried not to look too disappointed at the prospect of not having Bess with her during the summer months.

"Volunteers are important, Mother, you know that. So many of the nurses are with the troops that there is a real need for those of us in our last year of schooling to do what we can. Besides, it will be great experience learning how to deal with different sorts of problems. I know that my first rotation will be at a public school in the nursing office. I'm anxious to be a help to the one nurse who is only part-time there. She travels to three different schools, spreading herself thin. Bonnie and I will be there when she is not, and when she is, we will learn and assist her. I'm not sure what other places Bonnie and I will be sent, but don't worry, we are assigned in pairs and have to travel back and forth together. Anyway, rotations stop at the end of August, and I'll be able to take the train to Stone City. I'll have about ten days before school begins in mid-September, and I'm looking forward to being in that house for a time, especially if you do decide to sell it."

They spoke more about the summer plans as Greta began to clear the table. Soon the three of them were in the kitchen, washing and wiping the dishes, wrapping the remainder of the food, talking about Bess's school, the goings-on in their neighborhood, in the city, in the world. As they enjoyed each other's company, as they relaxed in the coziness of their Chicago home, as they reveled in the familiarity of their close, small family unit, there was no thought of what fate might have in store for them; of what part circumstance and chance would play in their lives in the following months. And years.

***

War was coming. For years before the attack on Pearl Harbor, citizens discussed the inevitability of it, argued about remaining neutral, commented about the problems during the last conflict, hoped that what was happening in Europe would remain there, and finally, became saddened by the December, 1941 reality that it would not. When the abstract became concrete, when FDR created the War Production Board, when factories stopped making home goods and commenced making war supplies, Chicago was among the first cities to support the effort. The plant which made stoves switched to making armored personnel carriers. Farm implement production became army tank assembly. The factory which used to make curtains began producing mosquito netting to protect those soldiers sleeping in the mosquito-filled areas in the Philippines. Experts at the musical instrument workshop developed sound-detecting devices for use in ships and airplanes. Automobiles were no longer made, but airplanes were rolled out by the dozens. Producing and supplying needed goods and parts to win, win, win this conflict was uppermost in everyone's minds.

Chicago hotels became barracks for soldiers and sailors who were waiting to ship out. Chicago high schools gave up their football fields to the military so that important drills could be held. Movie theaters entertained the men who were waiting for deployment, in an attempt to keep them from considering what was waiting for them in war zones. The Chicago Civilian Defense League organized and taught citizens what to do if the unthinkable, a foreign-enemy attack, was to happen. There were War Bond Drives, parades down Michigan Avenue, and blood donations sponsored by various hospitals. Victory gardens became popular once again, as did *Victory* songs, *Victory* scrap metal collections, *Victory* hairstyles, *Victory* posters, *Victory* cartoons. Perhaps repeating the term would help the US and her allies attain *Victory.*

Labor shortage was an issue. Factories and small businesses were subsidized by the government to hire additional workers because single, young men who worked at these places flocked to military recruitment stations to sign up and fight. Women were hired. Older workers came out of retirement. Men with families, following the dictates of the Selective Service, offered themselves for the war and were told to remain alert to the possibility that they would be needed. Many merchants closed their business doors and went to work in the factories, offering their expertise and experience for the war effort. The effort on the home front was significant and critical, and once the fighting in the towns of Europe and the forests of Asia was over, was won, things could get back to normal and their businesses and shops could resume their work. One of the businessmen who closed up shop and went to work at a Chicago factory in the attempt to help the war effort was Thomas Allerton.

In 1942, Thomas Allerton was thirty-nine years old, and when the Selective Service amended its rules to include men up to the age of forty-five, he signed up and waited for the national lottery to take place in March of that year. He and his wife, Lina, discussed the possibility of his being selected for military service.

"But our Clara is eleven and Joey is only nine," worried Lina, "What about them? What if you are called up? I'm fearful, Tom. What will we do?"

Thomas reached over and took his wife's hand. Yes, he was worried but would not show it. "We will do what everyone else is doing: I will serve. Then I will return home. You'll be fine because between you and Mrs. Kupper, the children will be taken care of. Lina, you will continue to work, and I promise you I will not attempt to become a hero. You know we are not the only family in this situation. Our business does not have that much work right now, and you should know that if I'm not called to serve, I intend to find another way to help," and he smiled at Lina. She wasn't fooled. She knew he was just as concerned.

It was providence. Thomas was not selected. Lina was relieved. Frankly, so was he. The decision to close his carpentry business was made, and he began to search for a way to help the war effort. He was experienced and capable and knew woodworking. He was able to repair and build and restore, and in April, he found and began a new job. Closing up his store, even temporarily, was a sad business, but the sign he taped to the front window of the building assured the customers who were looking for his expertise that he would return:

Helping the War Effort.

Can still work on weekends.

Telephone for assistance.

Will reopen once WE WIN THIS CONFLICT!

Thomas began work at the *Hammond Musical Instrument Company,* located on Chicago's north side on Western Avenue. Because of gasoline rationing, he could not drive the car to work but walked two streets to wait on the corner and board a city streetcar to the factory, about a twenty-minute ride. He worked long hours because of the labor shortage, and it was not unusual for him to work six days most weeks. He was adept at creating and making the needed supplies for the war, and because of his prior practice and experience, rose quickly to a managerial position in the company, beginning as a worker on the floor, advancing to floor supervisor, and within a short time, becoming assistant manager.

Thomas continued to work on the production line, demonstrating to the other men, many of whom were new to the work, what to do. Of course, the Hammond Musical Instrument Company was no longer using the precious wood to form the beautiful handcrafted organs made before the war. It was needed for other necessary war supplies, and Thomas knew what to do and how to do it. After all, when he was young, he had helped his father in their woodshop; he knew how to take the planks of wood once used to form lovely musical instruments and, instead, create durable caskets; he understood how to measure and cut and nail what his father called *eternity boxes*. At the factory, once the caskets were completed, he supervised their loading onto transports which were sent to the war zones, arriving in an empty state. Soon, too soon, they were filled and closed and sealed and returned to waiting families. Sometimes victories are defeats.

Mid-Summer, 1943

Bess and her nursing school partner, Bonnie, waited on the corner for the streetcar which would take them to their second summer rotation assignment: a north side Chicago factory helping the government by making necessary war supplies. Each young woman had a sweater around her shoulders covering a uniform, with a small white Flossie, a nurse's cap, placed in the tote bag next to a paper sack lunch. This was their first day for this job, and they were nervous and excited. The crowded streetcar was full of Chicago citizens traveling to jobs, to shops, to appointments of various kinds, and the two women were holding onto the overhead straps while talking to each other above the roar of the morning noise.

"Working with adults will be different than working with little kids," said Bonnie, "and hopefully none of them will throw up on your shoes!"

They laughed at the memory of Bess's first week in the rotation at a public school. This factory assignment didn't sound very interesting, but they needed to spend their weeks volunteering there before going on to the third rotation, the one they were looking forward to: Swedish Covenant Hospital. They assumed there would be the usual bedpan emptying, emesis basin cleaning, linen changing, but they hoped for some real patient experiences in the emergency room, the obstetrics ward, the operating theaters. They were ready to put into practice what they had been learning from their classes during the past two years of schooling. One more year, and much of that year completing actual hospital practice, was what they were anxiously awaiting. During this final year, they would study hard, then take the *State Board Examination,* hoping to pass it and receive the desired designation of *RN: Registered Nurse.* But for now, for the next few weeks, they would volunteer at the factory where they would patch cuts, pull splinters, and dispense headache medicine. Anything more serious would require a doctor to be notified.

They got off the streetcar, found their way to the large four-story building where the letters: **Hammond Organ Company** could be clearly seen across the front. They had been told to enter the main door and find the receptionist who would advise them where to go next. They walked in and saw completed organs lined up against one wall with pictures of various instruments hung along the extended hallway. Bess and Bonnie were directed to the end of the hallway where an elevator would take them to the third floor. Once they exited the elevator, to their right was a small office which they entered and announced themselves to the man seated behind a desk. He came out and shook their hands and introduced himself.

"Good morning. I'm Robert Holden. Let me show you where you'll work. The assistant manager, Mr. A, is at some meetings, so he is not here today, but said he would stop and introduce himself to you when he returns. In the meantime, I'll take you around to this floor and the second one and give you a tour of the place."

The three of them walked down a hallway and entered another small office where there was a desk with a telephone and some papers, a few chairs, a sink with running water, and two cots against the back wall. One cabinet stocked the minimum necessary medicines and provisions they might need while another cabinet was available for their sweaters and tote bags and personal items. Bess and Bonnie placed their effects into this cabinet, removed their caps from the tote bags and adjusted them to their heads, glancing into the small mirror on the inside of the cabinet door. Then they followed Mr. Holden outside to the factory floor. He showed them the various stations, explaining what was being created, took them to the second floor where a lunchroom and a small bathroom for women was available, and then came back to the third floor and their assigned room.

"There is a small canteen next to the lunchroom if you would like to purchase a lunch one day. We have informed the workers that you are available in case of small injuries. Honestly, there aren't many. Just mostly cuts and splinters, especially from the new guys who are not so careful. We are building caskets here, but there is some additional research going on the fourth floor…war research, and I don't know much about it, but you are asked to stay off that floor. Mr. A needs both of you to fill out the papers I left on the desk. It's mostly basic stuff, just some personnel requirements. I'll show you how to use the phone if you need to call me or call out, and I'll give you the list of available office numbers should you need them. Any questions you have, let me know." He completed instructions and left.

Bess and Bonnie looked at each other. "Well,' said Bonnie," I think the time is going to travel by like molasses on a cold day. We should have brought a book to study for the Boards. Tomorrow we will. Do you think we should at least keep our door open so if someone needs us, they will know we are here?"

"That's a good idea," and Bess went to the door, finding a doorstop to do the job. "Let's at least organize this place and see what supplies there are. Then we can fill out the papers and get them back to Mr. Holden. We should have some sort of schedule for ourselves and alternate lunchtimes so someone is always here," and the two of them created work for themselves. No one needed their services that first day, and when their work day was over, they agreed that it was definitely a *molasses day*.

The following day they were needed to bandage a couple of minor cuts and remove a rather large splinter from a hand. One worker came to them complaining of a terrible headache, and some aspirin was issued. The most medical thing they did was to take two stitches in a deep cut. For the majority of the day, Bess and Bonnie moved the furniture around and polished and cleaned the room deciding to look for something at their dormitory with which they could decorate the desk area. They found some blankets and pillows which they removed from the cabinet, shook out, placed on the two cots, and decided to create an organization sheet to record the names of the workers who required their services and what the services were. They kept themselves as busy as possible, but they agreed that the weeks at the Hammond Organ Company would be slow moving. Much of their time was spend testing each other and preparing for their State Board Exam.

***

Mr. A, Thomas Allerton, was kept busy at meetings for a couple days, and when he did return, he worked at the production line instructing some of the new hires, so he did not get up to meet the additions to the factory for that first week. When the following

Monday came, he completed his usual daily morning rounds, and about lunchtime, made his way over to the room designated as the Nurse's Office. The door was opened, and he glanced in to see one of the student nurses seated at the desk writing something, and he knocked gently. Bonnie looked up, smiled, and inquired, "Can I help you?"

Thomas walked in and held out his hand to her while introducing himself. "Hello. I'm Thomas Allerton, *Mr. A*, and I'm sorry for not getting here sooner, but I had some other duties. How are things going? Is there anything you need?"

Bonnie shook his outstretched hand and answered, "It's good to meet you, Mr. A. I'm Bonnie Hester. I know you have been busy. Mr. Holden told us you would eventually be here. Actually, there were a few supplies needed, and last Friday we gave the list to Mr. Holden who said that we would get them either this afternoon or tomorrow morning."

"Good. I'll check on them when I get back to the office. I thought there were two nurses here. Are you the only one?"

"The other nurse, Bess, has a lunch break right now. We take turns so there will always be someone here and available. She just went to the lunchroom a few minutes ago and should return in about thirty minutes."

"Well, it's good to meet you, and thank you for volunteering. This room looks nicely organized, and if there are additional needs, please let me or Mr. Holden know. Maybe I'll take a walk to the lunchroom and see if I can meet your partner…Bess, right?"

"Yes. She would be the one in a nurse uniform," Bonnie joked.

Thomas smiled and left. He moved around the third floor, greeting workers, checking things, answering questions. When he approached the elevator, he opened the stairway door next to it and walked down the flight of stairs. The lunchroom was just to his left and mostly empty. Bess was not difficult to spot. Thomas headed towards her but then stopped. She was seated alone at a small table taking bites of her sandwich. There was a large book opened in front of her. He watched as she read, put the sandwich down, took a sip from her cup, and wrote something in a notebook. The sun was shining in from the factory windows which were stretched almost to the ceiling, and her hair was surrounded in its light. A vague recollection floated through Thomas. He recognized the shade of her hair which was like a stain he once used for a project. The color was called *burnt-umber*. He watched as she brushed back some strands, repositioning them behind her ear. He remained still, watching the young woman jot down notes, and then, shaking off a murky memory, continued towards her.

He stopped in front of her, a smile planted on his face and when she looked up at him, his mouth opened and he swallowed the air in front of it. There was a second of indecipherable recognition, but he did not allow it permanence. He reformed his lips into a smile and spoke louder than he planned to. "Hello. I'm *Mr. A.* I was just upstairs in your office and met Nurse Bonnie. She told me you were here on your lunch break. I just wanted to introduce myself. You're Nurse Bess?"

Bess looked up and smiled, and her chestnut brown eyes met his. "I am," she said, "Glad to meet you. Would you like to sit down?"

"I don't want to disturb you during your break. I see you are busy."

Bess tilted her head to one side, and there was something about the definition of her cheek that captured Thomas's notice. He could not determine what it was.

"I just thought I would write a few notes down. Bonnie and I will be taking the State Boards Exam early next spring, and we want to get a head start on it."

Thomas remained standing. He nodded his head and answered, "That's a wise thing to do. I won't take more of your time. Just wanted to meet you and thank you for volunteering. Like I told Nurse Bonnie, if there is anything you need, let me know."

"Thank you; we will," and Bess picked up her sandwich for another bite as he began to move away. Then she thought of something and called to him, "Mr. A…?"

He turned back to her.

"What does the *A* stand for? You didn't tell me your name."

He spoke. "Allerton. My name is Thomas Allerton."

Bess nodded, "Thomas Allerton." Her lips curled and her eyes softened as she said, "Thomas. I'm told my father's name was also Thomas."

Thomas Allerton froze before he remembered to nod. As he walked away towards the elevator, there was a clenching in his stomach and a picking in his brain, and he had to think carefully about placing one foot in front of the other to continue moving.

***

Thursday morning brought sunshine and summer heat with it, and both the office floor fans and the factory's large industrial fans were turned to *high.* At mid-morning, Thomas walked past Robert Holden's office and peeked in to greet him. A discussion about some factory issues took place, and once done, Robert pointed to a small table fan on the chair next to him.

"I pulled this out from the old storeroom and thought that it could go into the office with the student nurses. Got to be warm in there. I'll take it there when I make my daily inspections."

Thomas nodded. "Good idea. I'm sure they will appreciate it. Go on and get the inspections done, and I'll get it to them. I was going to stop by and check on them anyway," and he took the fan, wrapping the cord around it. As he turned to go, one of the women in a back office called to him, telling him a telephone call was waiting for him.

The call lasted longer than he expected, and then there was some paperwork which needed to be done. It was past noon when he finished and was finally able to take the table fan to the student nurses. He knocked gently on the open door, and Bess turned to look at him. She stood, holding a book, and the tableau she engendered formed an image, a faint but startling one which moved from the recesses of Thomas's brain to the forefront. He pushed it aside and managed to find his voice.

"Mr. Holden found a fan for this room. Hopefully it will help when it's so warm. I see you cracked the window. Does it help?"

Bess placed the book on the desk and looked at the window which had been propped open with a large piece of wood they found in the cabinet. She shrugged. "A little, but thanks for the fan. This will be great. We appreciate it."

Thomas looked around for a place to plug it in. Bess brought an extra chair over so the moving air would reach across the occupied space. He arranged the fan on the chair and tilted it up so that it would move across the room depositing a breeze wherever it landed. Bess sat down at the desk, and when the breeze moved some of her hair, she grinned.

"This will help. Thanks again, Mr. A. Sit there, and you can feel the breeze too."

Thomas moved a chair from against the wall and sat in it and nodded. "It does help. Is Nurse Bonnie at lunch?"

"Yes. She left about ten minutes ago. She'll be happily surprised when she returns."

"So how have things been going? Have you had many patients? Most of the workers are careful, and I haven't heard of any terrible mishaps."

Bess nodded. "There have been a few every day. Mostly cuts and bruises. A few splinters. Some headaches, but nothing awful we can't handle. We have emergency numbers if something happens which needs more than we are prepared to deal with."

Thomas nodded. They sat quietly for a while enjoying the fan's work. He glanced at Bess. "Where are you from? I know that many of the student nurses come from Chicago, but many also come from other states."

"Well, Bonnie is from a small town in Indiana, but I'm from Chicago."

"It must be difficult for Bonnie to be away from her home, but since you live in Chicago, I hope you get to see your family periodically."

"During the regular school year, I do, but my mother is spending the summer at our house in a small town about an hour or so from here. We talk every Sunday, and I try to write at least one letter a week to her. She writes more often. I think she misses me, and so does Greta. That's our housekeeper, but she's more like a second mother to me. Before classes begin in mid-September, I plan on taking a break and going to Bonneville for a week or so."

Thomas squinted his eyes and croaked out, "Where?"

"Bonneville," repeated Bess, "That's the name of the small town our other house is in. You've probably never heard of it. Actually, I lived there until I was about twelve, and then we moved here to Chicago. It's a great little town, and the house is a wonderful old Victorian, but Mother is thinking about selling it. I suppose two houses are not necessary, but…"

Thomas knew Bess continued to speak, but he didn't pay attention to what she was saying. He was examining her and looking at the contours of her cheek, the shade of her hair, the hue of her eyes. There was a familiarity about it all. A disturbing familiarity. Memories came flooding back, and he swallowed hard. He became lost in the past. A silence occurred in the present. Bess was staring at him. Her head was tilted; her brow was furrowed.

"Mr. A, are you OK? Do you need something?"

He gathered himself, exacting what he thought was a smile. "No, I just remembered what I need to do this afternoon." He stood up and pushed the chair back against the wall. "I hope the fan helps."

"It does. Thanks again."

He left.

***

Thomas walked quickly. He stopped to ask Robert Holden where the personnel papers from the student nurses were. A folder was handed to him, and he went to his office. There were things to do, but they must wait. He closed his door, sat at his desk, stared at the manila folder. The first sheet was removed, and he glanced at the information which had been filled in by Nurse Bonnie. It was set to the side. His heart accelerated when he saw the name on the second page: **Beatrice Vogel**. Beatrice. *Bess* was a nickname. Her date of birth was listed as: **November 7, 1922.** He didn't need to compute the math. Under *Emergency Contact,* he read a name he had not thought of for years: **Ingrid Vogel.** The second contact listed was: **Greta Anderson.** He took deep breaths. He ran his hand through his hair. He sat back in his chair, reviewing his past, analyzing his youth, reflecting on the time, two decades ago, when a winter ended and a spring began, and he was expelled from the comfort of an old Victorian house without any clarification or reason.

Late Summer, 1943

Mrs. Kupper put her coffee on the table and waited for the back door to open and Clara and Joey Allerton to enter. Summer break would be over in a couple weeks, and the fall schedule would start. Then their mother would get them ready for school, walk them to the corner, and wave to them as she crossed it to catch the streetcar to her job while they traveled down the street to their school. After school, they would join Mrs. Kupper in her kitchen and enjoy her homemade treats. When their mother returned just before five o'clock, they would go home, complete homework, and wait for their father and dinner. It was a schedule which worked for them all.

Mr. and Mrs. Kupper had known Thomas and Lina Allerton for years. Joseph Kupper hired Thomas to work at his furniture repair shop when he moved to Chicago looking for a job, and they worked together until the Depression forced a shut-down of his business. But in the years afterwards, after the worst of the difficult time was over, the shop reopened with Thomas as the proprietor and Joseph Kupper as his mentor and advisor. And when a small house became available down the street from the Kuppers, it was a natural move for Thomas and Lina and their two children. Joseph's death two years before, left a pall over the two families which was somewhat mitigated when Lina began her job working for the Chicago Office of Civil Defense in the typing pool, because she asked Mrs. Kupper to watch Clara and Joey. *Grandma K*, as they called her, was delighted to add additional grandchildren to her own. Neither Thomas nor Lina had living parents, and they were grateful for Mrs. Kupper's assistance and acceptance into her extended family.

***

It was a mild Tuesday evening, and Clara and Joey were outside playing with friends, attempting to extend the bit of summer left to them before school began. Their parents were sitting on the front porch watching them, periodically waving to neighbors who strolled past. From their vantage point, they saw Mrs. Kupper seated on her porch talking with a friend, and they waved to each other. Thomas and Lina were discussing something which had come up over the past weeks. It was about Bess.

"Tom, you continue to talk about this. It bothers you, and rightfully so. I know she is no longer volunteering at the factory, but you are still thinking about her. You should make up your mind. Are you going to travel to Bonneville or not? If you are, you should go soon, because once school starts, you know how busy we are." Lina was aware of Bess and her husband's speculation about the young woman. Nothing from their pasts had been hidden from each other. She knew about Bonneville. About Ingrid Vogel. And now, about his speculation concerning Bess.

"I know, Lina. I keep going over everything in my mind. How much she looks like her mother, and honestly, some aspects of her remind me of, I suppose, myself. What if she is my daughter? The thought haunts me. No information had ever been told to me, but even if it had, what would I have done? The way I was sent from the house, her actual name: *Beatrice*, the date of her birth…it all falls into place. What could I do now? She is an adult. Does it matter to her? What was she told about her father? Once she mentioned that she was informed that her father's name was Thomas. How could I help her now? What responsibility do I have?" Thomas sighed and shook his head.

Lina leaned against him. "Do you think that if you went to Bonneville and faced Mrs. Vogel, she would tell you the truth? And what would you do then? What would you say?"

"I'm not sure. I know that if I go, I need to do it now. Bess said she and Mrs. Anderson are there for another few weeks, and Bess will be visiting after her volunteering is done. I wouldn't want to be there when Bess is. I just don't know, Lina."

They sat for a while watching the impromptu game of tag half a dozen children were playing up and down the street. Summer duskiness was creeping in and momentary miniature flashes were noticed as lightening bugs began their nightly display. Lina sat up and took Thomas's hand in hers.

"I think you should go, Tom. I don't know what you will say or what she will, but you have a right to know the truth. I know this bothers you, and you should settle your mind. Perhaps this weekend you can take some time for a trip."

Thomas squeezed her hand and brought it to his lips. He nodded. "What if you and the kids take a ride with me?"

Lina looked at him and smiled. "No, Tom. This is your trip and your truth, and you need to go. I know you, and you won't rest easy until you find out."

Thomas looked at her and heaved another sigh. "OK. You're right. I'll tell Robert I have some important family business to take care of and go down there Friday morning," and he nodded, pointedly adding, "And you're right about the trip too. I need to do this by myself. This is my duty."

Lina nodded assent. They remained together on the porch until darkness claimed the day. Thomas called to Clara and Joey to come in, and the four of them went into the small Chicago bungalow. The adults, following their children, suspended their discussion, took their disquietudes inside, and closed the door against the flickering shimmers of luminescent beetles.

Eleven

Reacquainted: Bonneville

Monday

Greta continued her running commentary to Ingrid during their weekly trek to the Bonneville grocery store.

"…and not just that, but don't you remember the General Store changed to the *groceteria* and it's now that new *A&P Supermarket*? I'm telling you, Ingrid, this is not the same town we lived in all those years ago," and Greta maneuvered the car as closely to the entrance of the cemetery as possible.

"Of course it's not, Greta. That old General Store was here decades ago. You and I are now in our fifties and have changed too. Besides, I rather like the A&P. Those little shopping carts are clever," and Ingrid stepped out of the car, shut the door, and waited for Greta to step up the curb and join her on the sidewalk. They entered the cemetery for their visit.

Gas was still rationed, and they limited their use of the car. While in Bonneville, they drove into town every Monday, visiting the graves of their husbands first before completing the shopping for the week. Each weekend, they planned the following week's menu and made a list of needed supplies. Rationing continued, and they were careful in their use of stamps and points. This week they were canning tomatoes, and after the cemetery visit, they would walk to the hardware store for additional canning jars. Greta would go to the A&P for groceries, and Ingrid wanted to visit the newly opened *Jo-Ann Sewing and Craft Store* for some additional embroidery floss. They discussed stopping for a quick lunch at the diner on the corner which opened a month ago, but decided that there was too much to do this week, and they needed to get home and finish it. Bess would be in Bonneville the week after next, and Ingrid wanted all the canning done so she could work on embroidering the new towels she was readying for Bess. The canning, the cleaning, the bit of gardening meant there was plenty of work to keep both women busy.

It was not all work. There were visits to and from friends, social and civic activities, periodic trips to see a new movie at the Bonneville Movie Palace. Mr. Owens, the theater owner, died a few years ago, but Marion, his wife, continued to work behind the ticket counter while her youngest son, Ben, and his wife, ran the business. There were other changes. Doctor and Mrs. Marshall retired to Kentucky where two of their children and their families were living. Dr. Joseph now ran the Bonneville Clinic with his wife and another young doctor. Mabel McHenry was retired from the telephone company, but she worked three days a week at the A&P behind the cash register. She enjoyed her new job. It gave her plenty of time to talk to the customers and learn the latest news. Tony Jr. now ran *Tony's Filling Station*, but Tony Sr. was still there most days, straightening up the inside, sweeping the outside, continually instructing Tony Jr. what to do and how to do it. Even Harold Jones no longer completed any backbreaking work on his farm. His son, Raymond, had taken over, building a rather large farmstand just down the road from Ingrid's house. Most of the fruits and vegetables canned in her kitchen were purchased by Greta there. Summer time passed quickly for Ingrid and Greta. They were diligent and active and content. And there was no reason for them to expect that in a few days, the Past would march up to the sturdy front door of the old Victorian house, move the heavy door knocker three times, and wait, Fate's luminary, to enter.

Tuesday

They sat in the porch swing enjoying the slight breeze the darkening sky brought with it. It had been a long day, and they were tired. The canning of the tomatoes was completed and the dozens of jars were on the kitchen table resting, waiting for their movement to the cellar the following day. Greta pushed her hand through her mostly gray hair and sighed.

"I don't know about you, but I am done in. The canning is finished for now, although perhaps next week I will try that new recipe for zucchini pickle relish. I'll put up a small batch just to try it. What do you think?"

Ingrid nodded. "That sounds good. Is there anything else we should do before Bess gets here?"

Ingrid was quiet for a few seconds, recounting in her mind the work done over the past month. She used her fingers to name the sorts of foods canned. "Well, the strawberry and blueberry jams are done. The cherries and peaches are finished. We canned the green beans and corn and finished the tomatoes today. I'll do the relish next week, and a bunch of the herbs are hanging in the cellar drying. When we return to Chicago in a few weeks, I am hoping we can get a bushel of Hoover apples and maybe some early Rome beauties to take back. We can work with them in Chicago. Can't think of anything else, can you?"

"Only some cucumber pickles. We didn't do those yet. Maybe Bess won't mind helping out when she's here. Otherwise, it all seems to be done. I'm thinking about our trip back to Chicago and wondering how the car will hold all those jars, the three of us, and the luggage."

"We can leave some clothing here and return at the beginning of October to get it. You'll be ready for a break from school then, and we can make a quick trip down here on a weekend."

Ingrid pushed the swing gently. "Maybe. There's always the gas rationing to consider, you know."

Greta shrugged. "Oh, I think that can be worked out," and she glanced at Ingrid who gave her a knowing smirk. "And now, before bed, I'm going to have a bath and wash this hair, unless you planned to do that for yourself tonight."

"No," Ingrid shook her head. "I can wait a day or two to wash this hair. I think I'll sit out here for a time. Good night, Greta. See you in the morning."

"Good night, Ingrid."

Wednesday

The morning's brief rain cooled things off and kept the two women inside for most of it. When it stopped, Ingrid examined the wetness and decided it would not hamper her sitting outside. She took some rags with her, wiped off the porch swing, and sat down with a book. After a bit, Greta appeared holding two glasses of cold tea, offering one to Ingrid who smiled, put her book down, and took the glass. They sat in companiable quiet, sipped the tea, and watched as periodically a farm truck or a car drove past. Sometimes they recognized the person in the vehicle and waves were exchanged. Greta cleared her throat.

"I know you have talked about selling this house for a while, and if you do decide to sell it, I will miss the summers here. Have you made up your mind yet?"

Ingrid shook her head. "I intend to call Jason Adill this week and make an appointment with him. With the war on, I don't think this large house will sell quickly, but I'd like his opinion. We are getting older, Greta, and I will miss Bonneville too, but there is no reason to keep two houses. Of course, we will take trips here to visit the cemetery, visit friends, view the changes. But I like living in Chicago, and I miss the theater and musical offerings there. Hoping once this war is done, we can go back to the way it used to be. I'm anxious to attend the concerts and operas. You'll go to the theater with me, won't you?"

"Absolutely. I don't know much about plays or music and such, but this old dog can learn new tricks. Speaking of theaters, that *Casablanca* movie will be showing at the Palace this weekend. Why don't we go Saturday night? Or even that afternoon to the matinee? Mabel said it's a real tearjerker."

"Alright. We can think about doing that. It will do us good to get out. Listen, don't plan a big dinner tonight. Let's do something with the leftover tomatoes."

"Actually," said Greta, "that was my plan."

Thursday

"This may be the best tomato soup you've made, Greta. Really good," and Ingrid savored another large spoonful.

"Well, I needed to use up the rest of those tomatoes, and *lagom är bast*, as my mother used to tell us: *Enough is as good as a feast!*"

"You mother was right! The wheat bread is tasty with the soup, and tomorrow morning it will be great as toast."

They finished the soup and bread, and Greta removed the dishes. She busied herself making tea to go with the molasses cookies she made, and listened as Ingrid talked to her.

"…so when Jason and his family return from the visit to his father, I will meet with him. I have an appointment for Monday and thought that while I talk to him about the house, you can do the shopping. Will that be OK?"

"Yes," and Greta put the tea cups down. "If you do sell this house, I am guessing you will get a pretty penny for it. It's been kept up and renovated, and some large family will buy and enjoy it. What will you do with the profit?"

Ingrid took a sip of her tea and then broke off part of the large cookie. "I have thought about that. Of course, it will be a couple years at least, and I won't go anywhere until Bess has graduated and is somewhat settled, and she may not want to go, but I thought the three of us could go to Europe. What do you think?"

"Europe! Ingrid, there's a war there!"

"I'm talking about when it's all done. When things are back to normal in a few years. Fredrick and I planned a trip, but never did go, and I probably forgot all the German and French I knew, but it's a thought. What about it?"

Greta laughed. "First you are taking me to the theater and the opera in Chicago, and now to Europe! Sure, Ingrid, sounds great," and she dipped her cookie into her teacup.

Ingrid smiled. "Well, it's something to dream about, I guess."

Friday, August 20, 1943

The weather was temperate for an August day, and no laborious work was planned. Greta thought she would do a bit of gardening and wash the canning jars, getting them ready for next week's zucchini pickle relish. Ingrid was going to work in the library, sifting through Fredrick's books, deciding which ones to keep and which could be sold in Chicago. She would finish the letter to Bess and get it sent; it would firm up her travel plans. In about a week, Bess's summer volunteer rotations would be completed, and she would travel to Bonneville for a time. After the visit, the three of them would pack up the car for Chicago. The summer had been tranquil and relaxing, despite the worry about the war, the rationing, the lack of meat and dairy products, the changes in the town.

Ingrid woke early, and hearing no kitchen noises, assumed Greta was still asleep. She decided to take a bath and wash her hair and took her time doing it. Her hair had never been cut into a fashionable bob, and while most of it remained the burnt-umber color, there were observable strands of white in it. As she dried and combed through it, she looked closely at herself in the mirror. She was fifty-four, and there were a few lines around her eyes and a brown spot was noticed near the side of her face next to her right ear. *Well, those things do happen*, she thought as she patted her face and applied a thin layer of Woodbury face cream. She nonchalantly piled her almost dry hair on top of her head, the way she had worn it in her youth, took the jar of homemade rosewater and sprayed it on her face and arms. It helped to keep her cool in the heat. Turning her face to one side and then another she thought, *Not bad for an old woman*, then felt foolish. Deciding the day might turn warm, she pulled a light flowered summer dress from the wardrobe over her head and tied the belt into a bow on the side. She slipped into her shoes and walked downstairs to the kitchen to make morning coffee.

She set the kitchen table with coffee cups and plates, toasted the bread, and opened a jar of the strawberry jam which had been freshly made weeks ago. Ingrid was bringing the hot coffee pot to the table just as Greta was sitting down.

"A treat," she said, "I am served by the lady of the house. Thank you, Ingrid," and she readied her coffee and began to spread the jam on her toast.

"I was up early, took a bath, and decided to start the day. Here, have another piece," and Ingrid placed the warm bread on her plate. "We can rest today and do easy work. There's plenty of soup left, and I can make a green salad later. No sense in fussing for dinner. I have chores to do in the library, and maybe, after dinner, we can take a walk. How does that sound?"

"Perfect," answered Greta, and the two finished their breakfast in silence.

"Let me clean up, and you go on into the library. I want to get the jars washed for the relish next week, and I need to reread the recipe. Not sure we have all the ingredients. Then I'll begin the list of supplies needed for Monday's shopping," and Greta began to rewrap the wheat bread and move the breakfast dishes to the sink. Ingrid stood, stretched out her back, and left.

***

Sometimes the suppositions, the hypotheticals, the conjectures, the *what ifs?* of Life are too ferocious not to contemplate. *What if* Ingrid had sold the Bonneville house years before? She considered it. Had that happened, she would not have been in the library on Friday, August 20, 1943, working but unaware that her Past was coming closer. *What if* Ingrid and Greta had not spent the entire summer in Bonneville? Perhaps spent just a month there? Or a week? Or a weekend? *What if* Bess had decided to become anything else other than a nurse? There would have been no reason for her to spend time at the Hammond Organ Company. She would not have become acquainted with Thomas Allerton. She would not have filled out the personnel information sheet listing her name, her mother's name, the housekeeper's name. She would not have been in the factory's lunchroom looking over a book, sun streaming down on her burnt-umber hair, awakening a murky memory in Thomas Allerton's mind as he watched her. *What if* Thomas Allerton had been called up for active duty during the war? Then he would not have looked for another way to serve his country. He would not have gone to work at the Hammond Organ Company creating the wooden caskets which were sent empty and returned full. *What if* he had never asked Bess from where she hailed? He would not have summoned up youthful reminders upon hearing the name *Bonneville*. He would have had no reason to pull the personnel papers completed by Bess. He would not have read the name he had disregarded for years. *What if* his wife, Lina, had objected to his trip to discover the truth he suspected? *What if* she had been a jealous wife, forbidding him to travel to Bonneville? Raising the proverbial fuss when he took a day off to go there? *What ifs* clash with destiny, creating massive collisions, monumental confrontations, monstrous contests. Fate always wins. And on this Friday, with Ingrid sorting through books in the library and Greta sitting at the dining room table writing a list, the knock on the sturdy front door of the old Victorian house in Bonneville announced the Champion's arrival.

"I'll get that, Ingrid," called Greta as she put her pencil down next to the list she was creating.

Ingrid, standing, looking down at the two piles of Fredrick's books on the desk in front of her, did not hear or perhaps did not pay attention to Greta's utterance. She was holding a volume, lost in thought, remembering the day she and Fredrick purchased the quaint, ancient copy of Goethe's *Faust*. They were walking down New York's Fourth Avenue where all the bookshops were located, stopping at various stores, examining the offerings. Fredrick was delighted when he found the title. Ingrid smiled at the memory, wondering if she should keep it or attempt to sell it. It would be worth something. Neither one of them had ever actually read it, but she thought of that happy time and placed the book onto the "keep" pile. She was startled when Greta flung open the library door and stood there, eyes widened, mouth open, no sound coming out.

"Greta, what's wrong?"

"He's here. He is at the door and wants to see you. Wants to speak with you."

Ingrid shrugged her shoulders. "Who?"

Greta could barely get the name out, and when she did, it was a whispered tone, a sacrilege. "Allerton. Thomas Allerton. He is here. At the door."

Ingrid's mouth opened; oxygen halted in her lungs. Her hand clutched the flowered summer dress beneath which her heart beat a sudden, strange, undulating tremble. She eked out the words, "Why? Why is he here? What does he want?"

Greta shook her head. "I asked. He said he needs to speak with you. I can send him away. I will shut and lock the door. I will call… someone. Oh, I wish Lars was alive!"

The two of them stood for a full minute. Ingrid took deep breaths and calmed herself. She mustered fortitude and spoke in her usual tone saying, "Show him in. Whatever it is, I will handle it."

"Are you sure?"

"Yes."

Greta gulped in air and went to the door. Ingrid remained standing, picked up another book, opened it to the title page. She had no idea what it said, but was relying upon her youthful training on the opera stage to present a *tableau vivant*, a motionless scene: the library, the books, a woman in charge. Greta came to the door with Thomas Allerton standing behind her. She acted the servant and announced, "Mrs. Vogel, you have a visitor."

She moved away, allowing Thomas to enter the room, and closed the library door partway. Thomas stood looking at Ingrid, and after a pregnant pause of a good five seconds, Ingrid closed the book in her hands, placed it to the side, and looked towards him. It was not Fredrick standing at the doorway. There remained a look of him around Thomas's eyes, a minor hint of him at the contours of his shaved cheeks, a speckle of him in the notice of dark hair which contained a bit of early gray, but Thomas Allerton was not Fredrick Vogel. Both relief and retrospection flooded Ingrid's being.

How speedily do thoughts and memories occur? In which part of the brain do they reside? Do they hide behind wormy gray matter, peeking out only when nudged and jabbed, reluctant and hesitant to appear, unwilling and bashful of notice? There was no doubt about remembrances of brazen and blushing thoughts, of sensual actions and carnal deeds, of fleshy engagements and maneuvers not allowed to be considered during daylight. But certain former evocations cannot be allowed to emerge, to meddle, to muck around when they are no longer wanted. They must disappear; they are objectionable intrusions.

Thomas greeted her, "Hello, Mrs. Vogel."

And she answered, a command given, no salutation transmitted: "Thomas. Please sit down," and fully in control of her emotions, her role secure, Ingrid sat at the large chair behind the desk and, on cue, spoke her lines. "Why are you here?"

Thomas expected no niceties. The conversation would be formal and exact. He wasted no time. "I have met Bess."

Ingrid was shocked. It did not show on her face. A mask of nonchalance. Posing persona. She said nothing. She waited for additional information.

"The company I work for decided to give student nurses a chance to use their medical training. The nurse who was employed there enlisted with the army, and Bess and another nurse, Bonnie, volunteered at the factory for a month. I met her and spoke with her. Through her personnel papers, I discovered you are her mother. She told me you were spending the summer here. In Bonneville."

Ingrid raised her eyebrows. "So, this is a social call?"

Thomas would not play her game. He wanted to know. "Her actual name is *Beatrice. Bess* is a nickname. She was born in early November, 1922. She said she was told her father's name was *Thomas.*" He waited for admission. Acknowledgement. Confession.

"Yes. What is your point?"

Thomas was no longer a youth of eighteen. He was a man with a wife and a family, with responsibilities. He had a full and complete past, and honesty was required. It was demanded. He leaned forward, looked into Ingrid's face, and pressed, "Am I her father?"

Twenty years previously, when Greta explained the Plan to Ingrid, she was very clear that it must be considered valid forever. "There is no changing this, Ingrid. Lars and you and I know what the truth is, and tonight, here, at this time, we are agreeing to change it. The baby will never need to know. No one else will either. Do you understand? Do you agree to this?" Ingrid did. The only blunder she ever made was on the baby's birth certificate which was currently hidden upstairs in the middle drawer of her large dresser. It was under a doily, being guarded by a comb containing some dark hairs.

No emotion, no hesitation allowed. Ingrid looked at Thomas and provided a small, tight smile. "No. You are not."

Thomas sat back. He didn't believe her. "But her birthdate fits, the name *Beatrice*. We discussed that name my last night here. Her father's name was *Thomas*…"

"Bess is my adopted daughter. Her mother was my cousin, and she died soon after Bess's birth. I was with her, and named the baby *Beatrice* after her mother. Bess's father, whose name *was* Thomas, died before her birth. There was no one else to take her, and since I had no children, I adopted her. Bess knows this. She calls me "Mother" because I am the only mother she has known. No, Thomas, Bess is not your daughter, but she is mine by adoption."

"She looks exactly like you. The first time I saw her, I remembered, and thought it was you. Her hair…"

"…is a family characteristic. My cousin and I looked alike. We had the same coloring, the same hair and eyes. If this was what you came for, rest assured, Bess is not a product of…" here Ingrid paused, not knowing what to call it, "…our time together."

There was nothing else to say. The drama was convincing. Ingrid felt a lessening of the tightness in her stomach. This was the fitting libretto, and there was no regret. At least, not much. She eased up a bit and gave herself over to small talk. "Do you have a family, Thomas?"

Thomas nodded. "Yes. My wife and I have a girl and a boy."

Ingrid nodded. "And are you happy?"

Thomas smiled slightly. "I am. Lina and I are happy."

Ingrid pushed back her chair and stood up. Thomas did also. "I am glad for you, and I don't suppose we will ever need to see each other again. I'll call Mrs. Anderson to show you out."

"That's not necessary. I know the way out," but before he left, he reached into his pocket and took out a card. It was like the card that years ago, Greta had torn into a million paper snowflakes before allowing them to flutter into the trashcan, never to be reunited.

Thomas placed the card down on the desk. He looked up and said, "Just in case. This is where I can be found in Chicago." There were no parting handshakes, no farewell promises, no sentimental dialogue. The play was completed. Curtain down.

He stopped at the door and turned. Ingrid remained standing. Her hair was as he remembered it. The color was the same hue as the stain he had once used although there were beginning streaks of silver accenting it. He recalled its softness, its scent. She stood straight, not stooped; she was refined and elegant; a gentle grandeur emanated from her. Her performance was impeccable. He added, "Good-bye, Ingrid."

She said nothing.

***

Greta slid the hot tea over to her. "Drink this. It will help." She sat down across from her at the kitchen table and watched as Ingrid took a small sip. "You did the right thing, you know. Nothing good would have come of him knowing. Not for Bess, not for you, not even for him. Better stick to what was decided years ago."

Ingrid nodded. She was unnerved once he left; she was pale and weakened after she heard his receding steps, after she listened to the closing of the front door, after she noted the start of an automobile. When she got up the nerve to look outside and saw the empty driveway, she called for Greta who was waiting. She was too shaken to cry, and Greta helped her to the kitchen and obtained a cool wet cloth to place at the back of her head, at the nape, where tingling was absent, but pain was present. She made Ingrid lower her head towards her knees until the paleness disappeared from her face, and she was able to take steady gulps of air. Then the tea.

"I never imagined this would happen. I thought he was gone forever. Knowing that he met Bess makes me ill. How could we have prepared for this? Should I have done something different? Perhaps we should have moved back to New York when Bess was young. Do you think he said something to her? She never mentioned him. Should I ask? What do we do now, Greta? What do we say to her?"

Greta looked at her and slowly shook her head. "Nothing. We say nothing. We do nothing. If Bess mentions him or asks about him, we will deal with it then. I don't believe he did, or would, say anything to her. He wanted confirmation from you first. And you gave the right answers today. Bess is your adopted daughter, born of your dead cousin. We will forget today, forget this happened. Remove it from our minds. Are you feeling better now? Do you need anything else?"

"No, thank you," and Ingrid reached over to take Greta's hand. "I don't know what I would do without you. You are correct. Bess will be fine. She never mentioned anything in her letters or when we talked on Sundays. She does not suspect anything, and nothing will be said."

They remained like that, an altered *tableau vivant*: kitchen backdrop, tea cups, friends sharing confidences. Greta patted her hand and drank the remainder of her tea, as did Ingrid. They sat, screening thoughts, perfecting ordinariness. Greta gathered the emptied cups and took them to the sink. As she turned to wipe the table with a wet cloth, she halted and looked at Ingrid and asked, "Do you think you will ever tell Bess the truth?"

Ingrid looked out the kitchen window to consider. Then she answered. "No. I don't know. Certainly not now. Perhaps sometime. Maybe in the future."

Greta wiped the table while offering her take on the matter. "Well, I suppose *Det blir som det blir.*"

Ingrid nodded.

✳✳✳

Sunday
Early morning. Dawn appearing. Silence abounding.

Ingrid finished the letter. There were seven pages written in her careful cursive handwriting, perfected at the Bennett Academy for Girls years ago. She had three small white envelopes ready. Into one she placed the birth certificate. Into the second she slipped the card which had been placed on the desk. Into the third she moved the seven folded pages of the letter she had just finished. All were carefully and solidly sealed. On the front of the one containing the letter, she wrote:

Bess, read this first.

The three smaller envelopes along with a comb containing a few dark hairs were secured in a larger manilla envelope. Before sealing it shut, Ingrid reached in and removed the envelope with the letter. To the words already there she added:

My darling daughter, I love you. Please forgive me.

Once that was done, she replaced the letter, sealed the large envelope and wrote on the front:

To Beatrice Vogel.

From her mother.

She held the manilla repository, the faithful missive, the genuine epistle, weighing it in her hands. Portable truth. Ingrid opened the middle drawer of the desk where it would remain until Monday. She would take it with her and entrust it to Jason Adill, designating instructions. He would deliver it.

In the future.

Twelve

The Future: 1954

He walked to the stone bench where she was seated. The two small boys ran in front of him and down the cemetery path where they turned around and became interested in something on the ground. He watched them before placing his hand on Bess's shoulder. She looked up and smiled.

"How was the ice cream?"

"Messy," Brian answered, "Both of them will need baths tonight. But they enjoyed it." He squeezed in next to her on the bench, and they gazed at the second stone marker next to Fredrick's. It had recently been completed and set in place, and Bess wanted to take a ride to Bonneville and check on it. It was an agreeable late summer Saturday, and the four of them drove to the town where Bess had spent much of her early life. They traveled up and down the streets as she pointed out the old Victorian house in which she had once lived, the school she had attended, the stores she used to visit. Then they drove to Bonneville Cemetery and parked the car.

While her husband and sons walked to the newly opened ice cream shop just one street away, Bess entered the cemetery, visiting Lars' grave first, then moving to the others. She sat on the stone bench looking at the expertly chiseled gravestones in front of her. Fredrick's had been created by the memorial mason from Stone City, and the new one had been completed by his son. Bess wanted them to be authentically matched, to be harmonious, to be suitable partners. They were. The inscription could be clearly read:

Ingrid Winthrop Vogel

1889-1953

Wife of Fredrick

Mother, Grandmother, Friend

Loved by All

"It looks good, Bess," and her husband leaned over to kiss her burnt-umber hair. She wiped her chestnut-colored eyes and nodded.

"It does. Greta will be glad to know that. Hopefully next time she'll feel good enough to come with us, although I think she is fine. She was just too sad to travel here today. I know she misses Mother. I told her I was worried about her, but she said she is just old," and Bess gave a rueful smile. She turned around to see her sons watching a worm crawl across the path, attempting to burrow into the grass on the other side.

"I suppose we should start home. I do need to make one stop before we get on the road. Jason Adill said he has something for me which he forgot to give me at the funeral. I'll run into his office and get it."

Bess and Brian stood up from the bench. She turned to the boys and called to them, "Fredrick! Thomas! Let's go. We're going to leave now."

Fredrick, the six-year-old, looked up, then stood up. He started to walk towards his parents while his brother, four-year-old Thomas, ran past him to his mother and held his hands up to her. She bent down to pick him up and admonished him. "Thomas, you are almost too big for me to carry! You are growing so quickly."

Fredrick went to his father and looked up to ask, "Are we leaving now?"

"Yes, we are. Ready?"

"Yep," he said. He turned to his mother. "Mom, Grandma Greta said she was making those cookies for us. Can we have some when we get home?"

"I want one too," chimed Thomas.

"Yes, after dinner you can have a cookie. Let's go now. There is a quick stop we need to make before Daddy drives us home," and the four of them walked to the car.

***

That evening in Chicago, hands were washed, dinner was eaten, cookies were shared, baths were given, and finally, Fredrick and Thomas were settled in their beds. Greta claimed tiredness and said she was going to her room. Brian took the newspaper and went to the kitchen to read it and listen to a ballgame on the radio. Bess walked into the front room with the manilla envelope given to her by Jason Adill. She had not had time to open it, and in the quiet of the late summer evening, she would complete that task.

She sat in the chair closest to the window, and examined the front of the large envelope where her name was written in Ingrid's careful and refined handwriting. After running her fingers over the words, she carefully broke open the seal and poured the contents onto her lap. There were three small white envelopes and a comb. She looked quizzically at the comb, wondering if it was meant as a joke. She read the message written on the thickest envelope, then placed the other two unopened envelopes and the comb on the small table next to her. Reaching over to the lamp, she turned it on, adjusting the brightness so it would fall upon the words. Bess opened the thick envelope and removed the pages while she settled into the chair. She unfolded the letter and began to read.

Thirteen

At Last

It was six months before she ventured to contact him. They spoke on the telephone twice. The first conversation was awkward. The second, less so. They planned to meet on a Saturday because he worked only until noon that day, and they could have the shop to themselves once he closed up. She arrived early and sat in the car across the street. It was the same spot Greta had parked in years before.

She could see the shop which was housed between an empty building and a hardware store. The empty building was undergoing renovations, being readied for a new business. Old letters, announcing it had been a dentist's office, were being scraped off the front window, but there was no indication as to what business would take its place. She watched from her car, glancing back and forth at the work being done and the shop next door. Periodic movement in the shop's back room declared he was there. Just before noon, she left the car, holding a comb in her hand, walked across the street, and hesitated in front of the entry door. The hair on her arms stood up. There was a tingling at her neck. Her heart pounded. She turned the door handle. As she entered, a small bell above the door announced her. She walked inside, stood still, and waited.

He emerged from the back, recognizing her. They examined each other. The years were visible. Both were older. Faces had adjusted; bodies had shifted. His hair was gray, and hers was longer. She had pulled it into a knot at the nape of her neck, just as her mother used to wear hers. The color had not changed.

He greeted her, "Hello, Beatrice."

She smiled at her father. Thomas returned the smile.

Commentary:

The Internet, History, and Fate

Apparently, I owe a debt of gratitude to Vinton Cerf and Bob Kahn who, according to my research on the Internet, invented the Internet. Tim Berners-Lee is given credit, along with Radia Perlman, Marian Croak, and Elizabeth Feinler who are a few of the women who are due acclaim for their scientific prowess, and if I continue investigating and listing, I will never complete this meager note of acknowledgement. The Internet allowed me the comfort of my own home and favorite chair as I wandered the digital aisles searching for information to add credence to my books. If there was any impediment to completing research in this manner it is due to the miscellanea of topics which caught my attention and waylaid me for hours, reading and wondering about the garnishes which never gained a mention in the novels I write.

And then there is History itself, which I capitalize because I view it as a proper persona, deserving of uppercase. Historical mentions in all my books, but particularly this one, are meant to add accuracy and authenticity to the fiction. Oscar Hammerstein (grandfather to Oscar Hammerstein II of Broadway fame) and Heinrich Conreid were really friends turned enemies, and their very public spats entertained others for years. Oscar was a mythic figure deserving of more than a footnote in this novel, and I spent hours reading about his public and private adventures and misadventures. He was not the only historical figure with whom I spent time. The Steinway family: William, son of Henry (Heinrich Engelhard Steinweg), and his brothers, Charles and Henry created the renowned *Steinway and Sons* company whose musical instruments are still preeminently recognized and lauded. The creation of the Steinway Village in Astoria, New York began in 1873, before the 1879 Pullman planned community in Chicago and before the early 1900's Hershey, Pennsylvania town. Remnants of Steinway Village can still be found throughout the New York City area where it once stood strong. The mentions of Gustave Eiffel and his ill-fated bridge in Switzerland, the nineteenth-century New York opera wars, the rampart nationalism and food rationing during the World Wars, Chicago's patriotic actions during those wars, as well as the Hammond Musical Company's making of caskets, are real as are all historical events mentioned, and important to note. Some of the many available sites I owe thanks to are listed at the end of this commentary.

And Fate. I waffle in my belief. Or disbelief. But that is the exacting word to describe the interplay and effect the Internet and my meanderings through History have had on my invented characters. I looked for ways to connect the lives of Ingrid and Fredrick and Greta and Lars and Thomas and Bess, and there they were: Oscar and Heinrick, the opera wars, the faulty bridge on the Birs, nineteenth-century immigration and New York's musical institutions, the world wars, Steinway's Village, Chicago's early twentieth-century growth, Doctor DeLee and his gynecological inventions, and a dozen additional people and events. I drew the faces and bodies of the characters, but History provided the skeletal system which kept them upright. Serendipity and chance and connection. Or, as Greta might comment, "Whatever is going to happen will happen". And it did.

***

An informal listing of especially helpful sources:

A City at War: Chicago: (Produced by John Davis and Brian Kallies, narrated by Bill Kurtis) released 2018, and viewed on PBS: WTTW, Chicago

Tom Delgato: *Astoria, NYC: Everything You Didn't Know*, on *YouTube*, Aug. 3, 2022

Ruth Hume, *Oscar and the Opera* in *American Heritage* (February, 1973): https://www.americanheritage.com/oscar-and-opera

Steinway History: http://steinwayhistory.com/

The William Steinway Diary from Smithsonian Institution Libraries: https://americanhistory.si.edu/steinwaydiary/diary/

Wikipedia (source of all knowledge and bane of all teachers) for instant checks on multiple subjects.

Thomas Allerton's story is told in Tomas' Children

As Tomas watched his third child come into the world accompanied by screams and blood and puke, he wondered whether he should drown it in the same manner his father used to drown the kittens on the farm.

For generations, the Allerton family men worked as carpenters and furniture makers. They made bookcases and tables and bed frames; they whittled and carved keepsake boxes and whirligigs and canes; they repaired door frames and replaced rotted crates. And they made caskets and helped in the burial of the inhabitants when it was required. The family had settled in Levett, Illinois, a farming community with a middling town containing a post office, a general store and a hardware store, a church, a schoolhouse. This was the spot Tomas grew up, where he learned his trade, where he lived an austere and harsh existence.

This was the life Tomas Allerton left to travel to unknown places, new circumstances, strange locales.

About the Author

Susan M. Szurek taught in the

Chicago Public Schools for forty years,

embracing every day.

She is currently retired and

embracing every day.